A Matter
Of Control

John D. McCann

Copyright © 2014 by John D. McCann

Cover design by John D. McCann - Artwork by Jonas Doggart

ISBN-978-0-9905006-9-8

Dedication

As always, I dedicate this book to Denise, my beautiful wife and best friend. If it were not for her support, I would not be able to continue writing. I also dedicate it to Jonas, my step-son, who has much technical knowledge and artistic ability.

Table of Contents

CHAPTER 1
Solar Corp.

Phillip Parker was in the United States Marine Corps and commanded Force Reconnaissance, better known as Force Recon, during the first Gulf War in 1991. Phillip stood six feet tall, and for his age, still had the rugged look of a warrior and his gray hair was kept in a high-and-tight buzz cut. When wearing a t-shirt, you could see the bottom of a tattoo on his right bicep. It was a skull wearing a diving breathing apparatus over a pair of wings. At the top were the words "FORCE RECON" and around the bottom the words "Swift-Silent-Deadly." The smaller letters under the chin of the skull read "USMC." A set of paddles were crossed in the background.

A year after retiring from the Corps, with help from an officer he met during the Gulf War, and two young graduates from M.I.T. (Massachusetts Institute of Technology), he developed a solar panel that was cheaper to manufacture than those currently available at the time. He started a company called Solar Corp. and within ten years, he was worth millions.

Solar Corp. then developed a storage battery for solar systems that was not only cheaper than others on the market, but was half the weight with a life expectancy of twenty years. Those batteries provided a lightweight alternative for less money. They called it the Store-Lite Battery and interest for this product was immense.

Phillip Parker started getting multiple offers for him to sell Solar Corp. and the patent for the new battery, which he didn't want to do. Through various circuitous conversations he was told that his products would allow too many people to get involved with solar. Prices had always been kept high so this form of power would not cut into the profits of the oil and gas companies. Phillip explained that he was trying to provide products that would allow more people to get involved with solar. He was adamant in his view, and felt that the oil and gas companies were trying to control the options available to the people, for an alternative form of power.

Eventually, after offers from various power companies were continually rejected, subtle threats began. Becoming concerned and knowing that his son would eventually take over the company; he felt it was time to talk to him about the situation.

His son, Christopher Hughes, whom he always called Chris, was not his biological son, but Phillip always considered him his real son. He had met Chris's mother while stationed at Camp Pendleton, California. She was a beautiful petite woman, and her name was Carolyn. When they first started dating, Carolyn informed him that she had a young son. He learned that her son's father had also been a Marine but had died in a helicopter crash during a training exercise. They continued to date, fell in love, and married. He adopted her son, Christopher, and even though he loved him as if he were his own, out of respect for his real father and family, he never changed Christopher's last name, which remained "Hughes." When Christopher was in his teens, his mother was tragically killed in a car accident by a drunk driver. He, and his new father, became even closer and their relationship was always that of a real father and son.

After high school, having been awarded a scholarship, Christopher attended and graduated M.I.T. Although he spent some time working at his father's company, he had worked on a product of his own that he felt would revolutionize the ability to transport power, immensely reducing the cost for the people. He started his own company.

Phillip had his son stop by his home one weekend, and while both sat on the expansive deck off the back of his new country home, wearing jeans and sweatshirts, they drank a glass of wine. It was time for Phillip to pass on his concerns to his son.

Phillip started out with some small talk about what he had been doing lately; to include a tale of a recent hike he had taken whereby he realized his legs weren't what they used to be. They both laughed and continued with discussion involving recent news stories and how their respective companies were doing. The conversation was pleasant and they both sat comfortably sipping their wine.

When a break in the conversation presented a moment of silence, Phillip felt it was time to discuss the real reason he wanted to talk with his son. With a look of concern on his face he began.

"As you know Chris, I have been receiving many offers in regard to buying Solar Corp and I have rejected them all," Phillip started the conversation nonchalantly wanting to appear casual.

"However, lately I have also received some veiled threats," he continued

"What do you mean veiled threats?" Chris responded in a concerned tone sitting up straight in his overstuffed deck chair.

"It seems that there are some large companies that feel that the products of Solar Corp. will allow too many people to get involved with solar systems, and the concern is it will reduce the need for oil and gas."

"But that's a good thing Dad."

"I know son, but the oil and gas companies want to ensure that people remain dependent on their products. Unfortunately, large companies don't care about the people, only profits. They are not interested in losing profits to people who are going to collect their own power, free from the sun, and cheaper than they could before. Apparently, prices have been kept high in the past intentionally to discourage the use of solar as a means of energy for the common people."

With a look of disbelief on his face, Chris said, "But solar power is the future. You don't really think someone would try to harm you just because you won't sell do you?"

"Let me explain something to you Chris. There will always be those who want to control the people. They do it for power, greed, and profits. They don't concern themselves with the needs and wants of others because they only care about maintaining their position. If you are smart, and I know you are, you will never get involved with those in power. Avoid them like the plague, as the only thing they want is to control others."

"Well, I must admit, you are scaring me a little. Isn't there someone we can go to and report this?"

Phillip refilled both of their wine glasses and continued.

"Chris, you are very intelligent, but naive in the ways of the world, and I'm at fault for that. I have tried to keep you from the more unsavory and gruesome aspects of reality. The world can be an ugly place. Countries and governments are run by the powerful. They control those who wish to stay in office, and to go against them could be very dangerous."

"Well what do you suggest? Should I just sit around and wait for somebody to hurt my father? You are very important to me Dad, and I love you more than you know."

"I know you do son, but this is not your fight. Continue with your work and your new company; watch your six and I'll watch mine. I just want you to be aware of the situation as you will inherit my company, and then the decisions will be yours. It will be up to you if you want to sell Solar Corp. But it will be based on YOUR needs and wants, not MY bullheadedness."

"If anything were to happen to you dad, I would be devastated." Chris looked down embarrassed at his words.

"No son, you would deal with it as you did with your mother's death when you were just in your teens. You are strong inside and you will handle it like a man. But if you ever need help for something serious, you should contact a marine that served under me in the Gulf War with Force Recon. His name is Robert Armstrong, but he goes by Bob, and I trust him with my life, as should you."

Chris's father didn't tell his son about the pact that he, Robert, and another individual had made to each other one dark night in a sandy land, but that was one pledge he knew the three of them would never break.

His father continued, "One last thing son. Never trust those who want to control others, or who want to deny the people the things they control. They destroy the very fabric of our society."

"Can we change the subject Dad, I do not like where this is going."

"I'm sorry son, I'm just glad we got a chance to visit. It has been a while. Maybe someday soon you can go fishing with me on my new fishing boat. It has everything we need for a fun filled day on the water," Chris' father stated.

"It's a Hatteras 45 foot Express Sportfish, and it has a full tower, outriggers and a ton of other amenities. It was really set up for fishing and is equipped with an array of rod holders and even a fighting chair. It has an electric grill built into the starboard bait and tackle center. We can cook what we catch right there on the boat. The main cabin has really nice sleeping quarters so we could actually spend a night out there", his father continued sounding excited. "Just so you know, I named her 'Carolyn' after your mother."

"That was a really nice thing to do Dad, and it sounds great," Chris responded with a smile, knowing in his heart that he didn't really care to go fishing, but it would be a chance to spend some time with his father.

They both sat on the deck watching the sun go down and finished their wine. When they had both emptied their glasses they stood and Chris gave his father a manly hug, before he departed.

* * *

After darkness on the same night that Phillip Parker met with his son, two men slipped into the McGregor's Marina where Phillip Parker kept his new fishing boat. They were dressed in black trousers and turtle neck sweaters, and wore night vision goggles over a black balaclava. Together they approached Parker's boat and climbed aboard.

One of the men stood guard while the other unsnapped a small portion of the rear covering to the cockpit on one side. He entered and was surprised how beautifully the cockpit was adorned for a craft of its size. He approached the main control console and removed a panel. He then placed something inside, and after connecting several wires, replaced the panel. After exiting the cockpit and re-snapping the covering, the two men left the marina as inconspicuously as they had come.

* * *

Two days after Philip Parker had spoken with his son, he took "Carolyn" out for a little jaunt on the bay. He was alone and enjoying the weather. He had hoped his son could join him, but unfortunately he was busy with his new business.

He never heard the sudden explosion that completely destroyed "Carolyn" and him with her, exactly thirty minutes after starting the engine, and having travelled about seven miles out to sea from the marina.

When Chris learned of the explosion, he realized that the conversation he had with his father several days before, would be the last he would ever have. The initial investigation had indicated it was a suspicious explosion because of the size and the damage. But, later a report was released that explained it was merely some type of a gas leak which was ignited by an electrical spark from a faulty twelve volt circuit. Although it could never be proven, Chris knew in his heart that his father had been killed for not selling his company.

CHAPTER 2
Bob Armstrong

Bob Armstrong stood six feet tall with a medium build. He had a solid chest and small waist, and always looked to be in good shape. With long brown hair, normally worn in a pony tail, and a beard that was well trimmed but full, he looked older than his age, having only recently turned forty.

Bob lived in Peekskill, New York, a very exclusive and expensive area in the suburbs north of New York City. Most of the neighbors thought of him as some type of eccentric but nobody really knew a whole lot about him, and although he was always friendly, he kept to himself.

Years ago, he had invented some type of a device that could revolutionize the solar collecting ability of normal panels. A large company paid him an obscene amount of money for the patent (in the millions), then shelved the device. Bob had always suspected it had been a power company that bought the patent to keep it from being used.

Bob could care less, as his goal was to be independent of the system. The money he received was more than he would ever need, especially because of his self-reliant lifestyle. He used the money only in a manner that allowed him to reduce his dependency on others.

Nobody in the neighborhood knew that Bob had actually been in the military. Because of his present appearance, and the fact that he was an inventor who did well, even if by default, it never dawned on anyone to even consider he might be a veteran, and he never mentioned it. Actually, he had been in the United States Marine Corps, and served in the first Gulf War in 1991 as a team leader with Force Recon. He had gotten out after the war and never looked back. His father, Richard Armstrong, who had actually served with MACV-SOG (Military Assistance Command, Vietnam - Studies and Observation Group) during Vietnam, always told him to serve to the best of his ability, and then leave it behind. Bob did as his father had told him. Shortly after giving his son that advice, his father died from cancer, believed to be the result of Agent Orange. His mother was an only child and had died from breast cancer the year prior.

Bob had come to realize that his first mistake was not leaving the area he was in. He had been brought up in the Peekskill area, and when he had attained his wealth at a young age, he just never left. However, a year earlier, an earthquake had occurred on a fault line that many people didn't even know existed. He was aware of it and had constructed his premises with that in mind. However, the surrounding area, including the roads, had received major damage.

There had also been a concern and report of a radiation leak from a local nuclear power plant that had actually been built directly on the fault line. Fortunately, the radiation leak had been a false alarm and hadn't occurred, but it was at that time that Bob decided he would start looking for another place, further north of this area.

Bob had always liked this piece of property. It was a large plot of land with a long driveway that led up to the house. He had a huge array of solar panels that could not be seen from the road, as they where shielded from sight by a small berm; but it didn't shield them from the sun. He had a large bank of batteries that stored the energy from the sun, and when the electricity went out, he still had enough power to operate most of those things in his house that required electricity.

He also had a large vegetable garden, as well as various landscaped areas in which he grew all kinds of flowers that were either edible, medicinal, or both, as well as various types of herbs. All of the downspouts on his house, a large four vehicle garage, a potting shed, and other various outbuildings had large barrels that collected the water when it rained. Some of these were directed to a cistern for storage.

The problem was there were too many people in both his neighborhood, and the surrounding area, that thought he was some type of an eccentric because of his self-reliant lifestyle.

Most people saw Bob drive his Smart Car, as this was his usual means of transportation, around the local area. Only on occasion did they see him in his Land Rover Defender which had safari racks on the top and sides. Bob usually only used this vehicle for trips outside of the immediate area, especially when he traveled up north to go camping.

He also had a 1970 Ford F-Series Ranger 4x4 pickup truck, which he never really drove. It was kept in pristine condition in the garage. He was asked once by a neighbor why he kept such an old truck and Bob had explained it was just in case of an

EMP. The neighbor didn't know what that was, so Bob had to explain it was an Electromagnetic Pulse, and then had to elaborate on how it would affect all electronic devices, including most modern vehicles. Older vehicles would not be affected as they didn't have electronic computers and that was the purpose for keeping the old pickup. The neighbor thought Bob was just kidding him.

Another vehicle he never drove in the area was his Chenowth Scorpion Desert Patrol Vehicle, which was originally designed as a Fast Attack Vehicle for the Navy SEALS. It was first unveiled to the public in Operation Desert Storm. Bob was fortunate to find one, without the weapons package, and he considered it his "shit-hit-the-fan" vehicle. In his heart he hoped it would never come to that, but if it did, he would be prepared. He had a special trailer made for it so he would never have to drive it in public. If he wanted to drive it for fun, he would transport it in the trailer, then take a run in it out in the woods. It would then be returned to his garage, using the trailer. He had only done this twice.

After the earthquake, Bob did some searching for property further north, away from the suburbs and further up in the country. His criteria called for a large piece of land with very limited access, and a running water source to power a hydroelectric generator, which would supplement electricity collected by solar panels.

Bob spent some time up and around the Catskill Mountains area hoping that he would discover that perfect location. It was a beautiful area with lots of mountains and large tracts of land. It also contained the Catskill Park which consisted of 700,000 acres of land inside of what they call the Blue Line. Inside the Blue Line were the four counties of Delaware, Greene, Sullivan, and Ulster. Forty-one percent of this land was owned by the state as part of the Forest Preserve, and was managed by the Department of Environmental Conservation (DEC), and another five percent was owned by New York City to protect four of the city's reservoirs which lay partially within the park.

Bob felt that the area around this park might be just what he was looking for, but if possible, he would avoid being within the blue line in order to avoid the DEC.

While searching the area, he visited with his aunt Martha, who lived on the fringe of the Catskill Park. She was his father's sister and had a different last name, Wagner, due to marriage, but she was now a widow. She was a petite, yet rough woman, who enjoyed tending her small vegetable garden. The beauty of her youth had faded, but she was still an attractive woman for her age. She was one of the few who understood his desire to be self-reliant and not dependent on others. When he was younger and visited during the summer, she had been the one who taught him how to garden and got him interest in his present lifestyle.

Martha lived in a small charming country home, close to the road, surrounded by a huge tract of land, including both forest and fields. She had several smaller outbuildings as well as a substantial barn. The barn was old but well enough maintained that it was still very useful.

During his visit, Bob mentioned that he hoped to move up into this area, and asked if she knew about any large pieces of property that might provide him with both privacy and various other specifics that he explained.

Martha smiled and said, "Why don't you just move in here and build your place?"

"That is a very nice offer Aunt Martha, but I need something very large. But you are a sweetheart for offering."

"Well Bob, my property may not be the largest around, but I think over twelve hundred acres should be more than adequate for your needs."

"You are kidding me right?" Bob said with an incredulous look.

"No kidding Bob, everything you see and saw when you drove up our road is owned by me. My late husband had done very well and like your father always told me, 'invest in land.' I did and my little house is all I need to keep me happy."

Bob couldn't believe his ears. He never would have thought that the entire surrounding area was owned by his aunt.

Martha went on to explain that there was a driveway that proceeded around to the rear of the house and then actually became an old loggers road. It went quite a distance up into the hills behind her house. If he wanted real privacy, he could use that road to enter the property and there would not be any other entrance indicating he was residing back there.

"You can't ask for more privacy than that," she said smiling. "Oh, and there are several strong streams up and around that area as well, which you indicated you needed."

Bob was beside himself. This was exactly the type of property he had been looking for and it was hidden right under his nose.

"Well Aunt Martha, I must say I am very interested in your offer. Would it be alright if I took a hike around the property and see if it is as good as it sounds?"

"Of course dear and I'm sure you will find it everything you need. Now let's have some dinner, you can stay in the guest room tonight. Tomorrow morning you can go inspect the property and hopefully find an area where you want to build your new place. From what you have explained so far, it sounds like you have some really unique ideas for constructing your new home."

Bob didn't sleep much that night as he couldn't wait to get going to inspect the land. He hoped it would be everything he was looking for.

Once he started hiking around the property, which was enormous, he knew it would take several days to examine it all. Of course his aunt was happy as she had him for dinner and company in the evening.

After spending days walking around the property and exploring every area of interest, he knew this was exactly what he was looking for, and he told his aunt so. She was elated of course and stated that they would discuss the particulars later that evening.

After dinner they both cleaned up the dishes with Martha washing and Bob drying. Martha was delighted to have her nephew visiting as they were very close because of their mutual interests. Upon completing the kitchen duties, Martha poured them both a tall glass of apple cider, and they proceeded out to the wrap-around porch that contributed to the country charm of the house. Sitting in matching rockers, Martha began the conversation.

"Well Bob, it sounds like you found what you have been looking for, and I must say, I'm happy that it is up here. From what you described it will provide for both your needs and wants, so this is what I am thinking," she said as she took a sip of her cider.

Bob took a sip of his as well, wondering what his aunt was going to propose.

"Now I know you want to stay anonymous, so the deal I'm about to discuss will remain between just us," she said smiling. "I'm not as young as I used to be, and I've never had any children of my own. You are my only nephew and I have always considered you," she paused, "well like the son I never had," she continued.

"You specify the piece of property you are interested in and I will lease you that portion for your life. It will be a one dollar lease, and of course I hate to charge you anything, but the dollar will keep it legal. We will make some legal arrangements so if something happens to me, you will inherit the entire tract of land I own. This will ensure nobody can build around your area."

"Aunt Martha, I'm really not looking for anything for nothing, I do have quite a bit of money myself," he interjected.

"I know you do Bob, and I'm not looking to make any money either. I just don't want the land to go to the damn state, if something happens to me."

Bob was a little surprised to hear his aunt swear as he had never heard her do so before. It actually brought a smile to his face.

"You really are my only relative," Martha continued, "And even if you weren't, you would, of course, be my favorite," she said giving Bob a sweet wink of the eye.

Bob couldn't believe his good fortune and arrangements were made. He began designing his new place and figured, with the right equipment, the project should take about a year and a half to complete.

Bob had chosen an area up and to the left of Aunt Martha's. Many years before it had actually been the site of an old logger's camp. What really sold him on the location was an old well that had to have been drilled for the old logger's camp many years ago. It was still active and the well had good water depth. His luck couldn't get any better he thought to himself.

Having selected the spot for his new homestead, he would do as his aunt had suggested and use her driveway as his own.

This would prevent the necessity for any additional access roads that would reveal his presence on the property. Because of the amount of land she owned, the nearest neighbor would now be several miles away. This would be so much better than his place in the suburbs.

CHAPTER 3
ZeRho

ZeRho was a company started by Christopher Hughes, who maintained complete control of the company and was the majority stockholder. He was in his early thirties and already worth millions. He stood five feet eleven inches and, although not fat, he was soft from not being very athletic. He had always been a studier, not a doer, and his body revealed his lack of exercise. He dressed professionally but lacked the panache of his contemporaries in the business world. Everyone called him Chris.

When Chris inherited Solar Corp., his father's company, he eventually sold it for much more than it was worth. Chris used the profits from the sale of his father's company to expand his own firm. But he made a pledge to himself, that the only way to get back at those who took his father was by joining them, and then destroying them from within.

During the negotiations for selling his father's company, the Vice President of Operations, Ralph Cummings, who had been with Solar Corp. since the beginning, had asked Chris if he might have a position available for him at his new company.

Ralph stood six feet tall with a slender but rugged build. Always well groomed, he dressed very conservatively. Chris smiled, and knowing Ralph had always been extremely loyal to his father, said, "You know, I have been looking for a good Vice President of Operations. Think you might be interested in that position?"

Chris's company name, ZeRho, was based on a new "Super Conductor" that he and his staff had developed. He was going to call his company "Zero" for the zero resistance in a super conductor. However, wanting to be creative, he started with the "Ze" from zero and then added "Rho," which is the Greek letter used to represent resistivity of a material. Resistivity, unlike resistance, is an intrinsic property meaning that anything made of the same material will have roughly the same resistivity. Zero resistivity means it doesn't oppose the flow of electricity at all, as in a super conductor. The company name, ZeRho, was still pronounced "zero", but actually described their product.

As indicated, super conductors are conductors, not necessarily metals, which have zero electrical resistance. Among other things, this means no voltage loss, regardless of cable or wire length, and that it creates no heat when current is passed through it. This also means that electronics, including the chips in computers, phones, etc., would not get hot from use, other than from the batteries. As there is no loss over distance power companies would have zero loss between the power-plants and end users, meaning more profit, because normally about 6% of produced electricity is lost in transmission lines.

Super conductors already existed today, but the problem was they only worked when super cooled (hundreds of degrees below zero) which made them impractical for everyday use. A super conductor had a critical temperature, which was the temperature at which it became a super conductor. Substances with high critical temperatures (around -328° F/-200°C) were called high-temperature superconductors.

Chris and his staff were able to synthesize a cuprate-petrovskite ceramic material containing Lutetium, which was more abundant than silver but not very common in the earth. It was mostly found in China, the US, Brazil, India, Sri Lanka and Australia. It was difficult to separate and prepare from the ore, and was therefore very expensive. The advantage, even though expensive, was that the "Super Conductor" worked at much higher temperatures, between ninety and one hundred degrees Fahrenheit.

Because of the ability to use this new super conductor at higher temperatures it could be used for pretty much anything electronic. The power companies would want this new super conductor to transport power to customers, which would add millions of profit dollars, as there would be no loss to resistance in the line. Christopher knew that this new super conductor would also create a sudden boon for mining and synthesizing Lutetium, and with the new funds he had, he also set up a mining operation.

ZeRho had been operating at enormous profits for two years since Chris' father died, and the expansion of their facilities was necessary. Up until that time, they were located in Westchester County, New York, and had their manufactured goods produced at various locations around the area. It had been difficult to coordinate the effort, and they really needed a facility that would encompass their entire operation.

Ralph Cummings, the Vice President of Operations, had become a great asset to the company and had found a place for their new facility. It was located further to the north of Westchester County in the southern end of Dutchess County, New York It was a large complex that formerly housed a semiconductor fabrication facility. He felt it was perfect for both the present and future needs of ZeRho.

Before any further steps were taken, Ralph would need Chris to see the place and make the final decision.

He had Chris take a ride up to the location with him, and Chris was as impressed as Ralph. They immediately began negotiations for buying the property, which because of the location, was very expensive. However, Both Chris and Ralph believed it would place them in a strategic location.

A deal was finally struck and plans were immediately started for construction. It didn't take long for construction to begin. Some of the existing buildings were modified for their needs and a new building for the Corporate Headquarters was designed and built.

The complex was everything they had hoped for. They had a headquarters building that housed the executive offices and those of the sales and non-production staff. It had a modern architectural appearance and presented the company as one that was successful.

The manufacturing buildings also presented a modern appearance, yet provided all the requirements to manufacture their product, all in one location. Of course, the mining operation had to be kept separate by necessity, but a large dock at one building enabled the receiving of the processed ore, allowing for it to be synthesized on site. Other buildings housed production lines as well as a research and development department.

Chris sat in his new office on the third floor of the headquarters building behind an oak desk that was becoming of his position. A large glass window at one side of his office allowed him to look down at the complex, he had worked hard to create. He knew he couldn't have done it alone, and reached down and pressed a button on his phone.

"Yes Boss," Ralph Cummings replied.

"Could you step into my office for a moment?" Chris asked.

Ralph walked down the hall from his office which was located on the third floor as well, known otherwise as Executive Row. He proceeded directly to Chris's office and entered without knocking.

"Have a seat Ralph," Chris said with a smile.

Ralph took one of the two overstuffed chairs that sat in front of Chris's desk.

"How's it going Boss? What's up?"

"Nothing in particular. I just wanted to let you know that I really appreciate the job you have done since you joined us. I know why my father thought so very highly of you."

"Just doing my job Boss," Ralph said looking embarrassed.

"Yes you are, but you do it with the rectitude of a man with principles. I respect that in you and it shows integrity, which is something lacking in today's business community. I want our business to be a large success, but I will never prostitute the ethics my father instilled in me for money. I can see you are the same type of man."

"Well I appreciate your faith in me, and not to be flippant, but are we going somewhere with this conversation?" Ralph asked looking a little uncomfortable.

"As matter of fact we are," Chris said with an expression of seriousness. "If something should ever happen to me, not that I plan on that happening, I want you to take over the company and run it as your own. As of today, you are the Senior Vice President of the corporation. I have also increased your stock options, and although I know you don't do what you do for the money, you deserve the same dedication that you give."

"Well, at least I'm not in trouble," Ralph said smiling, looking relieved.

Chris stood and reached out with his right hand and Ralph returned the gesture. They shook with secure grips and both felt the bond that had been established between them.

With a serious expression and sincerity in his voice, Ralph said, "Thanks Boss, I appreciate your generosity."

"Now get the hell back to work," Chris said with a wink. "I'm not paying you to sit around and bullshit."

"On it Boss," Ralph said turning on his heal and departing the office with a mock jog.

CHAPTER 4
The Membership

One day, while Chris Hughes was sitting at his large oak desk reviewing a status report on production, he was informed by his administrative assistant, Sheila, that there was an incoming call from an organization called CANE - the Consortium for the Advancement of Nonpartisan Equity.

"They indicate that you are being considered for membership, which they say could be an advantage for our business as well as other members of the organization that could use our product. If you are interested, an interview could be arranged." Sheila explained. "Would you like to talk to them?"

"Yes please, put the call though," Chris said in a friendly tone.

Chris took the call, and a professional sounding woman reiterated what she had told Sheila.

"Your organization sounds more like it has some type of political agenda as opposed to a business objective," Chris stated with skepticism.

"We truly believe that the best way to help the people is to help big business. After all, it is business that creates the jobs. Sometimes titles can be misleading, but our organization truly supports business and it could be very advantageous for you to join 'us' in our endeavors."

Although the statement made by the woman on the phone was innocuous, it didn't sit right in Chris' mind. Who was this "us" she referred to? His interest was piqued and he agreed to a personal interview. It was arranged for the following week.

The first interview took place at a Doubletree by Hilton Hotel in Tarrytown, New York, in a business suite, which was richly decorated. Upon entering the suite, Chris was met by a well dressed man who introduced himself only as Walter, and they shook hands.

Walter introduced Chris to an attractive middle aged woman, named Kristina, who was also professionally dressed and her scent exuded the fragrance of a very expensive perfume with just the right application. She stood by a counter that held a stainless steel coffee carafe, cups and saucers, spoons, and a selection of flavored creamers. To the right was an array of delicate pastries.

"Please feel free to help yourself," Kristina said with a pleasant smile, sweeping her hand from left to right in front of the offerings. "Walter will then start the interview in the comfort of the sitting area," she continued, indicating the adjacent area with a motion of her right hand.

Walter helped himself to a cup of coffee and placed an almond pastry on a small plate from a stack sitting on the counter as well. He carried both to the sitting area and placed his selections on the glass coffee table in front of a wingback chair upholstered with a rich burgundy tapestry fabric. He then sat down and waited for Chris to join him.

Chris poured himself a cup of coffee and joined Walter at the coffee table, sitting in a matching chair across from Walter.

Walter crossed one leg over the other giving the impression that this was a casual interview. When he smiled, his perfect teeth complemented his stylish apparel.

"It is my understanding that you have indicated interest in our organization, yet seem to be concerned with a possible political agenda," Walter said starting the conversation in a friendly tone. "Let me assure you that our organization certainly does not have a political agenda. We believe in equity for all, and also feel that we can do so while helping our members. Are you opposed to increasing profit margins, while at the same time helping fellow members do the same?"

"Of course not," Chris said with a smile, "But what does one have to do with another? Tell me more."

"Well Christopher, you don't mind me calling you Christopher do you?"

"I would prefer Chris, please continue."

"Well Chris, we specifically remain nonpartisan so we don't get involved with any particular political party or ideology. Our purpose is to increase profits for our membership, which consists of powerful leaders from various segments of the business community. It is our belief that the best way to help others, is to keep 'our' community strong. Our members provide many of the necessities that people have come to depend on. Of course, if those necessities were not available, the people would suffer."

"So basically, the consortium believes that in order to keep the country strong, business must be kept strong?"

"Yes Chris, and to do so, we must often ask for help from others. Others who can assist us in our endeavor to remain strong. Although these other people are not part of our organization, they are often in a position to help, if we can ensure that it is also profitable for them. Are you opposed to helping others who can, in turn, make our position stronger?"

Although Chris showed no outward indication, his mind spun and he wondered if this might be the opening he had been looking for. If not, what did he have to lose other than some time? If it was, he would become involved with those he wanted to destroy, but only until he could make them pay for his father's death.

"I have no problem with that at all," Chris responded with a smile. "I'm very interested. I understand that this is a very prestigious organization and certainly appreciate the consideration. It would be a great opportunity for both me and my company. Where do we go from here?"

"Of course, I'd like to sign you up today. But first we will do some normal background checks, not that we think there will be any problems. Normal vetting you understand?"

"Of course," Chris responded nodding his head.

"Once our membership committee makes a decision, you will be notified. If it is positive, and of course I'm sure it will be, you will meet with our Chairman, Mr. Mann, and he will complete your membership."

At that point, Walter stood and presented his right hand for Chris, who stood as well, and they shook.

"It has been nice to meet you Chris, and I look forward to seeing you again."

Walter then walked Chris to the door of the suite and opened it.

Kristina joined them, and smiling she said, "It has been nice meeting you Mr. Hughes."

Chris departed with his nostrils full of Kristina's scent and his mind in a whirl.

Exactly two weeks after his initial interview with CANE, Chris received a formal invitation to the CANE Headquarters to meet with Mr. Mann. His membership had been approved. The following week he traveled to the well know area of Purchase, New York. This was a wealthy hamlet in the town of Harrison, in Westchester County, New York, just north of New York City. Surrounded by exclusive Country and Golf Clubs, it was also a magnet for prestigious corporate headquarters who wanted a taste of the country yet be close to New York City. Being close to the Westchester County Airport, its location provided for convenient flights to and from the CANE Headquarters.

Finding the address on the invitation he had in hand, he drove between two large stone pillars which each held a brass plaque with the large capital letters C-A-N-E. He approached the barriers that were a short distance from the pillars and stopped at a small gate house. A well uniformed security officer greeted him, "Good morning Sir, may I help you?"

"Yes you can," Chris responded. "I have an appointment with Mr. Mann."

"Then you must be Mr. Hughes. Welcome to our facilities. Could I see some Identification sir?"

Chris showed the officer his driver's license.

"Thank you Mr. Hughes, that will be fine. If you will continue up this tree lined drive you will come to a fork. You will need to stay right, as the drive becomes a large one way loop at that point. You will see our facility directly ahead. As you approach the large portico, continue left under it and around the half circle. As you start back in the direction you came from, you will see a large parking area to your right. You can leave your vehicle there and follow the sidewalk back to the main entrance. When you enter the lobby, you will need to sign in and an escort will take you to Mr. Mann's office."

"Thank you sir," Chris responded, "That sounds simple enough."

A large arm, which had blocked the entrance, rose up automatically and Chris was able to proceed up the drive, and couldn't fail to notice how beautifully the property was landscaped. The 560 horsepower rear engine six-cylinder of his agate gray metallic Porsche 911 Turbo S hummed softly as he approached the fork in the driveway. He stayed right as directed and suddenly the facility came into view straight ahead of him. It was a sight to behold.

The entire building was made of flat faced stone, like the old mansions of the robber barons during the 19th century, but with a modern flare. The center, and largest section of the building, was a two story round turret type structure reminding you of a medieval castle. To both the left and right side of the turret, one story extensions spread outward like the wings of a raptor. The large front portico, with columns of stone, gave the appearance of subtle opulence. The various modern radio dish antennas on the roof of the main turret, almost hidden by the parapets, were a dichotomous sight.

Chris drove in a circular manner under and through the portico. He continued to the designated parking area and selected the first available spot he came to. As he exited his vehicle he could observe a large helipad on a grassy knoll to the rear of the parking area. He followed the sidewalk to the main entrance and was met by a large burly man who was well dressed. He had a bald head and broad shoulders.

"Good morning Mr. Hughes, my name is Boris and I will be your escort," he stated with a strong eastern European accent. "Please sign our visitor's log, and I will escort you to Mr. Mann's office."

Chris signed the visitor's log and was escorted through the main lobby, where he noticed that there was actually another round structure within the main structure. A circular hallway ran around the outer rim of this inner circle, and he was led to the left. One quarter of the way around the circular hall, they again turned left into the grand hallway of the left wing. Chris was surprised at how lightly Boris moved for a large man.

Although the wings were only one story, the walls of oak rose twelve feet in height, and meticulously crafted oak wainscoting embellished the lower portion. Like a gallery, and perfectly spaced, large portraits of famous business magnates adorned the upper walls. The original captains of industry from oil, steel, and banking were all there. New tycoons were also present and although Chris didn't recognize some of them, he would come to meet them soon enough.

Boris stopped in front of a large oak door on the right side of the hall near the end. He entered and Chris followed. They were in what appeared to be an outer office, decorated the same as the hallway.

"Good morning Helga," Boris said to the woman standing at a file cabinet alongside a small ornate desk. "This is Mr. Hughes to see Mr. Mann."

Chris could see that Helga was an alluring woman with an hourglass shape, wide hips, and an ample bosom tastefully confined. With blond hair and captivating blue eyes, she was impeccably attired.

"Good morning Mr. Hughes" she said in an accent Chris believed to be German, as she leaned over her desk and pressed a button on her phone. "Mr. Mann, Mr. Hughes is here," she said.

"Thank you Helga, please send him in," came a response from the small speaker on the phone.

"Mr. Mann will see you now," Helga said walking towards another massive oak door. "Right this way Mr. Hughes."

Mr. Mann's office was in stark contrast to the outer office and halls, and a distinct divergence from what one might expect. The dissimilar elements created an ambiance of both power and an obscure feeling of uneasiness. The walls were of brushed stainless steel, the floor a dark cherry wood, and the ceiling flat black. Although indirect lighting provided ample light to see clearly, it was dim enough to cause the furnishings to cast eerie shadows. There were no windows.

There was a magnificent heavily gilded Presidential Louis XV desk of maroon and gold, which sat upon a Bakhtiari Persian rug in muted tones of burgundy, gold and beige. Behind the desk sat a gilded Louis XV desk chair of maroon tufted leather, and in front, two Louis XV carved Fauteuil arm chairs.

The remainder of the room was sparsely furnished to include a Duncan Phyfe mahogany sofa, an antique coffee table, and two side chairs.

One of the brushed stainless steel walls, to the left of the desk, gave the appearance of a modern news studio. There was a huge flat screen monitor that was flush with the wall. On each side of that monitor were three smaller monitors over each other, flush as well.

As Boris led Christopher into Mr. Mann's office, Mr. Mann met them midway into the room with his hand extended.

Mr. Mann stood five foot, eleven inches, with a muscular build and large hands. A full head of thick gray hair imparted a feeling of paternal warmth, contradicted by the coldness of his gray eyes that seemed to lack any emotion. His attire was very well tailored although conservative in style. His only prominent feature was a jagged scar that ran from the jaw line just under his right ear to the center of his chin, in a lightning bolt pattern. Due to muscle damage, when he smiled, the right side of his mouth didn't move giving more the impression of a sneer than a smile. Nobody knew his age, but most would have guessed he was in his mid-fifties.

"Nice to finally meet you Mr. Hughes, I am Gray Mann."
Christopher approached and shook his hand.
"Nice to meet you as well Mr. Mann, let me thank you for the prestigious honor of being considered for membership."
"Well Mr. Hughes, the honor is ours and I welcome you to CANE Headquarters."
"That will be all Boris," Mr. Mann said, at which point Boris walked directly towards the brushed stainless steel wall to the right of the desk, and exited via a door that was so well concealed, that when it closed behind him, its presence left no trace.
"Have a seat Mr. Hughes," Mr. Mann said directing Chris towards one of the chairs in front of his desk. "Would you like a cup of coffee?"
"No thank you."
"Well then, let's begin."
Mr. Mann walked around to the back of his desk and sat in his thrown like chair facing Chris. He placed both elbows on his desk, and with the palms of both hands together, he touched his forefingers to the bottom of his chin.

After several moments of silence, Mr. Mann began with a voice that was firm yet amicable.

"Mr. Hughes, what if I was to tell you that up to this point we have not been totally candid with you. What if the name of our organization was purposefully misleading, to belie its true agenda? Might this alter your desire to become a member?"

Chris paused, as if thinking about the question, but sensed he was about to learn the truth.

"As long as the actual purpose will assist in the advancement of my company, it actually might enhance my desire."

"Well let me start at the beginning. As you know, membership is by invitation only and limited to those that have been thoroughly vetted, for both, having a company that they control, and for their proclivity to keep both their company and themselves obscure from the public eye. You have met those qualifications."

Placing the palms of both hands on the desk, Mr. Mann continued.

"CANE is made up of the most influential and elite members of the business community to include banking, oil, utilities, agriculture, pharmaceuticals, micro-chips, software, and others that provide goods or services that people depend on. Membership is shrouded in secrecy for the protection of both the membership and the organization. Members must pledge their loyalty to the organization, and for this pledge, they are allowed to dominate certain industries as a reward.

"The acronym C-A-N-E has a cryptic meaning only known by the members. As you know, a 'cane' is something a person needs to lean on, and that is what CANE actually stands for. We endeavor to utilize our immense influence to ensure that the people remain dependent on the commodities which our membership controls. The more dependent the people become, the more control the consortium wields. It is all about a matter of control Chris.

"In order to maintain our ability to control, we must use our immense influence on members of government. Although there are no members of government invited into the organization, there are employees of our members' companies that are often plugged into government positions. These positions assist in our influence over legislation to protect the needs of both our members and CANE.

"Most of our friends were not wealthy when they started out in government. However, when they get in a position to be of assistance to our needs, they soon start accumulating wealth. The government doesn't do that, we do. Therefore they are dependent on us for their continued prosperity. Like most people who become dependent on others for their needs, it is a hard habit to abandon.

"In all business there are unsavory aspects, but it is the ultimate goal for profits and control that drives us. Don't you agree Mr. Hughes?"

"Yes Mr. Mann I do," Chris responded. "It would appear that the initial deceit is to safeguard both the members and the organization, which shows the protective qualities of CANE. I applaud those efforts and I have no reticence in becoming a member. I look forward to membership, as well as a mutually beneficial relationship with the other members."

"Well then Mr. Hughes, I personally welcome you to CANE and look forward to you attending your first conference with us, which will take place in two months."

"Boris," Mr. Mann said out loud, at which time Boris reappeared from behind the concealed door of the brushed stainless steel wall.

"Yes sir, Mr. Mann?" Boris replied.

"Boris, would you please escort our new member back to the lobby where he can sign out?"

Mr. Mann stood and walked around to the front of his desk.

"Again Mr. Hughes, it has been a delightful meeting and I hope that our relationship will be helpful to all involved."

"Right this way Mr. Hughes," Boris said leading Chris out of Mr. Mann's office and back to the lobby.

Two months later Chris attended the CANE conference and got to meet with the members for the first time. He was on his best behavior and endeavored to ingratiate himself in their favor. However, personally, he was appalled by the posture, demeanor, and arrogance of the membership. These were the type of men who would stop at nothing, including killing, to control others. He knew what he had to do, the question was how.

CHAPTER 5
Bob's New Place

When Bob first started laying out the new homestead on his aunt's property, he determined the area he felt would be the most advantages for both, providing enough open space for gardens and solar, and yet concealment from the outside world. He had selected an area that was on a plateau higher than the surrounding community, which was heavily forested, including many coniferous trees. This shielded his main area, even in the winter when the leaves fell leaving the non-coniferous trees bare.

The only area higher than the main plateau was on the north side. This higher area of the property had been instrumental in choosing the plateau. There was a large stream that ran down from that higher part of the property and to the west of his chosen site. This provided more than adequate water flow for a hydroelectric power system, which would supplement the solar system, except in the winter when the water was frozen. However, in the winter, Bob planned on supplementing the solar energy with a wind generator. The additional advantage of the north side being higher than the rest of the plateau was that it would not shield the property from the sun, which was essential for his proposed gardens and solar panels.

The property on the north side did not rise in a steep slope, but gradually at first resulting in a large berm. This berm provided the ideal spot for Bob's main structure. He would build a passive solar residence into the side of this berm with the front facing south.

Bob didn't want any contractor's on site in order to maintain the secrecy of the location. Of course, this meant he would have to haul all the supplies and construction materials in by himself. He would also have to do almost all of the work himself, but time was one thing he had plenty of, and he did enjoy building things. However, Bob had a friend down in the area of his present house that he trusted implicitly. Bob hoped that he might be able to get his friend to travel up to the new property occasionally on weekends to help with some of the heavier work.

For starters, Bob would need a means in which to improve the road into the site he was going to build on, and dig out the area for his new home including some other trenches that were in the plan. He didn't want to dig all that by hand, so he figured he better purchase a small frontend loader and backhoe.

He had been driving a four wheel drive Nissan Xterra that he had purchased since he started looking for the property, and used that to travel back and forth between his home and the building site. However, he felt he needed something a little bigger for hauling construction materials as well as the small backhoe.

Bob discussed his needs with his Aunt Martha. He explained that he would leave all the new vehicles and equipment he purchased on the premises, using his Xterra to travel back and forth from his present residence. He wanted to store them in the big barn on her property so they would be out of site when not in use. Of course his aunt saw no problem with that and indicated there was plenty of room in the barn.

After the discussion with his aunt, Bob purchased a new Ford Super Duty F-250 XL crew cab with a 6.7 liter Power Stroke V8 Turbo Diesel engine. He liked that it was all black with the trim and grill being flat black. He also got the optional electronic shift on-the-fly four wheel drive system, as he never cared for the manual locking hubs which were standard. The hauling capacity was more than enough for what he would need.

In order to haul construction supplies, and not advertise what he was moving, Bob also purchased an enclosed Halmark utility trailer. But before he could start construction he would need to get the frontend loader and backhoe, so he could improve the road into the building site.

After doing some searching, Bob found a Kubota dealer that was down south of the Catskills, which would keep the neighboring community from hearing about some local guy buying a tractor. The less people who knew about what was going on here, the better it would be for him in the long run.

Bob travelled south to the Kubota dealer and selected an "L" Series Kubota diesel tractor with a frontend loader and backhoe. Having been designed for everything from estate maintenance chores to commercial landscaping and small farming, it would be ideal for Bob's needs. It was also much smaller than other types of tractors and much easier to transport. While he was there he also ordered a trailer to haul it on.

Bob had to wait several days for the trailer to arrive so he spent that time at his main residence checking on things, and playing catch-up. He had been spending a lot of time at the new property and he was only staying at his main residence a couple of days here and there. He had a feeling things would get worse before they got better, but he really wanted to get the new place completed to a point where he could move there permanently.

Upon receiving a call that the trailer was at the dealership, he travelled to his aunts, dropped off the Xterra, and picked up his new F-250 Ford pickup. He then went to the Kubota dealer, attached the trailer to his truck, and loaded the Kubota. Heading north, he drove back towards his new property.

When he arrived at his aunt's with the new Kubota, he stopped alongside her house seeing her sitting on the front porch.

"I'll be right over after I put this in the barn," he said smiling as he waved at Aunt Martha.

After securing the Kubota and trailer in the barn, Bob came walking around to the front porch of his aunt's house.

"How about some lemonade?" Martha asked.

"That would be wonderful," Bob replied while dropping down into a chair next to his aunt.

"I see you got some new equipment there. That should help you improve the road where it enters your property as well as dig those holes you need."

"It should do the trick; down here it is fine and shouldn't need any work. Where it enters my property, it just has to be good enough for me to get in and out of. Have to keep it low key you know?"

Martha smiled and said, "Low key is the plan."

"One thing I do need to get is a towable cement mixer as I will be mixing a lot of cement and I obviously can't call a cement truck. That is next on my list of equipment to buy."

Bob took a big gulp of his lemonade and said, "Aah, that just hit the spot."

"You looked like you could use a cold drink. Now skedaddle back to work and be back down here around six for dinner," Martha said with her usual smile.

The new home Bob was gonna build would be a passive solar home. He would use the berm on the north side of the plateau and dig into it so he could build the structure underground for the most part. It would be a long structure with the west, north, and east walls inside the berm, and then covered with a minimal depth of dirt. However, the depth of the dirt on top would be adequate to grow plants on the roof. The rooms of the structure would be lined up in a row, side by side with a hallway on the south side providing access to all rooms.

Being this structure only had to house Bob, and maybe someday a lady friend, it didn't have to be expansive inside. He wanted it to contain, from west to east, a small living room, an eat in kitchen, a bedroom with master bath, that could be accessed from the bedroom and the hallway, a small utility room, and a small office/library. The walls between all the rooms would be load bearing to support the large timber roof and dirt.

The south side would be open to the sun, with windows along its full length, which would allow for passive heating of the structure during three seasons. There would be an overhang designed specifically to shield the southern windows from the sun during the summer, reducing thermal temperature.

Heating, only for the winter months, would be provided by a wood burning masonry heater between the kitchen and living room wall, heating both rooms. A masonry heater was much bigger and more efficient than a regular wood stove, and therefore more capable of heating large rooms. The flue gases being forced to take a circuitous route before escaping, travelling through the mass of the stove, caused them to give up much of the heat, which is absorbed by the mass and slowly radiated into the room and so could last for hours. Although they were rare in the United States, they were extremely popular in Europe where being frugal was still admired. It would be fed from the kitchen but would radiate heat into the living room, as well.

The kitchen would also have both a wood burning cook stove, which would supplement heating, as well as a propane stove. Even though the temperature should not get extremely cold during the winter, as long as there was sun, he would also install a small wall mount propane heater in both the bedroom and office/library.

A solar water heater would be installed above the structure on the berm, which should provide all the hot water Bob would need. However, a small supplemental on demand water heater would also be put in.

Bob had some other plans as well. Behind the main structure, to the rear of the kitchen he would dig further into the berm. This would provide for a large pantry and supply room, small wine storage area, and a root cellar. This area would be concealed by a camouflaged door in the rear of a very small walk-in pantry in the kitchen.

To the right of these concealed rooms, another small room would be constructed, with a concealed entrance from the large pantry. This room would be for his two large gun safes, and his communications equipment.

Being the large berm extended all the way to the tree line on the east side, Bob wanted an alternative exit from the house. He knew it would take a lot of extra work, but he decided to dig a trench from the gun room behind the main structure, thirty-five feet to just inside the woods line east of the house. He would then construct a tunnel in the trench. The tunnel would exit through the top, via a short ladder. The exit would be concealed by a large fiberglass rock, like those used over wells, which would be on a hinged platform over the tunnel exit.

Bob realized this would be a formidable task, but it wouldn't get done by itself. The entire structure was laid out and the digging began using the Kubota. With all areas designated, the next step was to build footings for all outlined walls and the tunnel.

Bob spent an excessive amount of time mixing and pouring the footings, but within a couple of weeks the footings were complete and it was time to start the walls. In order to construct the walls, and to reduce additional labor involved in insulating a concrete foundation wall, Bob decided to use Insulating Concrete Forms, known as ICFs. They were permanent polystyrene forms that were then filled with concrete and reinforced with steel rebar. They used much less concrete than a conventional concrete wall and yet provided superior insulation. Being Bob was mixing the concrete on site, the use of the ICF's would significantly reduce the amount of concrete needed. The other advantage was he could purchase the interlocking ICF panels in four foot by eight foot sections which could be brought to the site in his trailer.

At that point Bob could really use help filling the walls. He called a good friend that he could trust with knowing the location of his new place. Arrangements were made for his friend to take a two week vacation and come up to the new site and help him fill the walls, and pour the floor. Bob knew it was an aggressive undertaking for only two weeks, but felt the two of them could complete the task, which they did.

It had been good seeing his friend again and Bob had missed their spending time together. When it came time for his friend to leave, Bob thanked him, stating he couldn't have done it alone in such a short time.

While waiting for the walls and floor to cure, Bob mixed and poured a concrete footing and a pad a short distance from the house on the west side, which would become a four bay garage.

After the walls were set, Bob used heavy timber for roofing material, which was covered with Building paper, then polyethylene sheeting, and finally with dirt.

Bob had been working on his place for just over a year and had accomplished a tremendous amount of construction, as well as other projects. His good friend had been able to come up occasionally on weekends to assist Bob with various tasks.

Both the solar panels and solar water heater had been installed. A hydroelectric generator had been put in using the stream west of the property, to supplement the solar system from spring to fall. A wind turbine was in the plans for supplemental power in the winter, but Bob was still designing a collapsible tower. For now, he would use a gas powered generator in the winter to recharge the battery bank when the sun wasn't sufficient to do so.

The inside of the house had been mostly completed and all heating systems were functional. A well pump had been installed and water was connected to the house, with plumbing to both the kitchen and bathroom.

The rooms concealed behind the main structure in the berm had been outfitted as required. The garage had been completed as well as a potting shed.

During visits at his home in Peekskill, Bob had brought up two vehicles, one at a time, using a trailer. His Land Rover Defender and Chenowth Scorpion Desert Patrol Vehicle were now tucked away in the new garage. He would still need to bring up the 1970 Ford F-Series Ranger 4x4 pickup truck. When it came time to move up to his new place he would sell the Smart Car, as he wouldn't need it up there. He also contemplated selling the Nissan Xterra before moving up, as he had the new pickup, which he kept in his aunt's barn when not in use. He would make that decision when the time came.

During his trips bringing up the vehicles, he also transferred some of his weapons from his old gun safe to the new ones in his concealed room off the hidden pantry.

Bob wanted to install a satellite dish for both television and internet. He spoke with his aunt and made arrangements to bill the service under her name and address. He didn't want anything that might reveal his living at this new location. His aunt was more than amicable, understanding his reasoning. It was placed on a mast and tuned making the correct elevation and azimuth corrections. He was surprise at the good reception he received, which then provided him with the needed service.

Bob spent additional time putting up antennas for his various communications equipment which had all been selected because they would function on twelve volt DC. He strung a long wire antenna for his ham radio and installed a mast mounted wideband Discone antenna providing excellent omni-directional reception for his various scanners and an AOR wideband communications receiver. Another mast was erected for a Sirio Gain Master fiberglass base station antenna for his Galaxy DX-2547 AM/SSB CB base station.

Lastly, Bob planted two large posts, one to each side of the entrance from the logging road, into his property. He then strung a cable between them, whereby it was padlocked on one side. He hung a metal sign, he had made, from the center of the cable that read "Keep Out - Private Property." He knew it wouldn't prevent people from entering if they really wanted to, but at least it was a warning that the property was inhabited. When he entered, he could simply unlock the cable and pull it to the side of the entrance, and put it back up when he left.

Things were looking good and the next step would be cultivating the gardens. Bob knew that in a very short time he would be moving there permanently.

CHAPTER 6
CANE Conference

It had been a year and another CANE Conference was only a week away. Chris received a small package at his office from a company called Intel-Tech. He told his administrative assistant, Sheila, not to disturb him and sat at his desk opening the package. He examined the device that he had custom made to help him accomplish his plan. Only one more week and this device should serve his needs well.

The night before the conference, Gray Mann checked with Boris to ensure that the TSCM (Technical Surveillance Countermeasures) team was scheduled to conduct a sweep of the meeting area, as they always did, to ensure that it was free of any electronic intercept devices. Boris ensured him that it was on schedule. Upon completion, the sweep team would place seals on the doors to maintain the integrity of the area until it was time for the conference. The team would depart the premises before the sun began to reveal its first rays of light.

On the day of the conference, Chris took his device, got into his Porsche 911 Turbo S, and headed towards the CANE Headquarters building. Upon arrival, he noticed that as usual, most of the members were chauffeured and dropped at the semi-circle at the main entrance. The drivers then departed with the vehicles, having been given specific instructions on when to return for pickup. Chris was one of the few who drove themselves to the conference, and he'd had members comment on it. "In your position," they would say, "you should have a driver." Chris would always tell the person that it was not a matter of money; but that he simply liked to drive himself. He was in close proximity to the headquarters building and he enjoyed driving, so why have a chauffeur?

Chris was amazed again at the security precautions taken at the conference, and the actual conference room they used. Upon entering the building you were required to give all cell phones, tablets, and other electronic devices to security personnel where they were locked up in cabinets. They were not returned until after the conference. Before entering the actual conference room, everybody was required to go through walk-through metal detectors. Any change, keys, etc., were placed into a dish and walked around the metal detectors and returned to the owners on the other side.

The actual Conference Center was inside the round section of the building inside the larger circle. The outside wall of this inner circle was covered in the same flat stone as the exterior of the facility. In order to enter the inner circle, you walked in either direction around the outside circular hallway to the entrance that was on the opposite side of the circle from the lobby.

When you entered the inner circle, you could notice that the walls were much thicker than most rooms, and the doors were extra thick as well. The walls of the entire room were covered in brushed stainless steel, with a flat black ceiling, the same as Mr. Mann's office. The circular floor was covered in a gunmetal gray carpet. There was a huge brushed stainless steel conference table that was shaped much like a crescent moon, but the ends did not come to a point. There were black leather inlays on the surface of the table at each seating position. The chairs were modern, high-backed, and were upholstered with horizontally ribbed black leather. On the floor, where the chairs sat, there was a black marble crescent, inset level with the carpet, on which the chairs could easily roll.

In front of the conference table, in the center of the floor facing it, there was a large podium, again made from brushed stainless steel. It was the spot at which all speakers must address the membership with their presentations.

The lighting in the room was indirect and low around the perimeter, and other than a small shielded lamp at each seating position at the conference table, and on the podium, the room remained mysteriously ominous. The room, from within, seemed to radiate a sense of sinister power, a feeling that was only heightened with the members assembling.

Upon entering the room, members would shake hands, and engage in small talk. Eventually each would find their nameplate on the conference table and take a seat at their assigned position.

Chris found his nameplate, which was near one of the ends of the table, and took his seat. Rolling his chair up to the table, he placed his keys on the leather pad and waited for the conference to begin

When all members were in their position at the table, Gray Mann suddenly appeared and stood behind the podium.

"I welcome all our members to the annual conference of CANE," Mr. Mann started with a sneered attempt at a smile. "After having spoken with those members who wish to present a position at this conference I can see that we have an agenda that is important to those members, and therefore important to us all. The concerns for this conference all seem to revolve around the proclivity for some people in our country wanting to be more self-reliant, and thus, less dependent on us. I ask that all members listen carefully to these concerns as this type of behavior might eventually affect any one of your businesses. As usual, we will allow members to present their concerns one at a time here at the podium. If there are any questions or suggestions, I ask that members hold them until each member has finished."

Clearing his throat, Mr. Mann said, "First I would like to offer the podium to Mr. Wellington from PETRO."

Gray Mann then took his place at the conference table, which was the center seat and the only one unoccupied.

The company name "PETRO" was an acronym for Petroleum Extraction Technology & Refining Operations. It was a multi-billion dollar company that was run with an iron fist by Randolph Wellington. They extracted and refined oil and gas and designed technology that allowed them to do so cheaper than their competitors.

Randolph Wellington was a very powerful man, in his early sixties, and stood six feet tall with extremely broad shoulders and a solid chest. Although he walked with a slight limp, it didn't diminish the dynamic stature he projected. He wore a well trimmed silvery mustache and goatee on a square face, with hair that was short but thick. His speech was normally resonant, and when he spoke, people listened.

Randolph Wellington proceeded with his slight limp up to the podium and faced the membership.

"I would like to welcome all our members to the CANE Conference as well, and good morning to you all," he started. "As you are all aware, we depend on the people of this country relying on our goods and services. For my business, that means that the people must remain reliant on oil and gas for heating, transportation, etc. But I have two issues," he said holding his right hand up with his index and middle finger pointing at the dim ceiling.

Continuing, he indicated that his first issue was the use of solar panels not being tied to the grid which keeps them from feeding energy back into the system. His second complaint was the use of Wood Burning Stoves which do not use oil or gas as a means of fuel, denying him and his company profits.

"First of all, having a solar system that is not grid tied is a problem. When a system is grid tied, the customer may use less power from our company, but is feeding energy back to us to sell to others. Also, even though these grid tied customers pay less for their power, they are still charged for the line, meter etc. Even if they owe nothing for their power usage for a month, they still get a bill which is free money for us. Many of these self-reliant type individuals are also utilizing solar collection to recharge their own battery banks for later use, not requiring them to purchase fuel oil or gas for a generator.

"These same 'prepper' type individuals use wood stoves to heat. Although it is not a large number yet, the number is growing. This growth denies us profits. We need legislation that outlaws the use of solar panels that are not tied to the grid and wood stoves for heating or other purposes," Randolph stated vigorously.

"This should be an easy sell. We convince the public by explaining that those independent solar systems, that are not grid tied, are also not inspected for safety issues. Also, they can be used by domestic terrorists to hide from the system. In regard to the wood stoves, we will get the backing of those who believe that they contribute to green house gases, even though we know they don't. We again push the idea that wood stoves can be used by those who want to hide from the system, which means they have something to hide, and therefore might be domestic terrorists. As always, we use our friends in the government to do our bidding. If they push the agenda that these types of devices are not only dangerous to society, but are used by those who wish to harm us, the people will buy it."

When Randolph Wellington completed his presentation, and although there were not any questions, the concerns were discussed between the membership and found to be valid.

The next member to be introduced by Mr. Mann was Jacques André of Mysticorp.

Mysticorp was a multinational conglomerate with its headquarters in the United States. Although the company name was not recognizable by most consumers, their brand names were, and the breadth of its holdings was significant. Having been in business for only a little over twenty-five years, and starting out only selling coffee, through the acquisition of other food, beverage, and tobacco companies, they were able to expand exponentially and ultimately dominated the industry.

However, their major expansion had been into bottled water, and that required a source of water.

Mysticorp was controlled by Jacques André. He was a slim man who appeared taller than his five foot ten inches. He always wore a welcoming smile, and seemed charismatic in nature, but he was not someone to antagonize. His piercing blue gray eyes could produce a stare that would cut through you like a knife. Always meticulously dressed, he was quiet and reserved.

Jacques André approached the podium and welcomed everyone to the conference as well. He then began his presentation.

"As I have indicated previously, Water is a major profit center for our company. Like Mr. Wellington from Petro, I have two issues as well." Jacques also raised two fingers but pointed them more sideways than straight up.

"My first issue is the collection of water by these prepper people, we have spoken about previously. Every drop of water that they collect in barrels or other systems does not return to the aquifer, which is where we get our water to bottle. Although we are already buying water from various community sources, we can't have people just taking water for free.

"Secondly, many of these survivalists are diverting running water from creeks and streams to create power off the grid. Although this should concern Petro as well, every bit of water that is diverted from the aquifer is water we are denied.

"Like Mr. Wellington's concerns, this should fit well into the 'Domestic Terrorist' agenda we wish to create. Our friends in the government can easily indicate that water is actually owned by them, and by taking that water for yourself, you are denying others its use. The water must be regulated in order for it to be available to all. In regard to the use of water for power, Petro can utilize the same issues as with solar, because if these individuals are using it to make their own power, they are not using oil or gas. Our friends can also indicate that the use of water for creating power is regulated by the Water Power Regulation Agency and therefore must be inspected and approved before use."

Jacques' presentation created quite the discussion and some of the members had not been aware that water was being collected by some people without paying for it. They were all in agreement that this couldn't be allowed to go on.

The next speaker introduced was Maximilian Adler from SacreMont.

SacreMont was a multinational corporation that specialized in the genetic modification of seeds for growing food. They were not the first company to make genetic modifications but were able to steal formulas that allowed them to, first compete, and then dominate the field. During both world wars, they were a weapons manufacturer, dealing with everything from large weapons to small arms. After the Second World War, they started manufacturing gardening tools as they already had the machinery to do so. Gardening tools led to other gardening products, and eventually seeds. After obtaining the formulas for genetically modified seeds, they started experimenting on their own. Their goal was to develop seeds that would produce a larger quantity of food and larger crops, with the intent to make them sterile, after the first growth. Therefore, it would require that seeds be purchased each growing season. The sales pitch was always that the larger crops produced, more than compensated for the price of the seeds. However, they found that if heirloom seeds were grown in the same area as their genetically modified seeds, they would interfere with the modifications they developed. As they perfected their "Frankenstein" seeds, they quickly started buying up seed manufacturers so they could exchange the heirloom seeds for their own. Their long-term goal was to have heirloom seeds outlawed in order to dominate the industry. The byline for their company name was "Feeding the Future."

SacreMont was controlled by Maximilian Adler. He was a large man standing six feet four inches tall with a very erect posture. He was of German heritage, but with a rounded bald head and a thick handlebar moustache, he looked more like a Russian Cossack. He always walked with a swagger that gave one the impression of arrogance.

Maximilian Adler swaggered up to the podium, and standing tall, started his presentation.

"As many of you know," he began, "our products are important to the people. Some countries might not see the advantages of our products, but we understand their importance. We must maintain our dominance in this country, and we have already received assistance from our friends in the government. Having the president sign a bill instituting the 'SacreMont Safeguard Act,' it helps protect us from those who wish to besmirch our hard work by indicating that we are evil. We are not evil; we merely want to provide food for the people. But, to do so, we must ensure that only our seeds are used. We must convince our friends that the use of heirloom seeds, by these survivalists and preppers who want to be self-reliant, can be a threat to the people. These heirloom seeds are not inspected or approved for use, and therefore could crossbreed with our seeds. Who knows what could happen. Only those who wish to harm our country would use seeds that we have not determined to be safe, and these people should be labeled 'Radicals.'"

Maximilian Adler was so forceful and animated in his presentation that he actually received a small applause upon completion. The membership was with him and agreed something must be done.

The next speaker was Atwood Buckingham from UrBank.

UrBank was one of the largest bank holding companies with global services that included commercial banking, trust services, credit cards, mortgage banking, and other financial services. It was controlled by Atwood Buckingham, who was also on the board of governors at the National Reserve Banking System (NRBS). The NRBS was an independent agency, not a government entity, although most people believed it was. Some people had actually implied that the NRBS ran the government, but who knew for sure. The stated purpose of the NRBS was to maintain the stability of the banking system and ensure money was available if a bank failed. They had the currency printed by a government department, who then delivered it to the NRBS, who disseminated it to the banks and then charged the government interest for its use.

Atwood Buckingham was of medium height and had a lanky build. With a thin face and a well trimmed moustache, he would have reminded you of the British Field Marshall Montgomery. Known for wearing fine English tweeds, and carrying an umbrella, he was very articulate in speech.

Atwood Buckingham approached the podium looking as dapper as ever, and started his presentation. "Our concern at UrBank is the use of cash by people. As we know, we need to keep the people in debt. Like our government, as long as we can keep them in debt, they must continue to be part of the system, which we control. We also need to know where the cash is. If it is kept in banks, then we control it. The use of cash also denies us the ability to track purchases. We sell this information to companies for their advertising purposes, and using cash excludes us from that additional revenue."

He continued, "I agree that these survivalists, who think they can use cash and operate outside of the system we have designed, must be dealt with, and severely. Using the 'Domestic Terrorist' angle, we can indicate that those who use cash are trying to work outside of the system, which is in place to protect the people. Only those who are trying to avoid taxes, or want to keep their purchases a secret, would need to use cash. Only those who wish to harm our country need to stay hidden. This shouldn't be a hard sell to the public, if the government mandates it."

The conference went on like this for most of the day. There was a break for lunch which was an epicurean's delight and served in a plush dining room located in the extension on the right side of the facility.

Starting with a large shrimp cocktail with firm jumbo shrimp, it proceeded to a petite salad of fresh mixed greens. For the main course, members had a choice of herb crusted salmon or filet mignon medallions served with a rich béarnaise sauce. Sides of asparagus spears and baby red potatoes supplemented the entree. Both red and white wine was served, depending on your choice of entree. The meal was completed with a perfectly prepared crème brûlée.

Towards the end of the afternoon, Gray Mann spoke again with a closing to the conference.

"So what we need is for our friends to initiate some type of legislation, and then an agency that could implement that legislation to control these people who insist on being self-reliant. If we can get these damn 'Survivalists' or 'Preppers' or whatever they call themselves labeled something that will scare the hell out of others, they will insist that the government do something.

"With a good propaganda campaign, those who don't want to be part of 'our' program, and think they can be independent of our goods and services can be dealt with. They WILL remain dependent on the system we have created, or be dealt with in the harshest means possible. I'm sure that our friends will be able to help us in this effort. "

When the conference was concluded there was little small talk among the members. Most went directly to, and exited the lobby. Vehicles were already lined up with drivers waiting for their employers. The vehicles were pulled up one at a time, and doors were opened for the employers. The vehicles would then drive slowly up the exit lane and disappear around the corner, towards the main entrance gate.

This activity continued as Chris walked slowly towards the parking area to retrieve his vehicle. Although he was nervous on the inside, he remained cool on the outside. He had much to think about.

CHAPTER 7

The Recording

Upon leaving the conference, Chris drove directly to his house which was located in Yorktown Heights, in northern Westchester County, New York, 45 miles from New York City. It was a beautiful area with many exclusive residences.

When he entered, his heart was beating so hard he could almost hear it. He proceeded directly to his home office, and sitting at his desk, he removed the key fob from the split ring that held it attached to his keys. He extracted a small screwdriver from his desk drawer and removed a small access panel from the rear of the key fob, which revealed a micro USB port.

With his hands slightly shaking he attached one end of a adapter cable to the micro USB port on the key fob and the other end to a USB input on his computer. This provided him access to the custom key fob recorder that had been built for him by Intel-Tech, a company that had shortened their name from Intelligence Technologies. The recorder had a built-in 2 GB

Flash memory with an AGC (Automatic Gain Control) ultra sensitive microphone that provided a 25 foot pickup distance, and 15 hour recording time. It had been a good choice, as a key fob was not restricted at the conference, and Chris was actually able to lay it in plain sight on the conference table without suspicion.

Upon opening a special program for listening, and copying, audio recordings he found that the device had worked exceptionally well. He had the audio from the entire conference and the clarity was almost as if you were actually in the room as the conversations were being held. He was especially pleased with the introductions of each member before they spoke. It would be difficult for the members to deny what they said.

The question Chris now asked himself was how he could secure the recording until he could find a way to reveal it?

He knew he could keep a copy saved on his computer, but that probably wouldn't be safe. He would copy the recording onto a flash drive, encrypt access to it, and conceal it in his home office. He transferred a copy of the recording to a miniature flash drive, encrypted the access, and started to look around his home office for a place to hide it.

After further thought, and knowing that he needed to be careful, he realized he would need to hide a copy outside of his home for safekeeping, just in case. In the morning he would take another copy to his office and put it in his very secure and concealed safe there. Someday I really need to get a safe for my home office, he thought to himself.

Just to be careful, he decided to hide one more copy. Chris grabbed two more mini flash drives, copied the recording to them, and encrypted access.

As Chris looked around his office he remembered that there was an actual space between the drawer dividers and the drawers in his desk. He pulled one of the drawers out all the way and found that the small space was just perfect to conceal small flash drives. He placed two of the flash drives in the small space, slid them all the way to the rear of the area, and replaced the drawer. He would retrieve one of the copies in the morning and take it to the safe at his office. He then erased the recording from the key fob and put it in the top right desk drawer.

For the third copy, Chris had another idea for concealment. He had been involved with geocaching with some of his fellow students when he was at M.I.T. This was an outdoor recreational activity where those who are participating use a GPS (Global Positioning System) to both conceal and locate small waterproof containers called "geocaches." Oftentimes, the small waterproof containers are buried in the ground. Geocache data, known as waypoints, are provided to the searchers along with the actual coordinates of its location. Although handheld GPS units have traditionally been used for the concealment and location of such caches, there were now some mobile applications available for some smart phones that allowed them to be used as a mobile GPS device.

Searching around his office, Chris was able to locate one of his old waterproof caching containers made from red anodized aluminum that was just big enough to hold the third mini flash drive, after it had been inserted in a small waterproof bag, for additional protection. Upon securing the screw-on top, the next question was where to hide it.

After rejecting the thought of burying it on his own property, he decided that he would take a ride and find a wooded area that he could easily access, and bury it there. However, he would have to wait until it started to get a little darker, as it would be less likely that he would run into anybody else. Until then he would fix himself some dinner.

Upon completing his meal, Chris gathered together a small trowel, the container holding the flash drive, a headlamp, and a handheld GPS unit. He got in the Porsche and drove to a wooded area that he was aware of, a couple of miles from his house. It was ideal, as it had a parking area for hikers. It was not an official hiking area, as the property was privately owned, but people had been hiking there for years without a problem or complaint.

When Chris arrived at the parking area, no other cars were parked there. The sun had just set, and although it was just starting to get darker, he had plenty of light to complete his undertaking. He gathered together those things he needed and started to hike up one of the short trails. It was early autumn and the smell of the cool and refreshing air reminded him of pumpkins and apple cider. Although leaves had begun to fall, they had yet started to become dry and crunchy, so his footsteps along the path were soft and muted.

He was searching for a location that would provide a small clearing where he could bury the cache and mark the coordinates, so he could retrieve it if necessary, at a later date.

He didn't have to go far when he saw a clearing that was to the left of the trail. He carefully left the trail, first checking in front and behind him, to ensure no one else was around.

As he approached the small clearing he took out his trowel and checked various spots to determine how hard the ground was. He found an area that allowed him to dig a hole that he felt would provide adequate depth to both secure and conceal the container he had chosen for his cache. He buried and covered it, making sure that he left no trace that digging had taken place. He then took out his small handheld GPS and recorded the coordinates for the exact location of the hole, then carefully spread leaves over the area so there would be no indication that anyone had been there.

Having completed the job, he slowly returned to his car, enjoying being out in the countryside. He didn't spend enough time outside, he thought to himself.

When he got back in his car, he turned on his small GPS and looked at the coordinates he had recorded for the cache. He needed a way to safeguard them until he could write them down and put them in his safe at the office. For the time being, he decided to upload them to a network cloud with his smart phone, and delete all data from his handheld GPS. He may be a little paranoid, but if the GPS got into the wrong hands the coordinates could be found. When he got back to the office, he could retrieve the information from the cloud and secure it.

Chris pulled the Porsche out of the small parking area and proceeded back towards his house. It had now turned dark and a light rain had started to fall. It wasn't a hard rain, but more than a drizzle, and just enough to wet the leaves littering the road.

As Chris came around a tight corner on the country road, all he saw was headlights in his path and before he could react, the crash occurred. He never heard or felt the collision and the Ford 150 pickup, speeding on wet roads, nearly drove completely over the Porsche before sliding off the road and into a tree that failed to yield to its sideways sliding action.

When Ralph Cummings arrived at the hospital, the antiseptic smell invaded his nostrils; a smell he always hated. He proceeded directly to the emergency room and asked if there was any news on the condition of Christopher Hughes.

"Are you a relative sir?" the nurse asked.

"Not actually, but I'm the only family he has. I'm Ralph Cummings and I'm the Senior Vice President for Chris' company, ZeRho. Is he alright?"

"He has been taken to intensive care. If you would like to wait in the waiting room, it is on the second floor. Just follow the signs. I will have the doctor in charge come out and talk to you when he has more information."

Ralph proceeded to the cafeteria first, and although his stomach wasn't ready for any real food, he got a cup of coffee and continued to the intensive care waiting room.

Time passed slowly as Ralph sat and fidgeted hoping that Chris would be alright. After having perused all the magazines twice, a doctor finally entered the room.

"Is there a Ralph Cummings here?" the doctor asked.

"That would me sir," Ralph said as he stood.

"I'm Dr. Steinberg; let's take a walk."

Ralph followed the doctor out into the hallway where the doctor started to speak softly and sincerely.

"It is my understanding that you are the only family that Mr. Hughes has, so it is for that reason that I will provide you with his condition at this point."

"I appreciate that doctor, as I will be the person who will be taking care of him and his business. He will make it won't he?"

"Mr. Hughes was banged around quite a bit in the accident and has sustained various non-life threatening cuts and abrasions to his body, but does not have any broken bones or damage to internal organs. However," and the doctor paused for a moment and looked directly at Ralph and continued; "it appears that he received a traumatic blow to the head. As a result of the severe head trauma, Mr. Hughes has slipped into a coma. Now this could last for a short duration, or he could remain comatose for an indefinite period of time."

"Is there anything we or I can do?"

Dr. Steinberg cleared his throat and said, "Not really. There is no cure for a coma. Our options at this point are limited to preventing further damage, treating the underlying causes, and maintaining proper blood flow and nutrition. The rest is up to the patient. I wish I could be of more help."

"What are Chris' chances for recovery?" Ralph asked.

"The chance of recovery for a patient in a coma is dependent on the severity of the injury sustained and the amount of time spent in the comatose state. Oftentimes, patients with mild head injuries regain consciousness within a few weeks. Those with severe brain damage could slip into a more permanent vegetative state. At this point, we do not believe that any severe damage has taken place. But we are still doing tests."

Ralph pressed on with his questions. "If he does come out of this, will he be able to function normally?"

"That's hard to say," Dr. Stenberg replied. "Usually, patients who regain consciousness, also regain their cognitive and motor skills, but often need rehabilitation. Through various programs, physical therapists and doctors can help patients recover their normal skills."

"I thank you for taking the time to speak with me doctor. I will be here every day until Chris comes out of this coma. If there is anything else I can do, just ask."

"If you could take care of the paperwork for Mr. Hughes' insurance that would be a great help."

"I'll take care of that immediately," Ralph assured the doctor. "One other thing Doctor, I would like to arrange for a private room for Chris during his stay here. Not to be pompous, but money is not a problem. I would like to be assured that Chris will receive the best treatment available."

"That will not be a problem," Dr Steinberg replied.

As the doctor walked away, Ralph thought about the situation and was very concerned. He knew Chris was strong, and was certain that he would come through this. But, in what condition? He now had to run the company and be there for Chris, and he would do both to the best of his ability.

Chris had only been in the hospital for three days when Ralph received a phone call from the local fire department that there had been a fire at Chris's home. Although the central station alarm from his home had the fire company there in less than five minutes, the damage to the area of the house where his office was had been severe. Apparently, that was where the fire had started, and it appeared to have been a lightning strike, so it was not under suspicion. Ralph immediately got a crew over there to clean up the mess and smoke damage and secure the damaged area from the weather. He wondered to himself if anything else could go wrong.

The news about Chris' accident hit the papers, but always keeping a low profile, it didn't make headlines. However, it was picked up by Gray Mann, and he was concerned.

"Helga" he said pressing a button on his phone, "Have Boris come to my office."

"Yes Mr. Mann," she replied in her normal fashion.

A few minutes later Boris entered Gray Mann's office.

"It would seem Boris, that Mr. Hughes from ZeRho has been in an automobile accident and is in a coma. As you know, we are very interested in the super conductor that his company produces, and it is important for some of our members."

"Yes sir, I am aware of that."

"I would be very interested in knowing what is going on over at ZeRho while Mr. Hughes remains unconscious. Can you take care of that forthwith?"

"Not a problem sir, I'll get right on it."

CHAPTER 8
The Awakening

It had been almost six weeks and Ralph had been at the hospital every day. After coming out of intensive care, Ralph made sure that Chris had a private room and he would sit with him for hours and wait and hope. He was able to control the company through the assistance of modern electronic devices, and would have been lost without his smart phone and tablet.

Much of his everyday work could be accomplished from Chris' room, but he still needed to be at the office each day to take care of those duties and responsibilities that required his personal attention, as well as coordinate with the construction crew that he had repairing the fire damaged area of Chris' home.

The day before it would have been six weeks, Chris suddenly awoke from his coma. At first he was confused as to where he was, but then he saw Ralph sitting in a chair to the right of his bed.

"How long have I been here?" he asked with a perplexed look.

Ralph about jumped out of his chair hearing Chris speak.

"You're alright," he said excitedly. "I knew you would make it! You have been here almost six weeks," Ralph said finally answering Chris' question.

"Six weeks? What happened?"

"You were in a bad car accident and you have been in a coma. I'm just glad to see you awake. They say the longer you're in a coma, the less chance of coming out."

"Sorry, if I had known, I would have woken up earlier," Chris said with a groggy smile.

"Let me get the nurse and let her know you are awake. I'll be right back."

Ralph headed for the nurse's station with a smile on his face and relief in his heart.

When Ralph returned with the nurse, she smiled and said, "It is nice to see you awake Mr. Hughes. We have been worried about you. How do you feel?"

"Stiff, which I guess would come from laying here for weeks. I'm a little groggy, and I can't seem to remember any accident. Actually I don't really remember anything that would even explain why I was out in the car."

"What is the last thing you recall?" the nurse asked.

"I'm not sure," Chris responded with a frown. "I'll have to think about it."

"Well let me get the doctor on duty and we will take some tests and determine your condition," the nurse said smiling.

The nurse left the room and Ralph walked over to Chris' bed.

"I don't want to sound too emotional, but damn I was worried about you," Ralph said with a serious expression. "You really had me worried."

Chris smiled at Ralph and said, "How is everything at the office?"

"Things are going good and everybody misses you, but you have better things to concern yourself with right now."

"I'm sure you have taken care of things just fine, but you look like shit," Chris said with a smirk.

"Yea, well you don't look so wonderful yourself," Ralph replied with a grin.

After awaking from his coma, Chris was required to remain at the hospital for an additional week, so that tests could be conducted, and to ensure that there weren't any problems that were not readily apparent.

It was determined that Chris had only lost memory for about the last week or two before the accident. This type of short term memory loss was often the case after a coma caused by a traumatic experience, and the doctors felt that all memory would return eventually. It could be days, weeks or even months, but complete memory usually returned.

* * *

Boris entered Gray Mann's office and reported that the electronic surveillance at the offices of ZeRho had revealed that Mr. Hughes was out of the coma and would be returning to his home within a week. It would be several weeks until he would return to the office.

"Should surveillance be terminated?" he asked.

"It is my understanding that you are using a burst transmitter at their offices, which necessitates a repeater system to get the transmission down here. Correct me if I'm wrong, but this device records all conversation in the offices you have concealed a microphone in, and the information collected is compressed. Then once a day that information is transmitted to us in a single burst."

"That is correct Mr. Mann."

"Well, even if they did a sweep for radio transmitters, which they have no reason to suspect are there, the chance of seeing that burst on a spectrum analyzer is very low, unless they were watching at the exact moment the burst transmission took place. What have we got to lose? Let's leave it there. But, it seems like Mr. Hughes will be spending quite a bit of time at his home and I'm sure he will be conducting some business from there. This is what I want you to do. Get a team to his home before he gets out of the hospital and place intercept devices in his home office and anywhere else you deem prudent. Let's not take a chance of missing important business information because he is working out of his home."

"Yes sir," Boris said and departed Gray Mann's office.

* * *

Chris was finally allowed to leave the hospital and return to his home. It was at this time that Ralph told Chris about the fire, so he wouldn't be surprised when he got there. The reconstruction was still being completed, but the house was more than secure for Chris' return.

"What part of the house was damaged?" Chris asked.

"Just your home office and part of the area under it," Ralph replied."

"How much damage?"

"It was a total loss for everything in that area, but because of the quick response from the fire company, most of the actual structure was saved."

"Do they know what caused the fire?" Chris asked.

"It appears it was a lightning strike. They say it is unusual that such a strike would cause a fire, but on rare occasion it can happen," Ralph answered.

"Well if it wasn't for bad luck, I guess I wouldn't have any."

"You are still with us and that's what is important. As you will see, the house is being fixed and your office area should be completed in another month," Ralph retorted.

Having heard from the staff at the hospital that Ralph had been there every day, he said, "I really appreciate your standing by me Ralph, and especially taking on the additional duties at the company and getting my house repaired. You are more than an employee; you are truly a loyal friend."

"Well as far as the hospital is concerned, I'm also now family," Ralph said with a smile.

Upon returning home, Chris had a long series of therapy sessions ahead of him. He had physical therapy everyday for the first few weeks as a result of his body lying still for almost six weeks during the coma. He then had to attend various therapy sessions weekly to ensure his continued recovery.

Chris had accepted his situation and was anxious to get back to the office. He was also uneasy about the memory loss. He wanted to know why he was in the accident and what he had been doing the last few days before it occurred.

Finally, when Chris returned to his office, the entire executive staff surprised him with a "Welcome Back" luncheon ceremony in the cafeteria.

"Speech," everyone yelled, as Chris walked into the room.

Chris stood at the front of the room and raised his hands.

"All I have to say is, I thank everybody for their concerns and for the cards and flowers. I really appreciate how you have all been able to keep things running without my having been here. But then, if it were not for a leader like Ralph Cummings, things may not have run as smoothly. So I say, let's give credit where it is due, and that is with Ralph and his incredible managerial skills."

Chris began clapping his hands and the others followed. Ralph was embarrassed as was evident by his flushed face.

"OK everybody, let's get this show on the road so we can all get back to work," Ralph said.

Employees came up and shook Chris' hand and welcomed him back. A buffet had been set up and everybody eventually got a plate and sat at the array of tables. Chris spent most of the luncheon walking to each table talking with his staff. He was damn proud of all of them.

Upon Chris returning to his office after the luncheon, Ralph went to see him.

"Hey Boss," Ralph said walking into Chris' office.

"That was a great surprise Ralph. We have some great employees don't we?"

"We certainly do," Ralph responded.

"What can I do for you Ralph?"

"Things are going real well and you seem to be doing pretty good, even though I know you're not there yet. I have a favor to ask," Ralph responded as he dropped down into a chair in front of Chris' desk.

"Anything for my favorite employee," Chris said smiling.

"I was thinking of taking a short vacation to unwind. It's been a hectic couple of months and I could use the time off."

"I think that is a great idea," Chris responded. "What are you gonna do, if you don't mind me asking?"

"Not at all, actually I thought I might just go up to the Adirondacks, rent a small cabin, and do nothing for two weeks. Fish a little, hike a little, and generally just chill out."

"No problem at all Ralph. You have kept this place running since my accident, and as a friend, well I can't even begin to show my gratitude. When do you want to go?"

"Well, if you're feeling alright, I thought I might leave next Friday and I'd be back in two weeks or sooner if you needed me."

"Ralph, you are integral to our operation, and don't take this the wrong way, but I do believe we will make do for two weeks. As you see, we have a great crew here. Now you go find yourself a cabin and relax."

"Thanks, boss. But seriously, if you need me just call. That is, if my cell phone actually works up in the mountains," Ralph said with a smile and a wink.

"Get out of here and go pack your country best," Chris said.

"But if something comes up between now and next Friday, just let me know and I will cancel," Ralph said as he rose from the chair.

"Unless there is a catastrophe, you just plan on going," Chris replied waving him out of the office.

CHAPTER 9
Creating the DTTF

By the time Chris Hughes awoke from his coma and started on the road to recovery, the "People's Representatives" had been busy. They had a secret meeting of the Special Committee, which was held at a prestigious resort in the horse country one state over from the capital.

As the various members were gathering for the meeting, they all laughed when Ed Frendly stated, "I always like these meetings because we don't have to act like we oppose one another. I heard somebody the other day say that the two parties were basically just opposite cheeks of the same ass. I didn't like the 'ass' part, but the people don't know just how fucking accurate the statement is." he said with a laugh.

Ed Frendly had been around since his father, who was a member of CANE, got him elected. His cheeks and nose always had a red glow, and his first question at a special meeting was, "When are the cocktails being served?"

The meeting was chaired by Helen Ferguson. She had been a representative of the people for over 40 years and had lasted through many different administrations, having an innate ability to reach across the aisle when it served her to do so. However, she had been known to say ridiculous things. Once, during a hearing on alternative energy, she said, "We should not use wind turbines as the wind is a finite resource and if we use it up we will be without wind." However, she was very powerful in her position and at that time had the President's ear.

Joseph Mason was also present. He was a short robust man with thinning hair. A veteran, he had been around Washington since he got out of the service. Although he was a real war monger, he was always willing to help those that kept him in the position he had become accustomed to.

Barry Stewart was attending, as always at these special meetings, and he had a special talent for making things happen, even if rules had to be broken. He was small of stature with a weasel face and thin lips. He was always peering over his glasses which constantly sat at the end of his nose

Once everyone came to order, Helen Ferguson started the meeting without fanfare. "First of all, let me say that we are here at the request of our good friends at CANE. They have an issue that they find of great importance and therefore, as you all know, is of great importance to us as well."

She continued, explaining the specific issues brought to her by CANE.

"Our friends feel that this is an issue that must be handled as quickly as possible, if not immediately. They know that their continued friendship and support is important to us and also that our assistance with this matter will help sustain our relationship.

"It would appear that the best course of action would be to start a small agency that could handle the problems involved here, without all the usual formalities. This agency will deal primarily with the issues of our citizens trying to live off the grid, or trying to be self-reliant. The agency could use their position of authority to bring these people back into the fold and remain reliant on the goods and services of our good friends."

"This might not be an easy sell," Ed Frendly interjected. "This might cause some unknown issues with current agencies," he continued.

"Of course," Helen Ferguson continued, "We will need to sell this as a special agency dealing specifically with domestic terrorists. It would need to appear as though the purpose of the agency is to respond to those situations or incidents that represent a threat to our Homeland from within. It will be called the 'Domestic Terrorism Task Force' and it should not be made public by going through the House. We will need an Executive Order by the President, whereby the new agency will be concealed within an innocuous policy about immediate threats to our infrastructure and natural resources."

Joseph Mason interrupted, "We are going to have a major problem here with the FBI. They are already part of the Joint Terrorism Task Force (JTTF) and they will question why a separate agency is being formed to do the same thing they are doing. They will indicate there is duplication within the two agencies."

"I understand your concern Joseph," Helen Ferguson said, "But we will actually delineate the difference. As you know, it would seem that the FBI and the rest of the Joint Terrorism Task Force are more concerned with the violent aspect of terrorism as indicated by the literature they have promulgated."

As an example, Helen Ferguson showed a flyer that was disseminated by the FBI along with the Bureau of Justice Assistance, to gun stores. It showed potential indicators of suspicious activities that could "profile" someone as a suspected terrorist. It included:

- Provide identification that is inconsistent or suspect or demands identity "privacy."
- Significantly alters appearance from visit to visit (shaving beard, changing hair color, style of dress, etc.).
- Have missing hand/fingers, chemical burns, strange odors or bright colored stains on clothing.
- Make racist or extreme religious statements coupled with comments that are violent or appear to condone violence.
- Demonstrate interest in uses that do not seem consistent with the intended use of the item being purchased.
- Possess little knowledge of intended purchase items.
- Make bulk purchases of items to include: Weatherproof ammunition or match containers, Meals Ready to Eat, Night Vision Devices, night vision flashlights, gas masks, high capacity magazines, and Bi-pods or tri-pods for rifles.

"As you can see," Helen Ferguson continued, "these types of threats are considered suspect because they could identify a potential violent terrorist. Although the FBI doesn't seem to push the political agenda, it would seem that the DHS does. I received the following list of potential indicators of domestic terrorism from a retired law enforcement officer who explained he had received this list during a training course sponsored by DHS."

Helen Ferguson read the list of potential indicators.

- Expressions of libertarian philosophies (statement, bumper stickers, etc.).
- Second Amendment-oriented views such as NRA or gun club membership, or holding a CCW permit.
- Having survivalist literature such as "One Second After" or the "Patriots."
- Self-sufficiency to include stockpiling food, ammo, hand tools, or medical supplies.
- The fear of economic collapse including buying gold or barter items.
- Expressed fears of Big Brother or Big Government.
- Homeschooling.
- Declarations of Constitutional right and civil liberties.
- Belief in a New World Order Conspiracy.

"It is obvious that these indicators," Helen Ferguson continued, "reveal that the agenda is political. We will indicate that the DTTF is concerned with those situations where the activities deal with the misuse of property or resources which deny other citizens that use. We can label those persons as actual, not suspected, domestic terrorist, and therefore they fall under the purview of the DTTF. The violence aspect and political agenda will be left to the others.

"In regard to your concern about duplication, when was the last time that the government worried about duplication. The people see duplication in government and are used to having various agencies overlap responsibilities. Have people ever questioned having a Department of Environmental Conservation and a Department of Environmental Protection? I don't think duplication is an issue."

The representatives believed there was a concern that the FBI might try to pull the DTTF into the JTTF, so they discussed how it would have to be kept out of the hands of either the JTTF or the FBI.

Helen Ferguson indicated that Barry Stewart had been working on a solution. "Barry, would you like to provide us with your findings?"

"Yes, and thank you Helen. I have brought with me today a very trusted expert on our government organization. His name is Greg Bolton and he has done work for us previously so his loyalty to our group is unequivocal. He has conducted an in depth analysis of where this new agency might best be placed in order for it to remain somewhat obscure. He has come up with a suggestion and will now give us a presentation to explain his choice."

Greg Bolton walked to the front of the room. He didn't look like your normal analyst, standing six foot tall with a trim muscular build. His brown eyes were warm which was in contrast to his square jaw and military style haircut. His suit was tailored and his shoes highly shined. He spoke in a tone that, although not overtly loud, demanded attention.

Greg Bolton started his presentation by saying, "I know you are all familiar with the organization of the Department of Homeland Security (DHS). But please bear with me as I walk us through the various internal levels in order for you to see the depth in which we can bury this new agency."

Using a PowerPoint projector to show the various levels of the DHS as he spoke, he continued.

"DHS was established by the Security Act of 2002. Created in response to the September 11 attacks, its purpose was to consolidate U.S. executive branch organizations related to 'homeland security' into one Cabinet agency of the U.S. federal government. Even though the Department of Defense is charged with military actions abroad, the DHS works in the civilian sphere to protect the United States within and its stated goals are to prepare for, prevent, and respond to domestic emergencies, particularly terrorism.

"The DHS is the third largest Cabinet department of the government, with more than 200,000 employees. The only two departments larger are the Department of Defense and Veterans Affairs. We know that the DHS has received substantial criticism over excessive bureaucracy, waste, fraud, ineffectiveness, and as always, a lack of transparency. Even its information sharing centers have been accused of violating American civil liberties and targeting American citizens as potential threats to national security. What better place to hide a task force created to go after domestic terrorists?

"Now, as you can see here, under the DHS, a federal law enforcement agency called the U.S. Immigrations and Customs Enforcement (ICE) is responsible for identifying, investigating, and dismantling vulnerabilities regarding the nation's border, economic, transportation, and infrastructure security. ICE is the largest investigative arm of the DHS, and the second largest criminal investigation agency in the U.S. government, following the FBI. It is also the largest contributor to the nation's Joint Terrorism Task Force (JTTF). It has two primary components: Homeland Security Investigations (HSI) and Enforcement and Removal Operations (ERO).

"In my opinion, the obvious component is the Homeland Security Investigations (HSI). Within the HSI resides the National Security Investigations Division, which leads its effort to combat criminal enterprises by investigating vulnerabilities in the nation's border, infrastructure, economic, and transportation systems. It also prevents acts of terrorism by targeting people, money and materials that support terrorism and criminal activities. Its mission is strengthened by the unique investigative authorities that HSI commands.

"Now one of those authorities is the National Security Unit (NSU), which combines the HSI's national security and terrorism efforts into a single force. The unit has oversight of all counterterrorism investigations within ICE and works directly with the National Security Council and ICE senior leadership to carry out interagency policy.

"The newly formed Domestic Terrorism Task Force (DTTF) could be concealed within the NSU. Normally, the National Security Unit's Counterterrorism Section oversees all HSI special agents assigned to the JTTF, which is, as we know, a partnership between various American law enforcement agencies, to include the Federal Bureau of Investigation.

"However, the DTTF needs to be kept autonomous and not subject to any outside agency's purview. Hidden within the NSU, it would have its own organizational structure and report through channels eventually to those who controlled the purse strings. All special agents of the DTTF would be kept independent and isolated from other units. These agents would swear allegiance to the fighting of domestic terrorism and it will be recommended that they not associate with agents of other units or divisions, but not mandated. In other words, they will be considered 'special' and an elite group."

Greg Bolton concluded his presentation by saying, "As this analysis reveals, we can hide the DTTF in plain sight. Being creative and using the multi-levels that already exist within a huge organization, I believe the DTTF will be well buried in a wilderness of mirrors. This will also keep it from the prying eyes, and oversight, of the JTTF."

The people's representatives indeed found a place to hide the Domestic Terrorism Task Force in plain sight. Now they needed to find agents, and this task would be a very delicate process.

Upon all representatives agreeing with the creation and placement of the newly formed DTTF, Helen Ferguson indicated that she would get the President to sign off on this by executive order."

The President listened to the proposal and was more than eager to get involved. He believed that, even though these forms of domestic terrorism didn't involve violence, they were every bit as insidious and represented a clear and present danger to the economic stability of the country.

First he created preliminary regulations that declared the misuse of property or resources, denying others that use, without proper licensure, an offense under the new "Domestic Terrorism Act." Anyone convicted of an offense under these regulations would be considered a "domestic terrorist." Various specifics were delineated such as: Collecting water, or using it to produce power, without a permit, having a solar system off grid without a permit, inspection, and approval; using seeds that were not certified and approved before use. The use of wood stoves was still under review, but that also was being examined by the Environmental Protection Agency. However, the President wanted it under this regulation so those using them would need an approval and a permit, or be considered a domestic terrorist. He was also working on an angle to restrict the use of cash. As part of this Executive Order, not only was the "Domestic

Terrorism Act" established, but the "Domestic Terrorism Task Force" was created. All with a stroke of his pen.

Now that the DTTF had been created by a Presidential Executive Order, a Director had to be selected. After a thorough search was conducted, the position was filled by an individual by the name of Wolfgang Drescher. He was known for his no bullshit demeanor and unquestionable loyalty to his superiors. He stood five feet ten inches tall with an erect posture and barrel chest. A chiseled face, blue eyes, and close cropped blond hair, he reminded one of a figure from a recruiting poster for the Nazis.

Wolfgang Drescher had served as a Counterintelligence Agent with the U.S. Army Military Intelligence. As a Senior Counterintelligence Special Agent he was assigned to a U.S. Special Forces group where he successfully graduated both Airborne, and Ranger Schools. Upon leaving the Army he had been employed as a Diplomatic Security Special Agent with the U.S. Department of State. He had served in both, Iraq and Afghanistan, as well as other countries. He had both a TOP SECRET security clearance and Sensitive Compartmented Information (SCI) access, and had never been involved with U.S. Law Enforcement or The Department of Homeland Security. It was felt he would be a good choice for this new position.

Wolfgang Drescher, as the Director of the Domestic Terrorism Task Force had his work cut out for him. He needed a training facility and didn't want it in Virginia because the FBI Academy was in Quantico, Virginia, and he didn't want to be near any of their installations. Through some contacts, he was able to locate an adequate complex which would remain TOP SECRET.

Next on the agenda were agents. They would be drawn from various military and government agencies, but not law enforcement or DHS assets. All prospective agents would have to pass a series of psychological tests to determine if they had the mental capacity to be part of a "special" group that would be called upon to locate, and eliminate if necessary, domestic terrorists, as defined by their Directive for Operations. Once prospective agents had passed the psychological portion of the tests, and were found mentally suitable for the requirements, they would have to pass a physical fitness test, qualify with multiple firearms by shooting 90% or better in full tactical gear, and pass further oral interview processes. If they passed these stages, they were considered a "potential" agent and assigned to a "Yellow Team."

In a "Yellow Team' they would train with certified members of the unit and then proceed with specialized training in surveillance, counter-surveillance, intelligence collection, and counter-intelligence. Eventually, they would be sent to the Special Response Team (SRT) certification school at the U.S. Army base located at Fort Benning, Georgia, where they would obtain further specialized training to include sniper school. Upon the successful completion of their initial training "potential" agents would be considered "Agents" and become a member of a "Green Team" which meant they were ready for full time duty and operational.

The headquarters for the DTTF was housed in an innocuous facility near the Aberdeen proving grounds in Maryland. Satellite operational facilities were being placed in rural areas around the country where assets could be maintained. The east coast was completed with an office in the northeast in Albany, New York. This facility would be responsible for Pennsylvania, New York, Connecticut, Vermont, Maine, New Hampshire,

Massachusetts, and Rhode Island. Headquarters would be responsible for the mid-east coast and a facility in Huntsville, Alabama would handle the lower east coast. Further facilities were heading west at a fast pace. Things were going as planned and at an incredible speed.

Operations were already being conducted and funding, which seemed unending, had allowed for the procurement of several Bell OH-58D Kiowa Warrior helicopters for aerial reconnaissance and a dozen Sikorsky UH-60 Blackhawk helicopters for the operational insertion of agents if required.

* * *

Before a mission in the Mid-East Coast Sector, a briefing was being held by the Facility Commander, Chad Powers. Wolfgang Drescher attended, as he wanted to personally see how mission briefings were being handled. After hearing the mission, one of the DTTF agents, Craig Davis, asked, "Will we also be spending efforts on domestic terrorists that are violently trying to destroy the country, or just self-reliant type individuals?"

Drescher became enraged and immediately interrupted the briefing. Almost spitting while he spoke, he said "Apparently you don't fucking understand our mission. I will not tolerate anyone who questions it. Our purpose is to follow the directives handed down to us by our superiors. Ours is not to question those directives, but to perform our duties as prescribed. If you have a problem with that, you are in the wrong fucking place. You can turn in your god damn badge on the way out. What is your name agent?"

The agent quickly replied, "My name is Craig Davis, and no sir, I'm certainly not questioning our mission. I was just wondering if our mission might be expanded. I'm just happy to be here sir."

"Well stop wondering and start listening!" Drescher spat. "You are either a part of the team, or you are out."

Drescher then spun on a heal and went directly to the Facility Commanders office.

After the briefing, Chad Powers returned to his office and, upon seeing Drescher there, knew he was going to hear more.

Drescher slammed the door behind Chad as he entered his own office and immediately started, "I can't believe we have fucking agents that would question our mission. That son of a bitch Davis needs to be watched."

Chad Powers indicated that he didn't believe Davis was actually questioning the mission, but was just trying to sound patriotic. "Just sounds like he wants to go after the bad guys."

Drescher continued, "We have no place for fucking patriotism here. What do we know about this agent? I assume he has passed all training or he wouldn't be here?"

"He has," Chad replied. "He has been in the upper percentage of all the training and takes orders well."

"Is there anything we know about him?" Drescher asked.

"Actually he is rather a loner, but then many of these types of guys are. It is believed that he still has a friend that he went to college with, who is with the FBI. It is my understanding that they occasionally meet for a drink. But he doesn't try to hide the fact. Just two friends getting together."

"That is un-fucking-acceptable," Drescher sneered, "I want Agent Davis transferred to the Northeast Sector up in New York. That should keep him away from his FBI friend. And I want him watched. I'll fill in Max Archer, the Northeast Sector Facility's Commander, personally."

"Yes sir, I'll make it happen directly," Chad replied.

"You better," Drescher stated as he turned and left the office.

CHAPTER 10
Total Recall

Chris' recovery had been going real well, and he almost felt like himself. Of course the short term memory loss was still nagging at him and he hoped his memory would soon return. It had been several months and he was beginning to wonder if it would ever come back.

He was now working at his office every day and was getting back into his usual routine.

Almost six months later, Chris was sitting in his office comparing expenditures from the previous to the current year. He saw a charge from a company called Intel-Tech made in the past year. At first the name didn't ring a bell. Then all of a sudden, memory from the days before the accident started coming back. A few short flashes at first, but then his mind was flooded with precise images of those last few days.

It was miraculous how quickly the memories returned. The details became crystal clear which were a relief, yet frightening at the same time. He sat at his desk remembering the CANE Conference and the making of the recording at the meeting. He recalled making copies and hiding two of the flash drives between the drawers of his desk at his home office.

Suddenly a chill came over him, "the fire." he thought. The fire had destroyed his office completely along with the flash drives.

Pictures of that day months ago played through his mind like a movie; Him making a third copy and taking it to the woods and caching it in the ground. He remembered the approximate place, but not the exact spot. He also recalled using a GPS to obtain the coordinates and that it was on his return from caching the flash drive that the accident had occurred, the GPS unit having been in the vehicle. The car had been totaled. Then it became crystal clear. He had uploaded the coordinates to his cloud.

Chris accessed his cloud and found two innocuous numbers in a file with the name "cache." That would be the coordinates.

Chris could see the location where he had entered the woods in his mind and felt he could probably find the cache even without the coordinates. He would have to check it out. He thought he might be able to walk in and see if he could easily locate where he had buried the cache and maybe retrieve it with little problem.

Late that afternoon, he informed his administrative assistant, Sheila, that he would be out of the office for the rest of the day and would see her in the morning.

"See you in the morning," Sheila responded.

Chris headed towards the wooded trail and realized he had not been in that area since his accident. He was a little apprehensive driving on the road where the accident had occurred, but he fought the feeling and continued.

When he approached the area where the parking place had been, he was stunned. Instead of a small parking area and woods, he found a high chain link fence around the entire property with signs that indicated it was a construction site and there was no trespassing.

Chris, confused, continued past the site and turned around. He then proceeded directly to his house. Chris wondered when and how this had occurred. Maybe Ralph knew something about it he thought to himself. After all, he lived in the same area,

The following morning Chris called Ralph to his office.

"Good morning Boss," Ralph said as he entered Chris' office.

"Good morning Ralph."

"What's up?" Ralph asked cheerfully.

"Well, actually I have two things. First of all, my memory came back yesterday, and I seem to remember all the details from those last few weeks I was missing."

"That is fantastic," Ralph said sounding elated. "I know you have waited a long time, but the doctors said it would return eventually. I'm really happy for you Boss."

"Thanks Ralph, I know you went through a lot yourself because of this accident."

"That's what family is for," Ralph said smiling ear to ear.

"Yesterday I thought I might go to that place up the road from my house where I used to go hiking thinking the exercise in the fresh air would do me good. So I took the afternoon off and headed up there. I haven't been up in that direction since my accident as I don't need to for work or anything else. When I got over there I noticed that the wooded area where I used to hike is now a construction site. Any idea what's going on there?"

"Oh, they are building a new corporate complex for some big company, why?" Ralph said.

"I was just curious," Chris said trying not to sound as though he really cared. "I used to like to hike there as it was only a short distance from my house. It's a shame that it is all gone now," Chris continued

"They seem to be doing a nice job and are trying to leave the area natural. They even left a lot of the woods around the perimeter which will keep the property natural looking. But between the high chain linked fence and the security patrol, I don't think you want to try hiking there anymore," Ralph said jokingly.

"I guess not," Chris said with a chuckle. "Anyway, I was just wondering. I'm sure I will find another place to hike."

"Well if you need some suggestions, just ask," Ralph said getting up.

"I will," Chris replied.

Ralph smiled and left Chris' office returning to his own.

That evening, sitting in his home office, Chris wondered how he would get inside the chain link fence to retrieve the flash drive. He could see that the woods to the left of the construction site were still untouched, but it didn't mean it would stay that way. He knew he was no ninja and wasn't sure how he would retrieve the last remaining copy of the recording.

During dinner, he suddenly remembered what his father had told him about Bob Armstrong. If he ever needed help, Bob was the guy to go to. The only problem was he didn't know Bob or where he might be. He thought Ralph might be able to help.

The next day, Chris called Ralph to his office. Ralph entered and dropped down in a chair.

"What's up Boss?"

Chris wasn't sure how to approach this, so he thought he would just be direct.

"I need to find a guy that my father told me about," Chris said casually. "His name is Robert Armstrong, but my father said he goes by Bob."

"Bob Armstrong, you say. Any special reason why you need him?" Ralph asked.

"Just need to talk to him about something. Nothing special."

"I'm not familiar with the name; do you know anything about him?" Ralph continued.

"Not really, but I thought being he was a friend of my father's, you might have heard him mention the name."

"You know, I think he may have. Your father said something about him being involved with self-reliance. As a matter of fact, I belong to the National Council for Self-Reliance, known as the NCSR, and I believe there is a member by the name of Bob Armstrong. Of course I can't be sure this is the same Bob Armstrong."

"I didn't know you were interested in being self-reliant," Chris said.

"Oh I have always been. It's just a delicate balance between the corporate world and my private life. Actually there is an upcoming conference in Hartford, Connecticut and I believe a Bob Armstrong will be a speaker there. I have a brochure in my office. I will get it and be right back."

Ralph left Chris' office and returned to his. He grabbed the brochure for the NCSR Conference and Trade Show and headed back to Chris' office.

"Yup, I was right, there is a Bob Armstrong giving a seminar at the conference on Practical Self-Reliance. You want me to speak to him for you?"

"No, that's alright, I thought I might attend the conference myself and have a talk with him and determine if he is the one my father knew."

"I'll get you pre-registered to attend the NCSR conference and Trade Show as a guest of mine," Ralph said.

"That would be great, when is the conference?"

"It is on a Saturday and Sunday the second weekend of next month," Ralph replied.

"I won't be staying for the whole conference, as I just want to determine if this is the Bob Armstrong I'm looking for. I'll drive up by myself so you can stay for the whole weekend. Can you make reservations for us in the same hotel? We can go up Friday night, have a nice dinner together, and get into the conference first thing in the morning."

"I don't see any problem with that, I'll make arrangements. I already have a room booked, so I'll just add an additional room for you."

"And Ralph, I want to meet this guy by myself," Chris stated. "No offense, it's just a little personal and nothing you need to get involved with," Chris continued with a smile, hoping this would appease Ralph.

Ralph smiled back saying, "No problem Boss, your personal business is your business."

Ralph left Chris' office wondering what this was about.

CHAPTER 11
The Undercover

The Director of the FBI was not happy about the formation of the Domestic Terrorism Task Force and was suspicious of their purpose. He called a meeting of several of his top personnel to discuss the matter.

Harold Wolfson was the Director of the FBI and had worked his way up the ranks to this position. The Director of the FBI is an appointment by the President and confirmed by the Senate. It was unusual, at least in the recent past, for the Director to have come from within the FBI. He had been totally dedicated to the FBI since being recruited as a potential agent while still in college. He defended the Bureau's purpose, and was extremely protective of its position within the government.

Wolfson stood six feet three inches tall, and even though his position required him to spend too much time in the office, he stayed active playing golf, tennis, and racquetball. This kept his muscles toned and he was trim for his age of fifty-five.

The meeting was being held in the vast seating area of the Director's private office at FBI headquarters. The headquarters was housed in the J. Edgar Hoover Building located at 935 Pennsylvania Ave. NW, Washington, D.C. It had been designed as a concrete fortress to be a symbol of strength. However, over the years, it had deteriorated to a point that concrete was crumbling, fire alarms failed to function, and the buildings systems were badly out dated. It was estimated that it would cost over eighty million dollars for repairs and upgrades. Another problem was that the building was located in downtown Washington and couldn't accommodate all the employees of the agency in the region, so they were scattered among twenty-two annex buildings in the Washington area. Therefore a location was being sought for a new "Headquarters" building in either Maryland or Virginia and firms had already been selected to bid on the project. But a new building was still in the distant future.

Also attending the meeting was the Deputy Director of the FBI, a position just under the Director, and the Director's second hand man. His name was Michael Hernandez and after serving in the United States Marine Corps he had attended college. He had been with the Bureau ever since. Much shorter than the Director, he stood five feet ten inches tall with a stocky build. Even with his current duties, he had also kept in shape and often played racquetball with the Director. Although having been asked, he never played golf as he felt a golf course was a good waste of a rifle range.

The Director had also invited, Alaister Mitchell, the Director for the National Security Branch of the FBI. He oversaw the Counterterrorism Division, Counterintelligence Division, and the Weapons of Mass Destruction Directorate.

Alaister Mitchell was an Army Ranger and a member of the Los Angeles S.W.A.T. team before joining the FBI and had moved up quickly in the organization. He stood just six feet tall, and although he had a lean build, it was that type of sinewy physique often found in members of special operations.

Lastly, the Director had asked Jacob Cohen to attend, who was in charge of The Office of General Counsel. He was slight of build, and at five feet eleven inches tall, appeared shorter because of his hunched posture. He was, however, very well versed in the legal boundaries of the Bureau, and knew how to bend the rules if required, without putting the Bureau in jeopardy.

Once all attendees were present and seated, Director Wolfson began.

"As you all know, the Bureau is a member of the U.S. Intelligence Community and we report to both the Attorney General and the Director of National Intelligence. We are the leading U.S. counterterrorism, counterintelligence, and criminal investigative organization, and we have spearheaded the counterterrorist movement in this country for years. We are the leading member in the Joint Terrorism Task Force with others such as various components of the Department of Homeland Security, local law enforcement and some specialized agencies taking a back seat to us. Does anyone here disagree with this assessment?"

Wolfson looked around the room and everyone nodded in agreement. He continued.

"However, it would seem lately that everybody wants to get in on the act. First, all of a sudden, the President wants to create his own Domestic Terrorism Council within our own Department of Justice. I'm not sure what they plan to do. And now, we find out that a new organization has been created called the "Domestic Terrorism Task Force" to be regulated by a new "Domestic Terrorism Act." We had to find out about it from friends in the community, because apparently it is being kept classified. Has anyone here heard about it, other than my Deputy Director Michael Hernandez?"

"I have Director," Alaister Mitchell responded making a gesture slightly raising his right hand. "Apparently, this organization is being kept very hush-hush. But it is hard to keep a secret in our community."

"You are right Mr. Mitchell, and excuse my language, but this is freaking bullshit," Director Wolfson said vehemently, looking around the room at those attending. "They have buried this thing so far up the ass of the DHS it would take a proctologist to find it," he continued.

"I started poking around when this thing first started, but nobody wanted to talk," Mitchell threw in.

"I realize this," the Director interrupted. "But we need to know more about this organization. Damn, we are the top law enforcement agency in the world. Let's get some information about them and let's do it now."

"Actually sir, I have initiated an operation that I'm hoping will provide us with valuable information," Mitchell stated.

"An operation! What kind of an operation?" Wolfson responded looking directly at Mitchell.

"I have an undercover agent inside DTTF."

"You what?" Wolfson said, not believing what he had heard. "When were you going to say something?" Wolfson continued sounding annoyed.

"Well Director, this has only happened recently, and I thought I would wait until we found out if our undercover was going to be able to develop any valuable information," Mitchell replied. "When we heard through the grapevine that agents were being solicited for a new organization, which we were able to determine was the DTTF, I felt that if we could get an undercover agent inside at any level, we might be able to develop more information about the DTTF.

"It took a lot of time and effort to create a new background for our undercover agent that would not be penetrated by this new organization. We certainly wouldn't want the undercover traced back to us. Because of his short duration inside the DTTF, we haven't yet found anything of much value," Mitchell continued.

"Well I'll be a son-of-a- bitch," Wolfson said smiling. "Tell me about this undercover agent."

"Our undercover is in the position of an operational agent so he isn't yet privy to any information from the upper echelon, but he can provide information about their mission. It appears that the DTTF's main purpose is to target a specific segment of domestic terrorism. It looks like they are more concerned with citizens that have a desire to live off the grid, or be self-reliant from the normal system. They are particularly concerned with activities such as collecting water or using it for power, having solar collection systems not tied to the grid, using heirloom seeds for gardening, and things like that. We haven't quite yet been able to figure out why they have such a narrow mission."

Michael Hernandez, the Deputy Director interrupted.

"It sounds like they are being driven by a possible outside source that apparently has concerns in this area. Maybe this is a rogue agency being used for purposes other than to protect our country. Anyway, continue Mr. Mitchell."

"Our undercover is located at the DTTF Headquarters, housed in an innocuous facility near the Aberdeen proving grounds in Maryland," Mitchell continued. "That facility is also responsible for the mid-east coast. However, we have learned one interesting bit of information that I feel we may be able to exploit.

"Our undercover agent is using the name Clint Robertson, but his real name is Ethan Kelly. He is friends with another one of our agents by the name of Stuart McDonald. They went to the FBI Academy together. Before going undercover, Kelly was having lunch with McDonald one day and was told that he, McDonald, was still friends with a college buddy who was now an agent in an operational unit with the DTTF, his name is Craig Davis. McDonald indicated that even though it is frowned upon by the DTTF, both he and Davis decided to remain friends, but would keep it low key.

"Kelly knowing he was possibly going undercover with the DTTF, decided to write down the name 'Craig Davis' after the lunch. Of course, Kelly made no mention of his possible undercover assignment, and since going undercover has not had any contact with McDonald. However, since he has gone undercover, Kelly has run into Craig Davis during a mission briefing at headquarters.

"Kelly has kept his distance for obvious reasons, but thought we might be able to use the relationship between Davis and McDonald to carefully solicit further information. Unfortunately, Davis was transferred to a new DTTF facility in Albany. New York, before Kelly could attempt to get closer to him."

Wolfson cut in, "This might not be a bad thing. We have an undercover in the DTTF Headquarters. We have a DTTF agent in the northeast facility who remains friends with another one of our agents, what was his name, McDonald?"

"Yes sir," Mitchell replied.

Wolfson continued, "But maybe we can get Special Agent McDonald up in the Albany, New York area, say for some type of a law enforcement seminar. He could then use that opportunity to meet with his friend Davis for a dinner or drink. This would allow him to reestablish contact with Davis. If McDonald feels things are going good, he could mention that he might be getting a transfer up to that area. At that point we may even be able to have McDonald turn this Davis as an informant for us. Especially if we find that something illegal is going on. We can use that information to secure the confidence of Craig, ensuring him that we will keep him protected from prosecution.

"Of course, we need to be careful here. We will need to get with Special Agent McDonald to determine if he is both capable and willing to conduct such an operation. As a Special Agent of the FBI, I can't see him not being loyal to the Bureau. But first, we have him sign a special non-disclosure document, where under penalty of prosecution, even if he cannot accept the assignment, he can never discuss it.

"What do you think Mr. Cohen? Being from the Office of general Counsel, do you see any problem with this scenario?"

"No sir," Cohen responded. "If this does turn out to be some type of a rogue agency we can show that we were on top of the situation. This will strengthen our position in the law enforcement community as well as in the eyes of the people. Also, it is my understanding that this DTTF was initiated by an executive order by the President. Executive orders are subject to judicial review, and may be struck down if deemed by the courts to be unsupported by statute or the Constitution.

"If the agency is legit, no problem. We can always pull out our undercover with no harm, no foul," Cohen concluded.

"Thank you Mr. Cohen. Then let's continue with this Mr. Mitchell," Wolfson concluded. "And keep me in the loop; I want current updates on any new information."

With that, the meeting was concluded.

Less than a week later, Mitchell had Special Agent McDonald in for an interview.

"Good morning Special Agent McDonald, have a seat,"

"Thank you sir, am I in some kind of trouble?"

"Not at all," Mitchell replied smiling. "We just want to talk to you about a situation that we thought you might be able to help us with. But first, because of the sensitive nature of this situation, I will need you so sign a non-disclosure document in regard to our conversation here today. You understand its purpose, I'm sure."

"Of course sir, if I reveal anything from our conversation here forth, I will be prosecuted."

"It seems like you know the ropes," Mitchell replied.

Mitchell had Agent McDonald sign the document laid out in front of him on the desk.

"Now we can continue," Mitchell said.

Mitchell was careful, but explained about the known relationship between Special Agent McDonald and the DTTF Agent Craig Davis. He explained how they would like him to stay in contact with Davis. "We are very interested in this new DTTF organization and are trying to collect information that might not be available through normal channels.

"Possibly we could have you attend a law enforcement conference in Albany and you could arrange to have dinner with Davis," Mitchell suggested.

"Is Craig Davis suspected of doing something wrong?" McDonald inquired.

"Of course not, we are not specifically concerned with Davis. He just happens to be inside an organization we know little about. He might be in a position to provide us with valuable information."

"So you are asking that I use a friendship to gain information?" McDonald asked.

"We're asking that you do your duty as an FBI agent and obtain information that might be valuable to both the FBI and our country, by maintaining a relationship that already exists. We are not asking that you hurt your friend, only use him for information that he might, or might not be able to provide."

"I didn't mean to sound like I was troubled by the request sir, I was merely clarifying what was being asked of me," McDonald stated. "I will always perform my duties as an agent to the utmost of my abilities."

"So you would be willing to take on such an additional assignment?"

"Of course sir."

Mitchell outlined how he would make arrangements for McDonald to attend an upcoming law enforcement conference in the Albany area. It would be up to McDonald to make arrangements for a dinner, which he could try to arrange before the conference, to ensure that Davis was available. If Mitchell felt comfortable, and thought further meetings with his friend could be arranged, then he should tell Davis that there was a good chance he, McDonald, might be getting a transfer up to the Albany area. McDonald should try to get an idea as to how Davis felt in regard to that.

Arrangements were made for McDonald to attend the conference in Albany, and even before he left, his friend Davis confirmed their meeting for dinner, stating it would be great getting together once again.

CHAPTER 12
NCSR

The National Council for Self-Reliance (NCSR) was holding their Annual Conference and Trade Show at the Connecticut Convention Center in Hartford, Connecticut. With a large exhibit space and meeting rooms for seminars, it was the first time the conference was held in the northeast. It was always on a Saturday and Sunday, as many of the self-reliant attendees had a hard time getting away during the week.

Ticket sales had been good and it was expected to be a great conference. They had almost one hundred vendors for the exhibit space and speakers for several dozen seminars. Seminars would include topics such as Installing Off Grid Solar Systems, Water Catchment Systems, Square Foot Gardening, Food Preservation and Storage, as well as a new seminar called Practical Self-reliance.

The day before the conference, Chris and Ralph drove separately to Hartford, Connecticut and checked into the Marriott Hartford Downtown, an AAA diamond hotel that rose twenty-two stories above the Connecticut River in downtown Hartford. It was attached to the Connecticut Convention Center.

When Chris arrived he called Ralph on his cell phone and informed him that he was there. "Let's meet for dinner at 6:00 PM."

"That would be fine," Ralph replied. "I'll see you then."

After a pleasant dinner of conversation about work and the conference, Chris asked Ralph if he would like to have a night cap at the lounge before heading up to their respective rooms.

"I would love to Boss, but I have a couple of calls I need to make and I don't want to wait too late to do so," Ralph replied.

"No problem Ralph, and please start calling me Chris," he said with a smile.

"No problem Boss," Ralph replied with a wink. "I'll see you in the morning Chris," he said as he excused himself and rose from the table.

"Do we want to meet down here in the morning for breakfast before the conference opens?" Chris asked.

"That would be great," Ralph responded. "The conference check-in starts at 9:00 AM, so let's say we meet in the restaurant at 7:30 AM."

"I'll see you then," Chris said as he too rose from his chair.

They both proceeded to the lobby where Chris turned towards the lounge and Ralph headed for the bank of elevators.

The following morning Chris went to the front desk and requested a late checkout for his room, then met Ralph for breakfast. Ralph explained to Chris the type of vendors that would be present and he also had a listing of the various seminars that would be taking place.

"I see that Bob Armstrong has his seminar at 11:00 AM in meeting room three," Ralph indicated pointing at the itinerary for the seminars, which was laid out in front of him.

"I will be attending as I don't want to just stand outside waiting for him after he concludes," Chris replied.

"That works well for me," Ralph stated. "I am actually a Chapter Chairman for the Lower New York Area, and we have an executive meeting at 11:00 AM as well. When you are done with Bob Armstrong, give me a call on the cell phone. Maybe we can do lunch before you leave."

"That would be fine," Chris replied. "When we get checked in, maybe we can walk around to some of the booths and you can explain what I'm looking at. I'm actually getting interested in learning more about this self reliance stuff."

Chris and Ralph finished their breakfast and walked to the connected conference center. People were already lined up at the check in area. There were two lines. One was for those who had not pre-registered, and another for those that had. Ralph had pre-registered for both Chris and himself so they got in that line.

Check-in was painless, just presenting your pre-registration ticket, and showing a form of identification. An attendee badge was printed which was slipped into a clear flat pouch on a neck lanyard. You were informed that you must wear this in plain sight at all times in the conference and trade show area. You then moved to the line at the entrance to the conference and trade show.

Upon entering, Chris was rather surprised at the amount of vendors set up. Some of the booths were very impressive and some were just small mom and pop shops with a banner hanging at the rear of their booth.

As Chris started to walk through the aisles with Ralph he saw a wide array of products for the self reliant, preppers (a term he wasn't familiar with), and those who just wanted to be prepared for an emergency. There were various freeze dried food manufacturers, solar ovens, disaster preparedness products, emergency medical kits, water storage containers, canning and food preparation devices such as dehydrators, and many alternative power sources to include solar, hydroelectric, wind turbines, and generators. There were even various types of wood and pellet stoves. He was amazed at the selection of products, and he found himself picking up brochures for various products that interested him.

Chris and Ralph took a break at one of the side food vendor areas getting a cup of coffee and a pastry.

"I am actually surprised that I find myself very interested in some of this stuff," Chris said to Ralph. "I had no idea of the extent of this self reliant culture. I see people here that are not just farmers and country folk, but normal people."

Ralph laughed and said, "Chris this is not a bunch of crazies waiting for the Apocalypse, they are just normal people who want to be independent. In the 1950's most people were much less dependent on others, and it was just a way of life. Today, because of the direction our country has taken and the government creating an entitlement society, many people don't even understand being self reliant. It is a shame really, as they don't realize that they are dependent on a system, and if it fails, they will have a real problem maintaining their normal life."

"I agree with you Ralph. I haven't often thought about it, but we are very dependent on others for almost all of our needs. I think it is time for me to change some of my life's patterns."

"There is no time like today. It looks like you are enjoying yourself, and I'm glad you came. Even if this Bob Armstrong isn't the guy you are looking for, it would seem like your visiting the conference was a positive experience."

"Wow, look at the time," Chris said looking at his watch. "I better get heading over to the meeting rooms so I can attend Bob Armstrong's seminar. I'll call you when I get out."

"I have to head to the executive meeting as well; I'll see you a little later."

At that point, both Chris and Ralph got up and headed in different directions.

Chris got to the meeting room for Bob Armstrong's seminar in plenty of time to find a seat close to the front of the room and made himself comfortable. He could see that there was a row of tables at the front of the room with various objects laid out, some looking as though they were homemade.

Ralph attended the executive meeting of the NCSR which was only for officers of the organization and chapter chairmen. After the meeting was brought to order, minutes from the last meeting were read; the Executive Director opened the meeting to new business.

One of the members was concerned with new legislation and directives aimed at self-reliant people. It would seem that even the Department of Justice was now starting a division dealing with domestic terrorism.

A discussion ensued about how the government had really been trying to make, who they call "survivalists" and "Preppers" into some type of villains, or as they called them, "domestic terrorists." There was a time when being prepared, was something to be proud of. Now the government tried to dictate their agenda in order to make sure people stayed dependent on them. One agency said "you should have three days worth of food on hand for an emergency" and another said "if you have more than that you are a hoarder." "What will they be calling us next?" was a question asked.

Everyone agreed that the government was getting out of hand, but nobody seemed to have an idea of what to do. The discussion continued.

Bob Armstrong entered meeting room number three to a full house. He walked to the front of the room, and stood behind the row of tables. Bob was very casually dressed as were many of the attendees at the conference. Wearing a black Polo shirt with a red NCSR logo over the left breast, khakis, and beige light hiking boots, he presented a neat and professional appearance. Chris wished he hadn't worn the blazer. But at least he had donned a turtleneck instead of a shirt and tie, he thought to himself.

"Good morning, I'm Bob Armstrong," he said in a loud and clear voice.

"Many of the attendees yelled, "Good morning Bob."

"First of all, I am not an expert on this subject." Bob continued. "I just happen to be a person who tries to live a self-reliant lifestyle, and would like others to do so as well.

"I hear many people say they can't be self-reliant because they don't live in the country or on a homestead. Well let me tell you something. Yes you can!

"During today's seminar on Practical Self-Reliance I hope to show that whether you live in the city, the suburbs, or the country, there are many things you can do to reduce your dependency on others. Even if they are only little things, the more you can do for yourself, the less dependent you are on others."

Bob was a good speaker and spoke in a firm yet relaxed manner. He was knowledgeable yet able to interject humor into his presentation, and you could see that the attendees felt comfortable with him.

In Bob's presentation, he discussed food and how, even if you lived in the city, most people could at least grow a little. He described a friend who lived on the third floor of an apartment building yet grew tomatoes and herbs on his balcony. He talked about Farmer's Markets and Food Co-Ops, for those who really couldn't grow anything themselves. He discussed food preservation, storage and cooking options.

He then had a very interesting section about useful practices and skills that would help you in your efforts to being self reliant. Recycling, supplies, and even a short discussion on banks and investments was included.

Finally sections on water, light, alternative power, sanitation and hygiene, staying warm and cool, and transportation options were presented.

Chris understood that most of the topics were short and concise, as Bob only had an hour to present his seminar. However, the information provided was just enough to give you a basic understanding of the topic, and made you want to search for further details. What Chris really liked was all the objects that Bob was able to show to illustrate some of his points. Many he had made himself, such as a five gallon bucket clothes washer, a solar oven, and more. Chris was actually surprised when the seminar concluded, as he had thought this would be the longest hour of his life, but in actuality, time had flown by and he had enjoyed it.

Upon conclusion of Bob's seminar, he received a loud round of applause from the attendees, and many rushed to the front of the room to speak with Bob personally, or just shake his hand.

Bob was pleasant with each and everyone and at the same time collected his stuff from the table and placed it in a large box on the floor. Chris stood off to one side, by the door, so when Bob exited the room he could speak with him in the hallway.

As Bob finished with the last person, he placed his box onto a handcart. He then set the solar over on top of that and exited the room. As he started down the hallway, Chris walked up beside him.

"Excuse me Mr. Armstrong," Chris started in a low voice. "This may sound a little strange, but I am looking for a Bob Armstrong that knew my father Phillip Parker. Might that person be you?"

Bob Armstrong stopped in his tracks and looked at Chris for a moment before answering.

"So you must be Christopher," Bob replied with a smile.

"Yes I am," Chris responded very surprised that Bob knew his name. "But everybody calls me Chris."

"Well I have heard a lot about you, all good of course," Bob said outstretching his hand.

Chris reached out and shook Bob's hand and continued. "I have something very important to discuss with you, but I don't wish to do so in a hallway. I'm sure you understand."

"Well once I get this stuff to my vehicle I could meet you in the lounge area and we could discuss it there."

"I would rather not as it is very sensitive. I hate to sound mysterious or anything like that, and I certainly don't want to inconvenience you, but would you be willing to come to my room at the hotel where we might have more privacy?"

Bob thought for a moment and said smiling, "That would not be a problem at all Chris, and it would be a pleasure. However, there are several seminars I plan on attending this afternoon and I'm having an early dinner with a few friends I haven't seen in a while. If this can wait, I would be more than happy to meet you at eight o'clock this evening. If not, I could change my plans."

"Eight would be just fine Mr. Armstrong."

Bob interrupted Chris, "Please call me Bob. Everybody does."

"Well Bob," Chris said smiling back, "I really appreciate your being willing to meet with me later. I am in room 309 at the attached Marriott."

"I'm at the same hotel," Bob stated.

"Well I don't want to hold you up any further Bob, and I will see you at eight."

With that, Chris let Bob continue with his handcart which he had been holding during the entire conversation. I should have asked if I could help him with his stuff, Chris thought to himself.

Chris pulled out his cell phone and placed a call to Ralph, who answered on the second ring.

"Hey Chris, how did the seminar go? Was Bob Armstrong the one you were looking for?"

"It went well and yes, he was. Want to meet over at the hotel for a nice lunch, instead of the stuff they are serving here? I also need to extend my room for another night"

"That would great; I'll meet you over there in about fifteen minutes."

"I'll wait for you in the lobby," Chris replied and ended the call.

Approximately fifteen minutes later, Ralph entered the lobby and saw Chris sitting in an overstuffed chair reading through some of the literature he had picked from exhibitors booths.

Ralph walked over to him and said, "Let's eat Chris, I'm hungry."

"I am too," Chris replied.

They entered the restaurant and were seated at a nice table by the windows. They ordered from the lunch menu, which had a much more delightful selection then the food court in the conference area.

"So you found your man," Ralph said casually. "I don't mean to pry, and if I am just tell me to shut up," Ralph said smiling.

"Yes, I was surprised, but he is the 'Bob Armstrong' I was looking for. I'm going to be meeting with him this evening around eight as we couldn't really talk over at the conference."

"So you will be staying another night? That's great!"

"Yes I already extended my reservation for another day. I have to tell you Ralph, I'm actually enjoying this conference. I didn't think I would, but it is very interesting. I might even attend more seminars being I'm here."

"Well again, that's great! You not only found that Armstrong guy, but you're having a good time as well."

Chris and Ralph enjoyed their lunch having small talk about the conference and how being self reliant was not such a bad thing.

After completing lunch they returned together to the exhibition center.

"Believe it or not, I'm going to a seminar on Alternative Power Sources. As you know, I've always been interested in alternative power," Chris said to Ralph with a smile.

"I'm gonna wander around more exhibits. If you want to get together after the seminar, just give me a call. If not, I assume we will meet for dinner?" Ralph questioned.

"That's fine," Chris said. "If we don't meet up here later let's have an early dinner, say six o'clock."

"OK Boss, I mean Chris."

"Yea, yea, funny man," Chris replied with a smirk.

Chris and Ralph didn't meet again until dinner. Chris was getting real nervous and spent most of the afternoon trying to decide how to approach Bob with his problem. Would he be willing to help? He would just have to wait, but he didn't want to reveal his apprehension to Ralph.

Dinner went pleasantly with small talk about the conference. After dinner both Chris and Ralph went to the lounge for a drink. Chris felt a drink just might relax him before his meeting with Bob. After one drink, and some idle conversation with Ralph, Chris excused himself and started to leave the lounge.

"Want to meet for breakfast again?" Ralph asked as Chris walked past him.

"Oh sure, didn't mean to be rude, I just have some things on my mind," Chris replied. "Let's say the same time, same place," Chris continued trying to force a smile.

"See you then, Chris. Have a good night."

"See you then," Chris said as he left the lounge and proceeded to his room.

Chris was sitting in a comfortable wingback chair in the sitting room of his suite, when at exactly eight o'clock he heard a soft knock at the door. He wiped the sweat from his palms on his trousers as he rose and headed for the door.

Chris opened the door and Bob greeted him with a smile.

"Please come in Bob and make yourself comfortable", Chris said as he stood to one side so that Bob could enter the large sitting room of the suite. "Would you like a drink or cup of coffee?"

"No thank you," Bob replied as he chose a chair in the sitting room, and sat down lightly.

"I thank you again for coming, I know this isn't something you had planned on," Chris said sincerely.

"No problem Chris. First of all let me say that your father and I were very good friends and I was sorry to hear of his death, and of course your loss. Your father was a good man. I was out of town when you had the funeral, but I have visited his grave site since then."

"I thank you for that," Chris said softly. "So you and my father were good friends," more of a statement of fact than a question.

"Yes, we were, ever since the Marine Corps. I served under him and we maintained our friendship after getting out. Why exactly is it that you came to look for me? If you don't mind me asking."

"Not at all Bob. Before my father was killed, he told me that if I ever needed help for something serious, I should contact a marine that had served under him in the Gulf War with Force Recon. His name is Robert Armstrong and I trust him with my life, as should you."

"Excuse me, but you said killed. I thought your father died as a result of an accidental explosion?"

"I don't and won't believe that," Chris said curtly. "I'm sorry I didn't mean to sound rude. I must ask you Bob, can I be totally candid with you and can you assure me total confidentiality in all conversations between us?"

"Of course you can. You father already informed you that he trusted me with his life, and as his son, you can as well. Now tell me more about you believing he was killed."

Chris spent the next two hours explaining everything from his suspicion of why his father was killed, to why he had joined CANE. He explained his plan to hurt those who he believed had hurt his father.

Chris then told him about the surreptitious recording he had made and how. The details of the flash drives having been concealed in his desk, and the caching of an extra copy. But then the accident, the coma, and the memory loss. How the copies in his desk had been destroyed by fire while he was in the hospital.

Bob didn't interrupt, just listened. If this story came from anyone else, he would think they were crazy. But being Phillip Parker's son, he actually believed him.

"What is it you want me to do?" Bob asked.

Chris explained that the area where he had cached the last copy of the recording was now surrounded by a chain link fence and was a construction site. He knew he didn't have the skills to get inside and dig up the cache, but thought Bob might be able to do so.

"Doesn't sound like a big problem if done right," Bob said with a smile.

"Do you really think you can get it? It is the only copy left and without it I have nothing to go on with these people."

"Well Chris, I obviously can't make any promises, but if the site is as you describe I should be able to retrieve your cache. What I will need to do is a short reconnaissance of the area to determine my best plan of action. I will then contact you and we can meet. I will let you know if I believe it is feasible, and if so how I will proceed."

"Oh, that would be great. My father was right, I knew you would be the man for the job," Chris said feeling relieved and less nervous than when he began.

"I haven't done anything yet," Bob said smiling. "Let's take this one step at a time."

Bob got the address of the construction site and Chris and Bob exchanged cell phone numbers. Chris described the area on the left side of the property where he had buried the cache.

Bob promised he would contact Chris by cell when he had surveyed the area and indicated they could then meet and discuss going forward. Chris should expect to hear from him before the following weekend.

* * *

During the time that Ralph and Chris were having dinner at the hotel, and Chris' subsequent meeting with Bob Armstrong, another dinner was taking place in Albany, New York. Attending that dinner was Special Agent McDonald from the FBI and Agent Davis from the DTTF.

"It is really great to see you again my friend," Davis said as he met McDonald in front of Freeman's Steak House, a popular little establishment known for its succulent steaks and reasonable prices.

"You too Craig, It's been too long." McDonald replied extending his hand to Davis.

They shook hands and entered the restaurant asking for a private table in a corner if possible. They ordered a drink, made a selection from the menu, and began to talk.

"So, how was the conference?" Davis asked. "I don't really get to attend any since I started with the DTTF."

"It was really interesting," McDonald replied. "In one of the seminars, we had a speaker from the DHS Office of

Intelligence. He attempted to delineate the difference between groups considered right-wing extremists.

"The speaker indicated that one group is a hate oriented movement, and is made up of those who have a hatred of particular religions, racial, or ethnic groups. The other group is made up of those who are anti-government, rejecting federal authority in favor of state or local authority, or even rejects government authority entirely. Anyway, it was pretty interesting."

"Sounds like a hoot to me," Davis replied with chuckle.

Lowering his voice, McDonald said, "Anyway, it would probably be boring for a guy that was lucky enough to get hooked up with an exciting new organization like the Domestic Terrorism Task Force."

"I do miss hanging out with old friends, but it's a price one must pay to be part of an elite team," Davis stated, looking as though he was proud, yet somehow bothered.

"You are happy where you arc though, aren't you Craig?"

"Of course, of course, I really enjoy my job and we have the best of equipment. I just get a little tired of the continual warnings about not associating with agents from other agencies. That's why they won't authorize us to go to any conferences. It just puts a little cramp in your relationships. But at least we have been able to stay friends, and that's important to me."

Dinner was served and small talk ensued. The old days, good times, and memories. When the main course was finished and desert was served, McDonald thought he was in a position to continue.

"So Craig, I've heard rumors that I might be getting a transfer up to the Albany area," McDonald announced. "It should give us more opportunities to get together."

"That would be great," Davis replied looking pleased.

"I won't know for sure for a few weeks, but if I am, you will certainly be one of the first to know. Maybe we can even get together on weekends and go shooting like we used to."

"I can only hope it happens; it gets a little lonely up here at times. Anyway, let's hope for the transfer."

Completing their dinner, and having one last drink, Special Agent McDonald and Agent Davis went their separate ways.

* * *

Having interviewed Special Agent McDonald after his dinner with Craig Davis, Alaister Mitchell placed a call to Director Wolfson.

"Sir, I wanted to fill you in on the meeting between our Special Agent McDonald, and DTTF Agent Davis in Albany."

"Go ahead Mitchell."

"Well sir, they met for dinner and apparently things went very well. According to McDonald, Agent Davis likes his job, but, he seems a little disillusioned with the organization."

"And how is that?" Wolfson asked.

"Well, they are constantly warning their agents not to associate with agents from other agencies. They won't even let them go to law enforcement conferences because they might talk to other agents. He indicates it is very hard to have friends outside of the DTTF. Sounds almost like a cult. Anyway he was very pleased to hear McDonald might be transferred up to that area, so we are making arrangements for a transfer shortly."

"Good job Mitchell," Wolfson stated. "Keep me informed. This just might be the opening we have been looking for."

"Will do sir," Mitchell replied as the line went dead.

CHAPTER 13
The Plan

Chris had only been back from the NCSR for two days, when sitting at his home in the evening, he received a cell phone call from Bob Armstrong.

"Hello Bob," Chris said answering the phone.

"Hi Chris, I have done an initial survey of the area in question and I thought we might meet to discuss the situation."

"That would be fine; do you think it can be done?"

"Let's discuss that when we meet," Bob responded.

"Are you in the area now?" Chris asked.

"Yes, would you like to do it now?" Bob replied.

"Definitely, would you like to come to my home?"

"No problem, I'm on my way."

"Let me give you my address," Chris stated.

"I know where you are," Bob said. "I'll see you in a few minutes."

It wasn't long before Chris saw the lights from a vehicle coming up his long drive. It was a black Xterra and it stopped at the front of the house. Chris watched through the curtains and could see that it was indeed Bob Armstrong.

Chris met Bob at the front door and welcomed him in.

Shaking hands, Chris said, "Let's go to my office."

Bob followed Chris up a set of stairs to his home office which was well appointed with an oak desk and many book shelves.

"I see you like books as well as I do," Bob remarked.

"Yes, I always have, but many of them had to be replaced after the fire here. I actually used to have more."

"When did you have a fire?"

"While I was in the coma. But it wasn't suspicious and by the time I got out of the hospital, my Senior Vice President, Ralph Cummings, already had the place cleaned up and secured, and reconstruction was in the making."

"Sounds like a good man this Ralph Cummings," Bob stated.

"He is; I don't know what I would do without him."

Chris motioned to Bob to take a seat in one of the chairs that was on one side of a small square table with an intricate chess set on it. Chris took the chair on the opposite side of the table.

Chris sat nervously, slowly rubbing his hands together.

Looking at Bob he said, "Well, I don't mean to be eager, but do you think you can do this?"

"Well I checked the place out pretty good and the area where you say you buried the cache is still wooded and there is not any construction in that area. The fence shouldn't be a problem, but I do have to be concerned with the security patrol.

As long as your coordinates are correct, I feel pretty certain this can be done," Bob said smiling, trying to ease Chris' concern.

"That's great Bob, when do you think it can be done?"

"Well I noticed that the security patrol is rather lackadaisical and they don't seem to take regular patrols of the property. But I would like to be extra cautious and stack the deck in my favor."

"What do you mean by that?" Chris asked.

"I will attempt the retrieval on a night when there is a heavy rain. It lowers visibility, and most people don't want to go out in it. Even security personnel often shirk their duties to avoid getting wet. From what I've seen of the security there, I'm sure they will be in the security trailer drinking coffee until the rain slows down," Bob explained.

"That makes a lot of sense, but then you will get soaked as well," Chris stated.

"That's true, but as I'm sure your father told you, Marines don't melt," Bob said with a short chuckle. "I have already checked the weather for this week and we are in luck. Thursday night, the night after tomorrow, they forecast a heavy rain late, into Friday morning. That is when I will make my move."

"Wow," Chris said, "This is really moving fast."

"If you would like, we can put it off for another time," Bob said wondering if Chris was getting cold feet.

"No, No, that's not what I meant," Chris said quickly. "It's just been so long, and it seems like this is really gonna happen. I'm just both, excited and hopeful."

"Well then, give me the exact coordinates, and if you can, draw me a sketch showing where the walking trail was, and where you believe you left it for the burial of the cache. I believe most of the trail is still as it was," Bob said.

"Let me get you the coordinates and I will sit at my desk right now and draw the sketch. Would you like a cup of coffee or a drink while I do that?" he asked Bob.

"A cup of coffee would be great," Bob replied.

"I have a pot on in the kitchen, let me get a tray and we can both have a cup."

"Why don't we both just walk down to the kitchen and we can forego the tray," Bob said with a smile.

"Of course Bob, just follow me," Chris said feeling a little embarrassed.

Both Chris and Bob returned to Chris' office with a cup of coffee. Chris sat at his desk and pulled out an iPad.

"While you are doing that, mind if I peruse your books?" Bob asked.

"Not at all my friend, but I'm not sure they will interest you."

"You would be surprised what I'm interested in," Bob said smiling, already starting to scan the book shelves.

Chris used his iPad to retrieve the coordinates from his cloud and began hand drawing a rough sketch of the trail. He had hiked it many times and was surprised at how well he remembered the curves and topography. He had a good idea of the exact location where he left the trail and indicated that on the sketch.

While scanning the books on Chris' shelves, Bob spotted both *Currency Wars - The Making of the Next Global Crisis* and *The Death of Money - The coming Collapse of the International Monetary System* by James Rickards.

"Hey, Chris, I read James Rickards' first book *Currency Wars* but haven't read his new one *The Death of Money*. What did you think of it?"

Chris looked up from his desk and responded. "I thought they were both good, and the second was a very good follow up to the first. I liked his inflation-deflation paradox analysis and his views on the Fed. Would you like to borrow it?"

"No thank you," Bob replied. "I hate to borrow books because when I read them I need to keep them. Just a little quirk of mine. I will pick up a copy when I get a chance."

Chris took a few more minutes to complete his rough sketch. When he was done he called Bob over to his desk.

"I have the sketch drawn to the best of my memory," Chris began. "Here on the left you can see the trail and at this curve about here," he said pointing, "I went off the trail to the left a short distance. The cache was buried in this small clearing. I have written down the coordinates which should place you exactly over the cache."

"Well that seems pretty clear," Bob said looking at the sketch. "I have a handheld GPS that I use for Geocaching and this should hopefully be a pretty straight forward retrieval."

"You do Geocaching?" Chris asked.

"I've been known to do a little. I also have other experience using a GPS," Bob replied.

"I used to do some with my fellow students while at M.I.T."

"I have a question for you Chris," Bob said seriously. "I most likely will be going in just after midnight. If everything goes as planned, I should be out of there with the cache in about thirty minutes or less. However, after surveying the area, there is no place to park my vehicle in the vicinity where it won't look suspicious. Can you drop me just up from the site near the wooded area, and then come back to pick me up?"

"That would be no problem at all," Chris replied.

"I figure I can leave my vehicle at your house. You can take me there in your car. There is an all night diner about a mile up the road from the location." Bob stated. "You could wait there. When I have the cache and have exited the property, I will call you on the cell phone. I will wait just inside the woods on the left where you dropped me off. We can then return to your house and I can retrieve my truck."

"That would be fine. I never thought of where the vehicle would be parked," Chris said feeling naive at this sort of thing.

"OK, if it is raining on Thursday night I will get here about midnight. We can then get in your car and head to the location."

"No problem," Chris replied.

"I should be going as I have some things to prepare for Thursday night. Just so you know, if we don't have a heavy rain, I will put the retrieval off."

"Then let's hope for heavy rain," Chris said trying to be casual.

Bob returned to his home and thought about the retrieval. He didn't think he would need much. He would obviously take his Generation 3, dual tube, night vision goggles with custom head mount so he could wear it without a helmet, which it had been designed for. It had an integrated IR illuminator that allowed the use of the night vision goggles in "No-Light" situations. If the heavy rain came, the sky would be extremely dark. He might need the extra illumination back on the trail.

His handheld GPS would also be a necessity and he got that out and put the coordinates in it that Chris had provided him with.

The next day Bob selected some other gear to take with him. He grabbed a pair of folding bolt cutters, although he planned to scale the fence, not cut it. However, he always liked to have options. He took a small stainless steel trowel called the U-Dig-It and felt it would be adequate to dig up the cache. Chris had told him he had used a trowel to bury it. After further thinking, he also took a small Gerber Gorge Folding Shovel, just in case something changed and the digging was more difficult than expected. Bob hoped nothing had changed.

Other than his folding Benchmade knife, he decided not to go armed. He would leave his handgun secured in his vehicle at Chris' house. If somehow he was apprehended as a trespasser, a weapon wouldn't make things any better he thought.

A few other items were also selected and they were all placed into an old black Camelbak H.A.W.G. backpack. Then all that was left was to wait for the rain.

CHAPTER 14
The Retrieval

Thursday night at about ten o'clock it started raining. It wasn't real heavy but was expected to get much heavier around midnight. Bob Armstrong called Chris on his cell and said, "It's a go."

Bob was dressed in black Wrangler jeans, a lightweight black turtleneck sweater, and black Gore-Tex boots. He also had a lightweight black rain suit consisting of a jacket and trousers made by Marmot, a lightweight black balaclava, and a black wool watch cap. He would put these on when he got to Chris' house.

He grabbed his pack, rain gear, and headed to Chris' in his Xterra. Upon arrival, Chris was at the door. Bob grabbed his gear and ran up to the house.

"Good evening Bob," Chris said sounding a little nervous. "My car is in the garage; we get there just down the hallway," Chris continued, pointing in the direction of the hall.

131

"Just let me get into my rain gear and we will head to the site," Bob said showing Chris the raingear in hand.

Bob donned the rain jacket and trousers. He would wait to put the balaclava and cap on until he got closer to the site.

"Well let's get this show on the road," Bob said to Chris.

"Follow me," Chris said trying to sound calm.

Bob followed Chris to the garage and they both got in Chris' car. With the garage door opening automatically, Chris drove out of the garage, down the driveway, and they proceeded towards the drop-off point.

While Chris drove, Bob put on his balaclava and the wool cap.

"Doesn't that rain jacket have a hood?" Chris asked.

"Yes it does, but it blocks my peripheral vision," Bob replied. "That's why I wear the wool cap."

"Makes sense," Chris said. "I'm new at this," he continued trying to sound humorous.

After Bob donned his headgear, he pulled the night vision goggles out of his pack and tested them one last time to ensure they were working properly.

"Are those night vision goggles?" Chris asked.

"Yes they are," Bob replied. "They will make sure I can see without using any light source such as a flashlight. I certainly don't want to give myself away."

"Of course," Chris said. "I've just never seen a pair close-up, although we learned about them at M.I.T."

The last thing Bob did was take out his cell phone and put it on airplane mode. He couldn't take a chance of it ringing while he was inside the construction site.

"The location is just around the corner up here," Bob said. "But I want you to go by the place so I can see if anything appears to be going on. Don't go fast, but not so slow as we might seem suspicious. We will continue a distance down the road, turn around, and then come back. Once we pass the site, go just a short distance and pull over to the side of the road. I will quickly get out and head for the wooded area to the left of the site. You immediately drive away. And Chris, don't come back until I call you. If I don't call, you don't come back. If something goes wrong, I will handle it. We don't need you involved. You understand?"

"Yes, I don't like it, but I understand," Chris replied. "I got you into this and if something happens I should do what is necessary to help."

"The best thing you can do is let me handle it," Bob countered. "I know how to handle these types of situations."

"OK," was Chris' only reply.

"The rain is really starting to pick up. Here comes the place up on our left, just a nice normal speed now," Bob instructed.

They drove past the construction site but with the heavy rain it was difficult to see anything. The only lights that were on were in the security trailer which was permanently parked at the front of the building under construction, and they were dim and hazy from the heavy rain. Chris continued past the site as instructed, and after travelling a reasonable distance past it, he turned the car around. As they headed back, Bob again checked the site, as this time it was on his side of the car. There did not appear to be any change in the lights.

"Pull over here," Bob said when they were past the site by the wooded area."

Bob quickly jumped out of the car, his backpack and night vision goggles in hand, and immediately disappeared into the woods. Chris quickly, but cautiously, pulled away from the side of the road and continued to the diner Bob had suggested he wait at.

Upon arrival at the diner, Chris was nervous and it showed. He decided to sit in the car for a few minutes and calm his nerves. Eventually he went into the diner, ordering a cup of coffee and a piece of pastry.

Bob entered the woods and continued straight back for a distance that was beyond the lights of the security trailer. Turning to his right he cautiously approached the chain link fence. Even with the rain, the night vision provided him with an adequate view inside the compound.

He had no problem scaling the fence and dropped quietly on the other side. He easily located the old trail and proceeded to the point Chris had marked on the sketch, where he believed he had exited it to the left. Bob looked left and saw a small clearing. He walked to the clearing and took the GPS out of his pack. Upon turning it on, and waiting for it to fix on at least three satellites, he wished Chris had taken some waypoints on his way out. However, if the sketch was accurate, he should be able to find the approximate location and move back and forth until he was within a reasonable position to the cache.

Bob looked at the coordinates of the GPS and he appeared to be very close. He moved around slowly, waiting for the GPS to readjust. He believed he was damn close.

Chris had told him that the cache was not buried very deep, so Bob started feeling around and digging in a circular motion, working his way outward. It didn't take long until he hit something. He dug a little deeper at that point, but it was only a rock. Continuing a little further, he again hit something and this time it was a small red anodized aluminum container. This, as described to him by Chris, had to be the cache. He placed it in his pack and started filling the various small holes, trying to leave the ground look untouched. However, between the mud and wet leaves, he could only do so much. Bottom line he thought, it didn't matter now.

Bob quickly returned to the trail and headed back in the direction in which he had come. Suddenly he saw a light bouncing in front of him. It wasn't bright enough to affect his night vision equipment, but it definitely stood out. Damn, he thought, this can't be one of the security officers. Bob quickly exited the trail and went prone alongside it in the woods.

Lying alongside the trail, he watched as a young security officer walked by with a flashlight wearing a poncho. He didn't seem to be too motivated and appeared to be more concerned with the rain than looking around. Bob then heard a radio.

"Hey Dennis, how's the weather out there," somebody asked with a short laugh?

The security officer brought the radio up to his mouth, keyed the talk button and said, "You are a funny guy. The bottoms of my pants are soaked from this stupid poncho they provided us with. Nobody in their right mind would be out here in this rain tonight."

"Your right Dennis," a voice came from the radio. "Get back here and we will do a tour later if the rain slows down."

"On my way," the security officer responded.

The security officer turned around immediately and headed back towards the construction site. Bob waited until he was out of site, and then continued to the area of the fence where he had entered. He easily scaled the fence again and retreated into the woods outside of the fence line

Sitting in a crouched position, Bob couldn't believe how smooth this had gone. Thirty-five minutes and the operation was completed. He never had that happen in the Marine Corps he thought. All he had to do now was call Chris for pickup, handover the cache, and he would be back at his new place within a day or so, working on some final touches.

Taking his cell phone out of his pack, he turned off the airplane mode and dialed Chris' cell phone number. It was answered immediately by a very nervous sounding Chris.

"The chicken is in the pot," Bob said smiling to himself.

"The what is where?" Chris said.

"I got it, now come pick me up." Bob replied. "The same way you dropped me off," he added.

"On my way," Chris said.

Bob terminated the call, placed the phone back on airplane mode, put it back into his pack, and moved towards the road. He watched to see when Chris went by, at which time he would move closer for pickup.

Bob could observe Chris passing the pick-up point and knew it would only take minutes for him to turn around, return and pull over at the side of the road.

When Chris pulled his car over, Bob was ready and, opening the passenger side door, jumped in.

"Let's go," Bob said calmly.

"So you got the cache?" Chris said excitedly.

"I believe I do. Let's get to your house and open it," Bob replied.

"Did you run into any trouble?"Chris asked.

"None at all," Bob said smiling. "I was actually surprised yet glad it went so smooth." Some things I've done in the past didn't go nearly as well as this, Bob thought to himself.

Chris drove directly to his house and he and Bob proceeded straight up to his office. Bob took the cache out of his pack, which he had carried in with him, and handed it to Chris.

The cache was dirty and wet and Chris couldn't get the end cap unscrewed. Bob pulled out his Leatherman Tool from a sheath on his belt and handed it to Chris. "Try the pliers on this, it should work."

Chris unfolded the Leatherman Tool, apparently being familiar with them, to reveal the pliers. He was then able to unscrew the cap from the cache. He pulled the plastic bag out of the cylinder and opened it revealing a small flash drive.

"I have it," Chris said, holding the flash drive in his hand. "And I couldn't have done it without you Bob."

"After having retrieved it, I'm not so sure you couldn't have gotten it yourself, but I'm glad I could help," Bob said with a wink.

"I'm not good at that type of thing," Chris said. "I probably would have fallen while climbing the fence and broke my neck," Chris continued with a chuckle.

"Well now that you have it, what do you plan to do with it?" Bob asked casually.

"As I explained when we first met, I plan on destroying the members of CANE. Once I reveal this recording, people will see that CANE and its members are dangerous. Having an actual recording of the conference, those members who spoke will have a hard time denying their involvement. And they were introduced, so their names are also revealed."

"Can I be candid?" Bob asked.

"Of course, Bob, I respect your input."

"You do realize that this recording you have on that flash drive is very dangerous," Bob said looking very serious. "To have these powerful members of that CANE organization after you could be, not only dangerous, but deadly. Are you sure you want to pursue this? I'm not sure your father would want that for you."

"I am prepared to do what is necessary to expose them," Chris replied looking directly at Bob. "I may not be able to prove that they directly killed my father, but people like them did. They only care about power and profits. I only care about avenging my father's death."

"Well I'm certainly not in a position to stand in your way, but please give it some thought," Bob replied in a soft tone. "I know your father wouldn't want this for you. There might be a better way, without taking a chance on your life. I know these types of people and they will not deal with this lightly."

"Well, do you have any suggestions?" Chris asked curtly.

"No I don't, but time might provide an answer. I'm not trying to dissuade you, just asking that you think this out before you do anything. I'm a friend, remember, not the enemy."

"I'm sorry for my tone," Chris said, "But I have been waiting a long time to get back at these kinds of people. I will give it some thought before doing anything."

"Well the first thing I think you should do is make a copy and secure it at a different location," Bob said.

"I agree with you," Chris replied. "I plan on doing that tomorrow when I go to my office up in Dutchess County. I have not yet replaced my home computer as I usually just use my iPad when at the house. Of course I can't copy flash drives with it."

"With all you went through to retrieve this thing, I wouldn't take the chance of waiting until tomorrow," Bob said matter-of-factly. "You just never know what could happen between now and then. Last time you didn't bank on a fire. I have the capability to make copies at my house. If it is alright, I will take the flash drive to my house, make a secure copy, and return it and the original in the morning."

"I trust you of course," Chris said. "But I don't trust others. The housekeeper will be at my house tomorrow, and I don't want her to see you. Could I come to your house to get them, say about noon? I'm not used to staying up this late, so I'm going to call my Senior Vice President's voice mail and leave a message that I'm taking tomorrow off for a three day weekend. When he gets in the office in the morning he will get my message."

"That would be fine," Bob replied. "I'll have them ready. My address is number one, Bennett Road, in Peekskill. I'm the first driveway on the left, but it is quite the ways in from the deli that is at the intersection of Bennett Road and Route 9, which it is off of. Would you like directions?"

"No thank you," Chris replied. "I'll find it."

Bob took the flash drive and placed it in his front trouser pocket.

"I'll guard it with my life," Bob said smiling.

"Please do," Chris returned the smile.

With that, Bob left with the flash drive and returned to his house. It was late, almost two o'clock in the morning, and he wanted to get a few hours sleep before five-thirty, when he always awoke automatically.

Bob went to his den. He proceeded to the far wall to a large floor-to-ceiling bookcase and reached for a large statue of an eagle that sat there. But instead of lifting it up, he turned it sideways and it rotated.

Bob then pressed on the bookcase and it opened inward, like a concealed door, revealing a small room. He flicked a switch and the room was lit by small LED lights that were powered by a bank of batteries that were kept charged by the solar panels. He opened the top drawer of a large fireproof file cabinet and placed the flash drive inside. He then went to bed.

CHAPTER 15
Making Copies

The next morning, Bob awoke as always at five-thirty. He rose and put on a pot of coffee. While the coffee was perking he took a quick shower and put on a pair of jeans, a sweatshirt over a-shirt, and a pair of light hiking boots.

Returning to the kitchen, Bob fixed himself a cup of coffee and carried it into his den, placing it on his desk. He turned on his computer and then proceeded to his concealed room to get the flash drive from the file cabinet. While in the cabinet, he also grabbed two new IronKey secure flash Drives.

The IronKey was an extremely secure USB flash drive and was more than adequate for the purpose of carrying confidential information. It was the only USB flash drive validated to meet the stringent Security Level 3 requirements of the FIPS 140-2 standard. Additionally, the IronKey Basic S200 protected data with strong AES 256-bit hardware encryption. It had "Always-On" Data Encryption whereby all user data was encrypted with AES CBC-mode hardware encryption. Unlike software-based encryption, this "always-on" protection could not be disabled. In addition, since the IronKey Cryptochip generated and stored strong, random encryption keys, encryption routines ran faster and more securely than on any software-based encryption system.

What Bob really liked about the IronKey was that it was really physically hardened and its rugged metal casing protected it against physical damage, and the internal components were sealed to protect against tampering. Additionally, it far exceeded military waterproof requirements. It was actually "Self-Defending" and no one could access files stored on an IronKey drive unless they authenticated with the correct password. All encryption and password verification, was performed in hardware, and couldn't be disabled by malware or a careless user. Self-defending IronKey drives also provided hardware-level active protections against the spread of worms, crimeware, and other malicious code.

When an IronKey drive was plugged into a laptop or desktop computer, the user had to authenticate with a password before encryption keys were enabled and data and applications were accessible. Unlike software-based encryption, the IronKey Cryptochip did not export AES encryption keys to the host PC, thereby protecting against cold-boot and malware attacks. IronKey protected against brute force password guessing attacks by using non-volatile access-failure counters stored on the

Cryptochip itself. If a thief tried to break into an IronKey drive and entered ten incorrect passwords, the Cryptochip securely erased all encrypted data with patent-pending Flash Trash technology. This ensured no data could be recovered from the device. Also, and this is what Bob really liked, if the IronKey detected a physical attack, it would initiate a self-destruct sequence (kind of reminded him of the old Mission Impossible show).

With the IronKey, Bob thought it was nice to know that if this device was lost, the information on it would not get into the wrong hands. He felt it would be ideal for Chris' recording.

With Chris' flash drive, and the two IronKey flash drives in hand, Bob returned to the desk in his den, closing the concealed door to the room. The eagle automatically swiveled back into position securing the bookcase in place.

Bob sipped at his coffee while he copied the information from Chris' flash drive onto the Ironkeys. He then went back into his concealed room and placed Chris' original flash drive and one of the Ironkeys back into the file cabinet. The second IronKey he placed in his front trouser pocket.

Bob returned to the kitchen, poured another cup of coffee, and fixed a bowl of oatmeal with raisins. After finishing his breakfast, he dialed a number on his cell phone.

When the phone was answered Bob said "Hey Buddy, this is Bob. I need a favor."

"Anytime, what do you need?"

"I need you to safeguard a small item for me. When and if I need it, I will contact you."

"No problem Bob, where do we meet?"

"Well Buddy, if you can take care of it this morning, I will meet you in the old rest stop between the north and southbound lanes of the Taconic State Parkway, just north of Jefferson Valley. I'll be in a Black Nissan Xterra. See you there."

"I'll be there in an hour." The phone went dead.

One hour later, Bob sat in his Xterra with a cup of coffee he had put in a stainless steel insulated mug before leaving his house. Right on time, a vehicle drove past his, circled around and pulled up to the passenger door. A man got out and entered the passenger side of Bob's vehicle.

"Good seeing you again Buddy," Bob said with a grin.

"Yea, let's not wait so long next time. Now what can I do for you?"

Bob handed over the second copy of the IronKey. "I need you to guard this with your life. It might come in handy someday."

"No problem, it will remain safe until you need it."

The man got out of Bob's vehicle, returned to his own, and drove away.

Bob sat for a moment taking a sip of his coffee, then exited the parking lot, and returned to his house.

* * *

While Bob was making the transfer at the rest stop, Boris came into Mr. Mann's office, who had just arrived. "Mr. Mann, I have been reviewing the intercept from Mr. Hughes home for yesterday. It was unusual that there was conversation at the office very late at night. After carefully listening to the conversation, it would seem we have a problem."

Gray Mann said, "Fill me in Boris."

Gray Mann listened intently as Boris described the conversation that took place.

"How the hell did Mr. Hughes get a recording of the conference?" Gray Mann asked staring at Boris.

"I have no idea sir," Boris replied sheepishly.

Gray Mann sat with his elbows on the desk, his palms together and his finger tips under his chin thinking. Suddenly he said, "This is what we are going to do. You get one surveillance team setup at Mr. Hughes' house and another at the deli that Bob guy mentioned at the intersection of his road. When Mr. Hughes leaves his house, have the first surveillance team contact the second team at the deli by cell phone, describing the car Mr. Hughes is driving. We know where he is going so we don't have to follow him. Team two at the deli can verify Hughes arriving. Contact Pierre and tell him we have a job for him. Have him standing by near the deli as well. Give Hughes a few minutes to meet with that Bob character and then have Pierre go up to his house. Make sure Pierre recovers the recording and the copy Hughes is talking about. And Boris, make sure that Pierre understands that neither of them are to survive."

* * *

Chris left his house at eleven-thirty in the morning and proceeded out of his driveway. He drove past a phone repair truck parked at the curb midway down his road, where a repair man was working on the lines.

Chris was still getting used to his new Audi A8. He was done with his sports cars, but the twin-turbocharged V-eight gave him plenty of power, and the eight-speed automatic transmission and all-wheel drive provided him ease of driving and a safer ride.

The repair man working on the phone lines walked towards his truck and, opening the passenger's door, reached inside. Picking up his cell phone from the passenger seat, he dialed a number. When the call was answered he said, "Be advised the target is on the move and is driving a silver Audi A8 and should be heading your way. The personalized license plate says ZeRho spelled capital Z, small e, capital R, small h, small o."

"Confirmed, a silver Audi A8 with license plate ZeRho, spelled capital Z, small e, capital R, small h, small o."

The repair man placed the cell phone back in the truck and closed the door. He picked up the safety cones that had been placed at both the front and rear of his truck, and threw them into the back. He then got into the truck and drove away.

As Chris' car passed the deli and turned onto Bob's road, the surveillance vehicle at that location placed a call to Pierre. When Pierre answered, he was told the target was proceeding to the destination. The surveillance team then pulled out of the deli and terminated surveillance.

Chris proceeded directly to Bob's house. As Chris drove up Bob's long driveway, Bob was waiting at the front door.

Chris parked and walked towards the door.

"Been waiting there long?" Chris asked smiling.

"Not really," Bob replied. "I have a driveway alarm at the end so I knew you were coming in."

"I have the coffee on, come on in."

"That's great," Chris replied entering Bob's house. "I could use a cup."

Bob led Chris to the kitchen and poured two cups of coffee. He placed them on the table with a sugar bowl, a creamer, and two spoons.

"Have a seat and fix it as you please," Bob said. "I'll be right back with the original and the copy I made."

Bob went to his den, closed the door, and proceeded into his hidden room, retrieving the original flash drive and the copy he made. Returning to the kitchen, he placed them on the table and prepared a cup of coffee for himself.

"Wow, your flash drive looks a lot different than mine," Chris said picking up the IronKey.

"Yes, these are extremely secure. Let me tell you about them, as I highly recommend you get some for further copies."

Bob started to describe the advantages of the IronKey to Chris, when he heard a "Ping Pong - Ping Pong."

"What is that?" Chris asked.

"It's somebody coming up the driveway," Bob replied as he started to standup.

"Are you expecting someone else?" Chris asked.

"No I'm not, wait here," Bob said as he headed for the front door.

As Bob approached the front door, he could observe a black Cadillac CTS-V sedan pull up alongside Chris' Audi. A man about six feet tall got out of the vehicle wearing a well tailored blue suit. As he proceeded towards the front door, Bob took notice that he was lean, yet muscular, and walked with confidence. He had well cropped brown hair parted on the left side, and a thin well trimmed mustache, the type trimmed down away from the nose and up from the lip. Bob wasn't sure who this guy was and was immediately cautious.

The man approached the front door and rang the bell. Bob slowly opened the front door just about a foot.

"Can I help you?" Bob asked.

"Yes, my name is Irvin Slansky," Pierre said smiling graciously. "I'm running for City Counsel and I would love to talk to you about some of my proposals should I be elected."

"Don't you politicians normally do this on weekends?" Bob asked.

"Often," Pierre answered still smiling, "but I find if I do some during the day, I get to talk to the wives."

"I'm not really interested in politics," Bob responded.

"That's not a problem," Pierre responded as he took a step closer to the door. "Just let me leave a flyer which has my proposals on it."

At that point Pierre reached into the left side of his jacket. As he did so, he immediately kicked the door with his right foot, knocking Bob back, withdrew a suppressed Colt 1911, and entered the living room all in one smooth move. As Bob recovered from being knocked back, Pierre pointed the gun directly at his chest, only a foot from him, and asked where Mr. Hughes was.

Having heard the noise, Chris came around the corner into the living room, from Bob's left. Pierre glanced towards him, taking his eyes off Bob for just a moment.

Bob immediately moved left, and bladed his body to the left of Pierre's. At the exact same time, Bob reach straight out with his left hand open, grabbing the gun at the top rear portion of the slide, wrapping his hand around the slide and Pierre's gun hand, pushing the weapon left, just as it went off. At the same time, Bob's right hand grabbed the front of the gun under the barrel ahead of the trigger guard and in one swift motion spun the gun up and back towards Pierre's chest. As he did so, he could hear Pierre's trigger finger break and with the gun now pointing at Pierre, Bob pulled the gun back and down, breaking it free from

Pierre's hand. This entire action happened in a split second. Bob stepped to the left of Pierre, and bringing up his right leg, he thrust the outside edge of his right foot down and out into the outer right side of Pierre's right knee. Pierre's right leg immediately broke at the knee and he went down hard. Bob, with Pierre's gun in hand, leaned down and used it to smack Pierre on the side of the head, knocking him out.

Bob's movements had been so instantaneous they appeared as one blur to Chris, who couldn't even register in his mind what he had just seen.

"What the hell was that?" Chris said frozen in place.

"I told you this could get dangerous," Bob stated soberly. "This guy was looking for you by name, so somebody has to know about the recording. How could that happen?"

"I have no idea; I thought only you and I knew about it. I haven't told anybody else, I swear."

"Well they found out somehow. These people are fucking serious Chris, as you can see. Are you sure nobody else knows?" Bob asked.

"I'm sure Bob, this is like a bad movie," Chris said looking both upset and nervous.

"If nobody else knows, then that CANE organization you told me about must have electronic surveillance setup at your house. Why would they do that?"

"I have no idea," Chris responded. "I know they are interested in my company, maybe they are trying to get information on that."

"That would mean they probably bugged your offices as well," Bob said, trying to figure out what to do.

"What do we do now?" Chris asked.

"Well first, let's take care of this piece of shit."

Bob, still holding Pierre's gun, told Chris to wait there, while he checked the perimeter to make sure nobody else was lurking around. When Bob felt comfortable that the assailant had been alone, he returned to the house.

Bob told Chris to keep an eye on the assailant and went to his den, placing the Colt 1911on his desk. He then approached the wall where there was another bookshelf, but this one was not a floor to ceiling unit. It started above the wainscoting that covered the lower portion of the walls all around the room. It was built into the wall, so that it was flush with it. Bob pressed on the left side of the bookshelf and the entire unit slid to the left, revealing a display of several weapons that were mounted on the wall behind the shelf.

Bob perused the selection and lifted a Browning Hi-Power from the display and a leather speed scabbard holster for it. He ejected the magazine from the gun and examined it to ensure that it was full with its 13 round capacity. He then returned it back into the magazine well, tapping it up with the palm of his hand to insure it was seated securely. He pulled the slide slightly to the rear; just enough to verify that a round was in the chamber, and pushed the slide back home. It was then placed on his desk with the holster. Grabbing two extra magazines for the Hi-Power and two boxes of Federal Premium Hydra-Shok 9mm cartridges, he placed them on his desk as well.

Bob slid the bookcase back into position and unbuckled his belt. He pulled it out of the belt loops on the right and back side of his jeans, wove the belt, first through the back slot of the holster, then under and through a belt loop, and last through the front slot of the holster. He completed the remaining belt loops on the right and front side with the belt and re-buckled it in place. He knew that going through the belt loop between the slots of the holster would keep the holster from pulling the belt down from the weight of the gun.

Bob then slid the Hi-Power into the holster, which road nicely over the right hip. He pulled the oversized t-shirt and sweatshirt over the outside of his trousers and over the holster. Because of the slim profile of the Hi-Power, it would be difficult to notice by the casual observer.

Bob then picked up the suppressed Colt 1911 off his desk and went to the living room carrying it in his hand. He told Chris he had to go to the garage and would be right back.

Exiting the side door of the house, Bob carried the gun to the garage. He went to a corner by a workbench and reached down and removed the lid from a five gallon bucket. The inside was three-fourths full with old oil which Bob had collected from oil changes on some of his vehicles and lawn equipment. He unscrewed the suppressor from the Colt and dropped them both into the bucket, the Colt still loaded. As they sank to the bottom of the bucket, he replaced the lid. He then grabbed a roll of duct tape and several large zip ties and returned to the house.

Bob took the duct tape and wrapped some completely around Pierre's head, covering his mouth. He then rolled Pierre over onto his stomach and pulled his arms behind his back. He used zip ties to tie his wrists together, and then wrapped duct tape around his wrists, over the zip ties. Lastly, he used duct tape to bind his ankles together. Chris watched the whole procedure in puzzled amazement.

"You're going to have to help me get this guy outside," Bob said to Chris. "We will carry him down the hallway and out the side door, where we will stick him in the garage. We don't want him dead; we just don't want him following us. This way, I'm sure somebody will find him eventually."

"This is really new to me," Chris responded, "But it looks like you have been here before."

"I read a lot of books," Bob said smiling.

Bob and Chris carried Pierre out to the garage and leaned him against a wall in a sitting position. Then they returned to the house.

"I hate to say this Chris, but we are going to have to get out of here and hide out until we can figure out what is going on. You can't return to your house."

"Can't we call the police or something?" Chris asked.

"That wouldn't be a smart move at this point. There would be too many questions, and as long as we stay here we are in danger."

Bob then directed Chris, who was standing in the kitchen, to follow him into his den. Bob opened a closet and pulled out a small black Camelbak MULE daypack. "This already has various minimal supplies in it, so I want you to keep it with you at all times."

Chris took the pack and noticed that there was a small zippered pouch built into the pack at the top. Chris unzipped the pouch and placed both flash drives inside, and then re-zippered it.

Bob then pulled out a larger pack. "This is my bug-out bag, so it has a lot more supplies than your pack. I will take this with us as it can provide for us both if for some reason we have to take to the woods. I'm hoping that doesn't happen.

"This is what we are going to do," Bob stated. "I want you to follow me up to Newburgh, New York, to the Stewart International Airport. I would really prefer going to the

Westchester County airport, but we would have to drive completely west across Westchester County and then back. I want to keep us going in a direction away from here on a northerly path."

"That sounds good to me," Chris said sheepishly.

"When we get to Stewart Airport, I want you to park your car in the long term parking area. Do you have a cell phone charging cord in your vehicle?" Bob asked.

"Yes I do," Chris replied.

"I want you to plug your phone in to ensure it stays charging, and make sure you leave it there. I then want you to go inside the terminal and purchase a first class ticket for the first flight going west, and use a charge card."

"Where west?" Chris asked.

"Anywhere west; California, Nevada, Arizona, I don't really care, just west. Once you purchase the ticket, come outside and I will pick you up with my vehicle."

"Why do I have to leave my car and phone there?" Chris questioned.

"If these people are as savvy as I think they are, once they realize that we aren't dead, they will start looking for you. If they are really clever, they will use the GPS in your phone to track you. Once they find your car at the airport they will also check to see if you booked a flight. Initially, they will believe you flew west. Eventually, they will determine you never got on the flight, but this all gives us time to get to my secure location to hide until I can figure something out."

"Won't they also be looking for your vehicle?"

"I'm taking the Xterra which is registered under another name. Also, I have a driver's license under that name so If I'm pulled over, everything will be normal," Bob replied.

"How did you do that?" Chris asked.

"I'll explain it to you later."

"I don't even have a change of clothes, or anything," Chris remarked.

"We will get you something on the way," Bob responded. "We have the advantage of time before they start looking for us, but it won't last long. Now let's get out of here."

With Chris carrying his small pack, Bob grabbed his bug-out bag, the extra magazines, and the two extra boxes of 9mm cartridges, and they went to their vehicles.

CHAPTER 16
On the Run

Bob placed his pack into the Xterra and Chris took his small day pack and put it on the front passenger seat of his Audi. Bob came over to Chris' car and said, "If I go through a yellow light and it changes to red before you can get through, I will pull over and wait for you. We want to proceed in a manner where we won't have any problems with the police."

Bob then returned to his Xterra and pulled out of his driveway with Chris following. Bob traveled north on Route 9, keeping a pace that allowed Chris to stay behind him.

When Bob reached Route 84, he took the on ramp for the west-bound lanes. Seeing the sign for Stewart International Airport, he exited Route 84 and preceded a couple of miles to the airport. He then slowed and pulled over just before the drop off ramp. Chris pulled over behind him. Bob walked back to the driver's window of Chris' car. Chris lowered the window.

"As we discussed Chris, I want you to proceed to the long term parking area. I am going to park in the short term lot which is directly across from the terminal. As you can see, this is a small airport, compared to those down in the city.

"Remember to leave your phone plugged in the car when you get out," Bob continued. "Make sure you grab your pack, and proceed inside and charge the ticket. When you are done, I will be waiting in the short term parking lot. The lot isn't that big so you should be able to see me when you come out of the terminal. Come directly to the truck and we will be on our way."

"Got it," Chris said looking a little tense.

"When you go inside, please try to remain calm," Bob said. "Don't act like there is a problem. They pick up on that type of thing. Just pull around my vehicle and I'll see you in a little while," Bob said with a reassuring smile.

Bob let Chris pull around his vehicle, and as he proceeded to the long term parking area, Bob drove forward a short distance and turned left into the short term parking lot. He was able to park in a spot facing the terminal. When Chris came out, he should have no problem seeing Bob's Xterra.

Bob waited about fifteen minutes, and was relieved when he saw Chris exit the front of the terminal with the pack over one shoulder. Chris walked across the three lanes at the crosswalk and as he did so, he spotted Bob's truck. He walked directly to it and got into the front passenger seat.

"How did it go?" Bob asked.

"Fine," Chris replied. "Not nearly as scary as I thought it would be. I'm heading to Vegas in thirty minutes," Chris said smiling.

"That's good, now let's start our adventure," Bob said smiling back.

Bob returned to Route 84 again and took the entrance ramp for the west bound lanes.

"So tell me about this fake ID," Chris said.

"Bob explained that his alternate ID wasn't really fake. It actually was real, as the person he got the date of birth from had been a real person, but had died at birth. He indicated that when you know how, the rest is easy.

"My other name is Robert Walker. I ensured that I kept the same first name as a person will automatically respond to that when called. However, the last name should not start with the same letter as your real name. Just a study I read. I have a birth certificate, social security number, and various school diplomas and a college degree under that name. I also register some of my vehicles under that name, such as this Xterra. The ones left at my house are under my real name.

"I also have a driver's license under both names. The one under my real name has a picture of me without a beard and my hair is in a pony tail so it looks like I have very short hair. I also wore glasses with large black frames, which were actually just plain glass. My alternate driver's license has me with beard, long hair down with a head band, like it is now, and no glasses. Facial recognition software would determine I was the same guy in both pictures, but the average person would not. Anyway, just keep calling me Bob and we shouldn't have any trouble," Bob concluded with his perpetual smile.

When Bob approached the exit for Middletown, New York he exited Route 84 onto Route 17 north. Shortly after pulling onto Route 17, he exited into a large mall.

"What are we doing here?" Chris asked.

"At this point, nobody really knows what I look like. Unfortunately, they do know what you look like. I want to change your appearance, so we are going to get you some new clothes."

"Whatever you say Bob."

Bob pulled into a small side parking lot, as opposed to the larger lots, and parked. He then leaned to his right, released the catch on the glove box, and as it opened it nearly smacked Chris in the knees.

"Sorry about that," Bob said, "But we will need some cash for shopping."

Bob pulled out the owner's manual. However, when he opened it, it wasn't exactly a manual. The vinyl cover for the manual was actually just used to conceal the fact that the manual had been hollowed out. Inside the hollowed section was a stack of twenty dollar bills. Bob extracted a handful, placed them in his right front pocket, then closed and returned the manual to the glove compartment.

"Let's go shopping," Bob proposed as he started to open his door.

Chris got out, grabbed his day pack, and the two of them went into the mall. While they were walking Bob explained what they needed.

"Chris, I want you to get several pairs of plain jeans, some underwear, socks, some colored t-shirts and sweat shirts without writing on them, a light polartec fleece jacket, and a Carhartt hooded work jacket. We will also need a pair or two of work boots and a ball cap without any insignia on it. And for the time being, stop shaving," Bob concluded.

"Am I really going to need all of this stuff?" Chris asked.

"Chris, please just do as I ask, I don't have time to explain everything right now. I will help you select the clothes and I will pay for them in cash. DO NOT use your charge card until further notice. I'm serous Chris," Bob stated.

* * *

While Bob and Chris shopped at the mall, Boris entered Mr. Mann's office at CANE Headquarters and told him that it had been several hours and he had not heard from Pierre, who was also not answering his cell phone.

"You better get over to Armstrong's place and see if you can find out anything," Mr. Mann stated. "And make it quick. If something went wrong, we need to find out."

"I'll head there at once," Boris replied as he left Mann's office.

Boris drove to Bob's address in his gray Lincoln MKZ, and cautiously advanced up the driveway. As he got close to the house he could see Pierre's car sitting out front.

Boris pulled to the right of the driveway and after looking around, got out. He walked around the house trying to peer into windows to determine if he could see anything unusual. He was able to observe that nobody appeared to be inside, then went to the side entrance and knocked. Then, after a minute without anyone answering, he kicked in the door. It took several attempts, but Boris was a big man.

Using caution, he entered the house with his 380 Walther PPK/S drawn. He searched the house but found nobody. He noticed that some of the furniture in the living room looked like it had been pushed out of place. Something had happened here, he thought to himself. But what? When he walked though the kitchen he saw a small stack of envelopes on the counter, which appeared to be bills. He picked one up and saw it was addressed to a Robert Armstrong.

He next started to examine the yard and out buildings. When he entered the garage, he found Pierre leaning against the inside wall. Boris went over to him and, with little compassion, ripped the duct tape off Pierre's mouth.

"What the hell happened?" Boris asked not sounding pleased.

Still a little groggy, Pierre tried to answer, but his words were slow.

"The guy who answered the door got the best of me. Who is this guy?" Pierre responded after moving his jaw back and forth before he could talk.

"Where are they now?" Boris barked.

"I have no idea," Pierre responded looking down at the floor.

"So they just kicked your ass and left?" Boris spat showing little compassion for Pierre. "Where are your car keys?"

"In my right front pants pocket," Pierre responded without looking up.

Boris looked around and found a large adjustable wrench on one of Bob's benches. With the wrench in hand, he came back to Pierre and said, "You're getting old my friend."

With that, Boris hit Pierre in the side of the head with the wrench, knocking him over. He then put the duct tape back on Pierre's mouth, and got the car keys out of his pocket.

Boris picked Pierre up and slung him over his shoulder and exited the garage. He walked directly to Pierre's car, opened his trunk, and threw Pierre inside. Closing the trunk lid, he walked to the right side of the car and placed the keys over the right front tire.

Before he pulled out of the driveway he placed a call on his cell phone.

"I need you to get over to number one, Bennett Road, in Peekskill for a pickup," Boris ordered. "It is a black Cadillac

CTS-V sedan. The keys are over the right front tire. Take it to the crusher and report back to me when it is done."

* * *

When Bob was sure that Chris had obtained all the clothing items he had described, he pointed out they had better get going.

"I'm getting real hungry; can we grab a bite while we are here?" Chris asked.

"I am too, but I'd rather not do it here in a crowded mall," Bob responded. "We have been here long enough. When we get back on the road, and a little further up Route 17, it becomes a little more rural than this area. We can stop at an old trucker's diner for some chow."

Bob and Chris returned to the Xterra with several bags of clothes and exited the mall parking lot, heading north on Route 17.

* * *

When Boris returned to CANE Headquarters, he explained what happened, and announced that he was able to identify Bob as Robert Armstrong.

Gray Mann was livid. "I want this Christopher Hughes found and fast. I also want this Armstrong guy. If we can make him a fugitive from justice and get everybody looking for him it will take less time."

Boris said, "Mr. Mann, while exploring this Armstrong's place I saw all kinds of things that would classify him as a domestic terrorist under the new guide lines. He has off grid solar panels, water barrels collecting water from his roofs, and various types of gardens. Maybe we can solicit the DTTF to help in our search."

"They would certainly have capabilities we don't. And I'm betting if they find Armstrong, we will find Hughes. Let me make a phone call and see if we can't use this new agency to our further advantage."

Gray Mann placed a call to a special number he was given after the creation of the DTTF in the event he needed a special favor.

The phone was answered with, "This is Drescher."

"Are we on a secure line?" Mann asked.

"Of course, who is this?"

"This is Mr. Mann and I need a favor."

"How can I help Mr. Mann?"

Gray Mann described the situation and what he needed done. He indicated the importance that this be done as soon as possible. He explained that, because of the various self reliant stuff Armstrong had on his property, it should warrant enough justification for a DTTF raid. While there, they could use the opportunity to gather information that would help locate him.

Gray Mann continued his conversation, but lowered his voice slightly. "In the event that Armstrong is found there, it would indeed be advantageous if he didn't survive while attempting to resist arrest. However, if he isn't there, make sure that something occurs that would cause him to become a fugitive from justice. He will be easier to find that way.

"And one more thing. It is our understanding that Armstrong is somehow involved with an individual by the name of Christopher Hughes, who owns a company named ZeRho. We believe Mr. Hughes might have some information in regard to how, and why, the DTTF was created, which he threatens to reveal. He apparently is using Mr. Armstrong to help him in some way. Of course we can't let that occur. If this Hughes was also located, and he may be with Armstrong, we would certainly like to make sure he can't talk to anyone."

"Not a problem Mr. Mann, we enjoy raids. I can make it happen Sunday, which is the soonest with such short notice."

"I thank you for your cooperation," Gray Mann said and hung up.

Upon getting off the phone with Gray Mann, Drescher called Max Archer, the Facility's Commander at the Northeast Sector facility.

Max Archer had also been a Diplomatic Security Special Agent with the U.S. Department of State, and had served with Drescher. He was a real warrior, but liked killing maybe just a little too much. He stood six feet two inches tall and had a firm build. With close cropped hair, he always looked like he was ready to go back to battle.

Drescher discussed the operation, and Archer assured him that the raid would take place Sunday, and he would handle the Armstrong situation, as well as the Hughes complication, if he was present.

"By the way, how is that issue with our agent being friends with the FBI agent?" Wolfgang asked.

"It is my understanding that he has continued to make contact with his friend. We have also learned that his friend was up in this area for a law enforcement conference and they met for dinner. Amazing what a little surveillance on your own people can develop. Anyway, I believe I may be able to handle that problem at the same time."

"Keep me informed," Wolfgang said.

"I will sir," and with that the conversation was terminated.

* * *

Bob and Chris discussed the current situation while driving north. Bob explained that they needed to stay hidden until Bob could find out what was going on. Bob saw the diner up ahead and pulled into the large parking lot. He drove around to the far side and parked by several large trucks. They both got out and entered the diner with Chris carrying his pack over his shoulder.

Bob approached the counter and told Chris they would sit there. They sat down with Chris to the left of Bob, and Chris placed his small pack between his feet on the raised floor in front of his seat, which was mounted on a single support, as was so typical of diner counters. They ordered lunch and ate with very little conversation.

After finishing their meal Bob leaned over to Chris.

"I'll be right back; I need to hit the head."

"The what?" Chris asked.

"The little boy's room," Bob said with a wink.

Bob got up and went to the men's room. At the moment Bob entered the men's room a woman wearing a short skirt and too much eye makeup dropped her purse on the floor behind and to the right of Chris. The contents of the bag splayed all over the floor.

"Oh my God," the woman said loudly. "My stuff is everywhere, this just isn't my day," she continued in a loud tone.

Chris turned and saw the woman on her knees trying to gather the stuff and put it back in her purse. Chris got up and bent down to help.

"It's OK ma'am, I'll help you get your things together," Chris said courteously.

As Chris bent down to help, a scraggly man who had been sitting to Chris' left reached down and grabbed Chris' pack and immediately, yet discreetly, walked out of the diner.

"I thank you so much," the woman said.

"No problem ma'am," Chris responded with a smile.

The woman then walked to the door and exited the diner. She walked directly to an old late model vehicle and got into the passenger side. The man who had grabbed Chris' pack was sitting behind the wheel going through it.

"There ain't shit of value in this thing," he said as she pulled the door closed. "A freaking waste of time and energy. He looked like he would at least of had a tablet or something or something of value in here."

"It ain't me fault, you're the one who pointed him out," the woman said.

The man drove across the parking lot to one of the trash cans at the end of the aisle, reached out and threw the pack in, and drove away.

As Bob returned from the bathroom he sat down next to Chris and asked if he wanted to get a cup of coffee to go, as they would be continuing directly to their destination.

"Sounds good to me," Chris said.

Bob happened to glance down and didn't see the pack between Chris' feet.

"Where is your pack?" Bob said suddenly.

Chris looked down and realized it was gone.

"It was right here between my feet," he said in disbelief.

"What did you do while I was gone?"

"Nothing," Chris replied looking scared. "I sat right here, except for helping some woman for just a moment. But she was right behind me there on the floor," Chris continued as he swiveled around on his seat and pointed at the spot.

"What woman?" Bob asked looking around.

"She was right here a moment ago."

"Well I don't see anyone now. Tell me exactly what occurred during the short time I was gone," Bob said quietly sounding aggravated.

Chris, using a low tone, explained how a woman had dropped her purse and he helped her pick up her stuff. He said he was only out of his seat for less than a minute, and only right behind it. He assured Bob it was less than a minute.

Bob looked around and said, "Where did the guy go that was sitting to your left? He had just ordered a cup of coffee."

"What guy, I didn't notice anybody?"

There was a scroungy guy one seat over from yours on your left," Bob said.

"I never noticed him," Chris said apologetically.

"I'm not mad Chris, I'm just upset. You really have to start being more aware of your surroundings," he said in a low tone.

"I am sorry," Chris said quietly.

"We will discuss this in the truck. Let's get out of here."

Bob got up, went to the register and paid, and he and Chris went to Bob's truck and got in.

"Before I pull out of here, I will drive around the parking lot and you look around to see if you can find this woman," Bob said.

"If I see her, I will know," Chris replied craning his neck looking around. "But she couldn't have grabbed my pack. I was between her and my seat."

"I realize that," Chris. But she probably had an accomplice to grab the pack while she kept you busy looking down at the floor."

"I am so stupid," Chris said sounding extremely upset. "And now, again, I don't have anything. I risked your life and all for nothing. And now somebody is trying to kill us."

"Just calm down Chris," Bob said. "First things first. Keep looking for this woman."

"I don't see any women at all," Chris said as Bob continued around the parking lot.

"I don't either," Bob replied. "She must have gotten out of here in a hurry. Her accomplice was most likely waiting for her when she came out and drove away immediately."

"Well, what the hell do we do now?" Chris retorted.

"We continue with the plan and get to my hideout. I still have a few tricks up my sleeve."

"What kind of tricks?" Chris asked looking confused.

Bob didn't want to get into it now and actually felt that if he let Chris stew awhile, he might realize he needed to get a little more serious about his actions, and become more aware of his surroundings and those around him.

"We will discuss it when we get to a safe place," Bob stated flatly.

Bob continued north on Route 17 until he came to Livingston Manor, which is at the southwest end of the Catskill Park. Taking various backcountry roads north, up and through the Catskill Park to the northern edge, he then proceeded in a northeasterly direction to his new place.

As Bob drove alongside his aunt's house, he could see a light on inside. He stopped and told Chris to wait in the vehicle.

Bob got out of the truck and went to his aunt's house and knocked. Aunt Martha answered the door and smiled when she saw Bob.

"Well I'm back for a short stay," Bob said casually. "I have a friend with me so we will be eating at the new place. By the way, I'm not here," Bob continued with a wink.

"Well have a good time, even though you're not here," Martha replied with chuckle.

Bob continued up the long logger's road and stopped when he reached his property. He got out of the truck, unlocked the cable stretched across the entrance, and pulled it to the side. After entering his property, he stopped again to stretch and lock the cable back in place.

Pulling in front of his house, he parked.

"Well, this will be called home for the time being," Bob said dryly to Chris.

"Wow, whose place is this?" Chris asked.

"It's mine," Bob replied. It is my new place and fortunately, nobody knows about it. Now let's get inside."

Bob and Chris grabbed the bags of new clothes that were purchased for Chris. Bob unlocked the front door and entered with Chris following.

"This is really an interesting house," Chris said upon entering.

"It is a passive solar house," Bob said. "I'll show you the whole place tomorrow, but first things first. Would you like a cup of coffee?"

"That would be great," Chris responded

Bob went to the kitchen and put on a pot of coffee. Chris joined him and sat at the small table in the kitchen.

Holding his head in his hands, Chris started, "We are so screwed. I have put both our lives in danger, and I don't even know how they found out. This wasn't supposed to involve you after you recovered the flash drive. I am so sorry, Bob. And now I couldn't even keep the recording safe. I'm a real asshole!"

Bob walked over to the table and set down two coffee mugs, a sugar bowl, a container of powdered coffee creamer, and two spoons.

"Chris, understand something," Bob said while still standing. "I am not upset with you; I'm just aggravated at the situation. You are new to all this and maybe I should have taken control of the flash drives myself. But they are your property, not mine. I warned you that this could become a dangerous situation. I just didn't think it would happen this fast, and while I was still involved. I owe it to your father to continue helping you in any way I can, and I will do that. But, you will have to start taking this seriously, and start thinking differently. It is no different than your company, which you have been very successful with. I'm sure, even if you don't understand the concept; you had to think tactically when making decisions. Who are my competitors, how might they try to hurt me, what can I do to prevent that, and so forth. We are now in a tactical situation, and I need to know that you will act seriously and stop acting like we have already lost. And most of all, I need you to stop whining."

"I'm really sorry about all of this Bob, and you are right. I was careless and that carelessness has put us in danger. I will do what you say, and attempt to better understand this new operational mindset that apparently I'm not real savvy with."

Bob heard the coffee finish perking and walked over to it and grabbed the pot. Carrying it over to the table he poured a cup for both Chris and himself. He then joined Chris at the table.

"Chris, I'm not trying to place blame here, or make you feel bad," Bob said as he put sugar and creamer in his coffee cup and stirred. "But we are in this together and I need to know that you have my back. We need to depend on each other. It is that simple."

"I will do whatever you need Bob," Chris said preparing his own cup of coffee. "I realize that I'm on a learning curve here, but I will take it seriously and learn whatever I can from you. My only problem is, without the recording, I have no way of trying to prove these people are after us and why. They think we have it and will pursue us, I would assume. How do we protect ourselves from them?"

"Chris, I haven't been totally honest with you," Bob said looking directly at Chris.

"Chris, looking directly back at Bob said, "What do you mean?"

"First of all, don't get upset by what I am about to tell you. When I made the copies of the recording for you, I made one additional copy on an IronKey flash drive. I put that copy in safe keeping, just in the event that something like this happened. I did it as an additional measure of protection for both you and the recording."

"I can't believe you did that," Chris said when Bob finished his statement.

"I said not to get upset," Bob responded.

"I'm not upset, I'm in disbelief. I trust you explicitly Bob, and again, you have saved the day. But how do we get this flash drive without getting caught?"

"I will have it brought to us by a friend," Bob said.

"Are we sure we can trust this person?" Chris asked, trying to think tactically.

"As you have trusted me with your life, I trust this person with mine," Bob responded.

"I don't know what to say Bob, but thank you for your expertise and loyalty. I don't know what I would have done without you."

"Let's not get sappy here," Bob said with a smile. "Now let's get you a place to sleep."

Chris smiled back at Bob hoping that everything would now be ok.

Bob got up from the table and told Chris he had to go to the garage for a minute and would be right back.

Chris picked up the coffee cups and spoons, carried them to the sink, and started washing them.

Bob returned a few minutes later carrying a long folded item that Chris didn't recognize.

"What is that?" Chris asked.

"This is your new bed." It's called a cot and being I don't have a guest room, you will be sleeping in the living room. I don't have a very large couch because the room isn't that big, and I'm not known for lounging. It definitely is not long enough to sleep on."

Bob carried the cot into the living room, unfolded it and put the cross braces in place.

"It certainly isn't what you are accustomed to I'm sure, but it will have to do for now," Bob said after setting it up. "I'll get you a sleeping bag and you can get comfortable for the night. First let me show you where the bathroom is."

Bob showed Chris where the bathroom was, which Chris indicated he needed to use. Bob returned to the kitchen. Opening the small pantry door he walked inside as a small LED light came on automatically. He closed the door behind him and pulled up on a coat hook on the rear of the left wall. As he heard a click, he pushed the rear wall of the pantry open and entered his large pantry and supply area. Going to one of the shelving units, he grabbed a sleeping bag and returned to the living room with it. Chris came back from the bathroom and Bob handed him the sleeping bag.

"Just like camping out," Bob said smiling.

"Well I'm not used to camping out, but I do believe I will be comfortable. This is an awesome place you have here."

"Thanks Chris, I'll show you more of it tomorrow. I'll see you in the morning," Bob said as he headed for the kitchen. He turned off the coffee pot, cleaned it out, and set it up for the morning. He then headed for his bedroom.

When Bob got in his bedroom, he sent a text message to his friend, "Expect a call early tomorrow morning at six o'clock on your alternate device. I will explain then." Bob then got undressed and went to bed.

CHAPTER 17
Hiding Out

Bob woke up at almost exactly five thirty. He headed for the kitchen and turned the coffee pot on. He then went to the bathroom and took a quick shower, got dressed, and returned to the kitchen.

When he entered, Chris had already poured himself a cup of coffee and was sipping it at the table. An empty cup and accoutrements were sitting on the table.

"Good morning Bob, I hope you don't mind. The smell of the coffee woke me up."

"Not at all Chris, I thought it might."

Bob grabbed the coffee pot from the counter and poured himself a cup and then joined Chris at the table.

"How did you sleep?" Bob asked.

"Better than I thought I would. I guess knowing we still have a copy of the recording relaxed me. Plus all the excitement yesterday, I was beat."

"Well we don't have it yet, but if everything goes as planned, we should have it today."

"I have to make a call in about two minutes and I thought I would make it outside, as I have better reception there. Why don't you enjoy the coffee, and I'll be back in a few minutes."

"No problem, I'll see you when you come back in."

Bob grabbed his coffee cup and proceeded out to the front of his house and set it down on a small table. He then went to the garage and returned with a folding Adirondack chair. Sitting down, he pulled out his cell phone and placed a call.

The call was answered on the second ring and Bob said, "Hello Buddy, I need a hand with a little situation."

"What can I do Bob?"

"I need that item I left with you and I need you to bring it to me. Can you rent a car this morning under your alternate identification?"

"Sure, no plans and no problem."

"I need you to drive up here and deliver it to my new place. Oh, and bring a pack and some changes of clothes. I might need you here for a few days. What time do you think you can rent the car?"

"I'll be at the rental place around nine o'clock. I should be out of there in no more than fifteen minutes that time of the morning. It takes about two and a quarter hours to get to you, so I should be there at around eleven-thirty or so. If there is any problem I will call you with an update. Need anything else?"

"Come armed," Bob replied. "I'll see you when you get here and I'll explain what is going on."

"See you then."

Bob grabbed his cup and went back into the house. Upon entering the kitchen, he poured himself some more coffee and sat at the table with Chris.

"Why don't you go ahead and take a shower, and get dressed in some of your new clothes. I have a few things to show you before I have to leave," Bob said.

"You're leaving?"

"Just for a short trip to pick up some food for us. I don't keep anything fresh here while I'm down at my old place," Bob replied. By the way, the recording should be here by noon if everything goes as planned," Bob continued with a smile.

"That is great," Chris said sounding relieved.

"While you take your shower, I'm sure I can whip us up something to eat."

"Are you sure it is safe for you to leave?" Chris asked.

"I have the alternate identification for myself and the truck. At this point, nobody is looking for Robert Walker. I should have no problem. I want you to stay here because you might be spotted and the only identification you have is yours. I can't take the chance of you getting caught. As long as you are here, you should be safe."

"I understand," Chris replied.

"Now go rinse off," Bob said smiling.

Chris got up from the table, placed his cup in the sink, and went to the living room. He rummaged through the bags of new clothes and grabbed a pair of jeans, some underwear and socks, and a t-shirt. He then headed for the bathroom.

Bob checked the pantry and grabbed some flour, sugar, baking powder, salt, powdered milk, and a package of "OvaEasy" egg crystals, placing them on the counter. He also grabbed a can of Red Feather butter, which he opened. Placing the appropriate amounts of the ingredients in a bowl, and adding some water, he mixed it all together with a large hand whisk.

He set a cast iron griddle over two of the burners on the stove, lit the burners, and added some butter.

As he waited for the griddle to heat up, he readied a fresh pot of coffee and turned it on.

When the griddle was hot and the butter had melted, Bob grabbed a ladle and started pouring circles of the mixture onto the griddle. As bubbles appeared, Bob flipped the pancakes with a spatula.

Bob set a pot on the counter, and as he removed the finished pancakes he placed them in the pot and put the cover on it to keep them warm.

Chris entered the kitchen wearing his new clothes. Bob turned from the stove and chuckled.

"Does it really look that bad?" Chris asked.

"No Chris, actually you look pretty good. But I probably would have removed the tags."

"I planned to, I just didn't have anything in the bathroom to cut them off with," Chris said defensively.

"I'm just kidding Chris, grab some plates from the cabinet to the left of me here, and set them on the table. Get some utensils in this drawer and we will have some pancakes."

"They sure smell good," Chris replied as he got a couple of plates from the cabinet and set them on table.

Bob went to the pantry and grabbed a jar of maple syrup which he added to the table setting together with the butter.

"Let's eat my friend," Bob said as he sat down placing the pot of finished pancakes on the table.

Both Chris and Bob were famished and ate every pancake from the stack in the pot.

"I can't believe how hungry I was," Chris stated upon finishing his last bite of pancake.

"I was a little hungry myself," Bob replied.

Once breakfast was finished both, Bob and Chris, cleaned up the dishes. Bob helped cut the tags off the clothes Chris was wearing and handed him the scissors. "You might want to get the tags off the other new clothes before you need to pack some of them."

"Where are we going?" Chris asked confused.

"Nowhere, but I want you to setup a small bug-out bag later today in the event we need to get out of here quick for some reason."

When Chris had removed all the tags from his clothes he returned the scissors to the kitchen and found Bob sitting out in front of the house enjoying the early morning sun, finishing his last cup of coffee.

"I got two more chairs from the garage, one for you and one for my other friend. Have a seat."

"This place is really awesome," Chris said looking around.

"Well, when all this is over, hopefully it will be my new permanent home."

"Do you really think we will get out of this?" Chris asked.

"Well, I don't intend to give up without a fight. Besides, I put too much work into this place not to be able to enjoy it," Bob replied with his eternal smile.

"You have a great sense of confidence Bob; I really admire that in you."

"Well I've been through a lot of shit in my day and I don't plan on this situation ending my track record of surviving. I do have an idea or two. Now let me show you around a little and then I'll head down to the small store to pick up some food. I'm sure my friend will be hungry when he gets here."

With that, Bob got up, and with Chris following, started showing him the basic structure of the house. He explained how he had dug into the berm so that only the south windows side was actually out of the ground.

"This took a lot of work, how did you get a contractor way up here?" Chris asked.

"I didn't," Bob replied. "I did it all myself with a lot of help from a Kubota and a little help from a friend."

"How long have you been working on it?"

"Just a little over a year," Bob answered.

Bob then took Chris down to the large garage and showed him how he had plenty of room for his vehicles and a small workshop.

"What the hell is that?" Chris asked pointing at Bob's Chenowth Scorpion Desert Patrol Vehicle.

"Oh that's just a little vehicle I bought in case things really go to shit in our country. I figured I might become the Road Warrior," Bob responded with a quick laugh.

Bob Walked Chris around the immediate property showing him the potting shed, garden area, and other features.

"I hope that when I can live here permanently, I will be almost entirely self-reliant. Of course you can't be totally self-sufficient in today's world, but being self-reliant is something I can aim for."

"Why can't you be self-sufficient?" Chris asked looking puzzled.

"The world has become too small," Bob replied. "Almost everything depends on something else. Even my solar panels. They can provide me with energy that can be stored for later use, and allow me to live off the grid. But the panels, controllers, and batteries are made by someone else. I can't make those myself. So, although some things can allow you to live a self-reliant lifestyle, being totally self-sufficient is unrealistic,"

"I get what you're saying," Chris said nodding his head.

"Well anyway, I'm going to take that short trip to the store and will return shortly. But let me show you one more thing before I go."

Bob took Chris back into the house and proceeded to the kitchen. He walked over to the pantry and told Chris to come over there. "I have a secret place hidden behind this small pantry." He opened the door and showed Chris the coat hook. He explained that you had to pull up on the coat hook which was the opening mechanism for the rear wall panel. As Bob pulled up on the hook, he pushed against the back panel, and it swung inwards. He had Chris follow him into the large storage room.

"I want you to be careful while I'm gone. Don't get complacent just because you think it is safe here. Keep an eye and ear out, and if you see anybody approaching this place, you come hide in here. Make sure you close both the pantry door and the secret back panel. And keep quiet until I get back."

With that, Bob and Chris came out of the hidden area and Bob secured the two doors.

"I'll be back shortly," Bob said as he went outside and got in his Xterra. He drove to the cable across the entrance. He went through the usual procedure so that as he drove down the logger's road the cable was back in place.

Upon getting to the bottom of the road, he stopped at his aunt's house and explained that he had another friend coming up around noon.

"He is the same guy who helped me with foundation and walls, but he will be in a different car. I'm just going down to the store to pick up some food and should be back long before he gets here. Need anything at the store?" Bob asked.

"No dear, I went shopping yesterday, but thanks for asking," Martha replied. "But here, take a few jars of my strawberry jam that I canned earlier this year," she continued as she went to a cabinet and came out with them. "I'm sure you and your friends will enjoy it."

"Thanks Martha, I appreciate it. I'll probably see you later as I might park my friend's car in the barn."

Bob returned to his truck carrying the jars of strawberry jam. He proceeded to a small grocery store and purchased some milk, eggs, sausage, hamburger, steaks, bread, and fresh vegetables. Throwing some other items in the cart, he thought to himself how great it would be when he could start hunting up here to put away his own meat and start gardening for his own vegetables.

Bob checked out, paying with cash, and returned back to his property with the goods he had purchased. Upon arrival, he left the cable down at the entrance after lowering it, so his friend could pull right into the property when he arrived.

Chris was sitting in front of the house and walked over to Bob's truck to help him with the groceries.

"We should be eating good tonight," Bob said with a smile. "Anything happen while I was gone?"

"Nope, everything was fine. I kept an eye and ear out, that's why I was sitting out front," Chris replied.

"Good, let's get this stuff into the kitchen because I have another little project planned."

Bob and Chris carried all the groceries into the kitchen and they put everything away where it belonged. Bob had turned the refrigerator on when they had arrived the day before and it was plenty cold.

"This is what I want to do Chris," Bob said. "I want to put together a small bug-out bag for you just in case we have to get out of here."

"Bug-Out means leave in a hurry right?" Chris asked.

"Now you're getting it," Bob replied.

Bob had Chris follow him into the hidden storage room behind the small pantry. He grabbed an old large empty cardboard box and started throwing some items from the shelves into it, handing the box to Chris, when he finished. He then selected an older Blackhawk HydraStorm Cyclone backpack from a shelf that had an assortment of packs on it. He threw that on the top of the box with all the gear.

"I want you to take this stuff into the living room and wait for me. I have a couple of quick things to do and I will be right out," Bob instructed Chris.

As Chris left the supply room, Bob walked to the right side of the storage room to a set of shelves that held supplies such as large packages of toilet paper, paper towels, various sizes of zip closure and garbage bags, packages of paper plates, and other type of soft goods. He pulled the unit and it hinged forward into the room. He then opened a metal door that hinged inwards, into another room.

He entered the comm room and proceeded directly to one of his two large gun safes. Twirling the knob with the correct combination, he pulled the unlock lever down, and heard the locking bars move. He then took the Browning Hi-Power, which he had been wearing constantly since he left his other place, and put it in the safe, along with the holster. Extracting a Beretta 92SF and a holster for it, he donned the holster, and after checking the chamber and magazine of the Beretta to ensure it was completely loaded, he slipped it into the holster. Grabbing six extra magazines from the safe, a dropped down leg holster, and two fifty round boxes of 9mm cartridges, he placed them all alongside one wall on the floor, where he would later set the bug-out bags.

Closing the first safe, he opened the other. He looked inside examining the contents, then reached in and extracted a semi-automatic Bushmaster M4 carbine, chambered in 223 caliber. Bob liked the firepower this rifle provided, but didn't want to carry two types of ammunition. He placed it back into the safe.

Bob next withdrew a KEL-TEC SUB-2000 carbine. Being chambered in 9mm, the same as the Beretta, he felt this would be a good companion for the handgun, as he would only need to carry one caliber cartridge if he had to bug-out. Bob also liked the fact that the carbine was configured to take the same magazines as the Beretta which was another big plus. Most semi-automatic carbines are long and therefore difficult to carry through the woods along with a pack and other gear. However, even though the KEL-TEC was twenty-nine and a quarter inches long, by rotating the barrel upwards and back, it was reduced to a size of only sixteen and a quarter inches long. Having selected the KEL-TEC, Bob grabbed four more fifty round boxes of 9mm cartridges.

Bob also grabbed a special pouch he had made for the KEL-TEC, that had MOLLE (Modular Lightweight Load-Carrying Equipment) straps on it, which allowed him to attach it to the PALS (Pouch Attachment Ladder System) webbing on the back of his pack. It made for a nice carry system when on the run. It also had a small pouch on each side for a thirty-two round Beretta magazine, so he grabbed two of those from the safe as well. He placed it all next to the other stuff he had put by the wall.

From the backside of the door, he grabbed a khaki colored tactical vest off a hook and placed it with the other gear. When he got a chance, he would fill the magazine pouches on the front of the vest, once the magazines were loaded. He then closed the safe, and left the communications room, returning to the living room where Chris was looking through all the gear in the box.

"Well, let's get started," Bob said as he entered.

Bob explained to Chris that the pack would be prepared and staged in the event they had to leave quickly.

"It should sustain you for a couple of days," Bob said. "Keep in mind that mine is bigger and I will be able to supplement your needs. You are not used to carrying a pack so I want to keep yours on the medium size. It will probably be larger than you are used to, but I'm sure you can handle it."

Bob had Chris make up two military clothes rolls for two sets of underwear. Basically that was a way to roll a t-shirt, pair of skivvies, and a pair of socks into a small self contained roll that took up very little space in your pack. He then had Chris work a sweat shirt with a pair of jeans into a roll as well, and had him place these items into the bottom of his pack.

"I wish we could have picked you up some 5.11 tactical trousers like mine, but they didn't have anything like that at the mall," Bob said. "Jeans, being cotton, aren't the best thing for the woods, but you will have to live with it."

"These are two Spec-Ops BDU tactical belts made from nylon webbing. I want you to start wearing one now on your jeans and rollup the other one for your pack. We will determine the correct length for your waist and I will cut them with a hot knife first."

Bob then started laying out the various items from the box on the floor.

"First of all you need fire," Bob said. "Here is a BIC lighter, a tube of windproof and waterproof matches, and a Ferrocerium rod with striker."

"What's a Ferrocerium rod?" Chris asked.

"It's an alternate way to start a fire, just not as easy as a lighter or matches. I'll show you later how to use that. It would be your last resort anyway. Use the lighter or matches and you will have a sure fire. I have also thrown in a fire blowing tube which is basically a small collapsible stainless steel tube with a flexible hose attached. I'll show you how to use that later as well."

Bob then threw an extra BIC lighter to Chris and told him to keep it in one of his front pants pockets at all times.

"I always believe in backups, and that is your fire backup.

"Now for shelter," Bob continued. "Here is a casualty survival blanket, which can also be used like a small tarp to make a shelter, a smaller emergency blanket, a 10 foot by 12 foot ultra light silicone impregnated tarp, a poncho made from the same material, and an Eagles Nest Outfitters (ENO) hammock with slap straps."

"That little tarp is 10 feet by 12 feet?" Chris asked looking surprised.

"Yes, as you can see, it rolls up into a very small stuff sack.

"This little stuff sack holds one of the smallest sleeping bags I have found. It is called the Snugpak Jungle Bag. Although originally designed for tropical conditions, I find it is more than adequate for three season use. When packed in the provided compression sack it only measures about five and a half inches around by eleven inches long. Another great feature is a concealed roll-away mosquito netting that can be zippered over your face. You will strap this sleeping bag to the bottom of your pack to save room inside. I have also included a small silk sack that can be used inside your sleeping bag which provides additional warmth and helps keep your bag clean. And this is a one hundred foot hank of parachute cord which should satisfy any of your cordage needs.

"Now for water," Bob continued.

"Your pack has a one hundred ounce hydration bladder built in the back, but it makes it heavy if you fill it, so leave it empty for now. We can always fill it in the field if need be, as there is plenty of water around these parts.

"Here is a forty ounce stainless steel water bottle. Make sure you fill it before you put it in your pack. This here is a titanium pot, and as you can see, it slides nicely over the bottom of the water bottle so it doesn't take up any extra room in your pack."

Holding up a small package of foil encased tablets, Bob continued, "This is a package of chlorine dioxide water purification tablets in the event we can't boil water to purify it. I have also included a small Frontier Filter which will allow you to drink water that is questionable, through it like a straw. For additional water collection you will carry this collapsible bag. We can purify it when needed.

"You have a Mora knife here with a Kydex sheath and belt loop. Outside of your brain and the knowledge it holds, this is your most important survival tool, so protect it at all cost. Place this in the top of your pack and if we have to go, once we are out of here, you will put it on your belt.

"This is a Victorinox One Hand Trekker which is a good folding knife that you can open with one hand if necessary. It will be a backup to your main knife. I have also included a small folding Silky PocketBoy saw, and a stainless steel U-Dig-It trowel. I have a small Gerber Gorge Folding Shovel in my pack just in case we need something bigger.

"This is a Leatherman Wave, which is a multi tool that you will start carrying on your belt as soon as we get your belts adjusted. It, and the BIC lighter I threw you earlier, should be on you at all times.

"Now for food, and we won't carry much. Here you have four MRE (Meals Ready to Eat) entrees and heaters. This is a small vacuum sealed bag of rice, a bag of beef jerky, and a bag of bannock mix."

"What is bannock mix?' Chris asked curiously.

"It is sort of like bisquick, but I mix it myself using flour, baking powder, salt, and margarine. It lasts a long time without refrigeration so it is great for the field. It can be used to make bread, and sometimes in the field in the morning, I make a little pastry and top it off with some cinnamon-sugar mix. By the way, I included some of that as well.

There are also several packets of instant oatmeal, cup of soup, small envelopes of tuna, and a dozen power bars. This is a zip closure bag that holds twelve coffee bags with sugar and creamer packets. Last, we got you several packets of bouillon cubes, salt, pepper, and peanut butter which all fit in this small heavy zip closure bag. All the food and the small zip closure bag should be stored in this large Aloksak which is water, air, dust, and humidity proof. I have also included a miniature gas cartridge stove that stores in this small plastic case, and two small gas canisters. Also you have a plastic Spork, which has a spoon on one side and a fork on the other, as well as a long titanium spoon. The long spoon makes it easier to eat an MRE from its pouch.

"For some extras, this is a small headlamp, and one short flashlight, with an extra pair of batteries for each. In this little pouch you have a signal mirror and whistle which I don't believe we will be using, as we will be hiding, not trying to be found or rescued. But you should have them in your pack, just in case. Last there are two drum liners which you can roll up and put in the bottom of your pack as well.

"Drum liners? What are they for?" Chris asked.

"They have multiple uses in the field. Most likely we will fill one with leaves and use it as a mattress when we are on the ground. You can always do the same with the other and use it over you like a quilt. You could also make a poncho with one, but you have a poncho."

"Damn," was all Chris could say.

"I have a small zip closure bag here that has a short toothbrush, a few individual sized packets of toothpaste, some dental floss, a little comb, a mini bar of soap, a packet of antibacterial hand wipes, and a compact roll of toilet paper.

"This mini hockey puck looking thing is called a Lightload survival towel, and is actually a super absorbent fabric that measures twelve inches by twenty-four inches. It is all compressed into this little disc, but when you open it, it acts like a sponge to absorb water. It takes up little room.

"I've included a small first aid kit with just some basic essentials. I have a larger one in my pack in the event we have a major injury.

"I'm not sure if you know anything about navigation, but I thought you should have this base plate compass. If I get a chance I'll show you how to use it. If nothing else, it is a backup for me.

"This is a small lightweight balaclava and a wool watch cap. You've seen me use these before. If you have any room left in the pack, throw in this shemagh, it has multiple uses as well.

"I have also included two cotton bandanas which have multiple uses, and a mini roll of duct tape, which does as well.

"Last but not least, this is a set of night vision goggles like I used when I retrieved the cache. You will strap this to the outside top of your pack so you can grab them off if we need to leave in the dark. Here are two extra sets of batteries for them so keep them in your pack.

"Well that about covers it. It is not a hell of a lot, but more than enough to keep you alive for several days at least.

"Now let's get those belts adjusted so you can get one on and the other packed."

"All this is going to fit into this pack?" Chris asked holding up the Blackhawk Cyclone.

"I could fit a lot more than that in there and have," Bob replied. "You just have to pack it all a certain way, you'll see. You should have plenty of room."

Chris followed Bob out to the garage carrying the two Spec-Ops belts. Bob had Chris put one of the belts on and determined where it had to be cut and marked the other one at the same length. From one of the drawers of a large roller toolbox, Bob retrieved a small gas operated hot knife. It measured only seven inches long and three quarters of an inch in diameter, so it was much smaller than a normal gas operated torch.

Removing the top cover, Bob twisted the bottom to high and pushed up on a sliding button on the side, which turned on the gas. Using a sparking wheel on the side of the cover, he lit the hot knife. He then sat it on the counter with the knife tip portion sticking off the counter.

"It will take a minute or so for the blade to get hot," Bob explained to Chris.

"We used to have a small gas operated tool like that at M.I.T. but it had a soldering tip on it," Chris responded.

"This one does too, as well as a small torch tip. But I use the cutting tip most often so I leave it on there. It is great for trimming parachute cord when you make a bracelet, like the one I'm wearing, or when making lanyards.

"So that bracelet is made from parachute cord, like the stuff you gave me for my pack?" Chris asked.

"Yes, same stuff. This way I always have at least a small amount of cordage on my wrist wherever I may be. The parachute cord has seven inner strands that can be removed providing you with even more cordage. You can sew with that, use it for fishing, or other things."

Bob picked up the hot knife and cut the nylon webbing belts to the proper length with a diagonal cut.

"Why do you cut them at an angle?" Chris asked watching Bob.

"It makes the ends easier to feed through your belt loops," Bob responded. "Here, put this one on," he continued, handing one of the belts to Chris."

Chris fed the belt through the loops of his new jeans and slipped it through the buckle.

"Boy, this is a lot more substantial than those small thin belts I wear," Chris said.

"When you are carrying stuff on your belt like a multi-tool, a sheath knife, and especially a gun, you appreciate the additional support. The belt can also be used as a tourniquet, a sling, or to lash things together. Truly multi-functional," Bob added.

"I like it already," Chris said admiring it on his jeans.

"Here is the other one," Bob said handing it to Chris. "Roll it up and get it in your pack."

Bob and Chris went back into the house and Bob knew it was almost time for his friend to arrive.

"If you don't mind, you should start working on getting your pack in order. I'm gonna put on a fresh pot of coffee and take a cup out front to wait for my friends arrival."

"I'm on it Bob," Chris said light-heartedly.

Bob perked a pot of coffee and fixed himself a cup. He yelled down the hallway to tell Chris it was done and to help himself if he wanted any.

Bob then went out front and sat in one of the chairs with his coffee. He had tried to stay upbeat all day while he was with

Chris. But he still wasn't sure what to do next. Hopefully he and his friend could come up with an idea.

CHAPTER 18
An Old friend

Bob had almost finished his cup of coffee when his friend drove in with the rental car. He pulled up alongside the Xterra and parked.

Bob got up from his chair and walked over to the car and as his friend got out Bob shook his hand.

"Hey Buddy, it's been too long."

"I missed the place."

Chris, while working on his pack saw the car drive in through the expanse of windows on the front side of the house. He rushed down the hall to meet Bob's friend and see if he had the recording.

As Chris came out front and started walking towards the car he couldn't believe his eyes.

"Ralph, what the hell are YOU doing here?" Chris said, with each word getting louder as he spoke.

"Hey Boss, glad to see you too," Ralph responded with a smile."

"Chris, I'd like to introduce you to my good friend, but it looks like you two are already acquainted," Bob said with a chuckle.

"How the hell do you know each other? What the hell is going on here; I'm confused?" Chris shouted, not understanding what was happening.

"Well, let's all go inside and get a cup of coffee, and maybe Ralph and I can explain it to you," Bob said.

Ralph walked over to Chris and gave him a light hug.

"You'll understand shortly Chris; it's not a bad thing. Now come have a cup of coffee and calm down. By the way, looking good in your new duds," Ralph said with a smile.

Chris was still confused but followed Bob and Ralph into the house. When they got in the kitchen Ralph handed Bob the IronKey flash drive.

"I assume we want to protect this with our lives," Ralph said flatly.

"Is that the copy of the recording?" Chris asked.

"That it is Chris," Bob stated.

"How did Ralph get it? I'm not understanding this."

"You will, you will," Bob said. "We will fill you in on how we know each other and then I need to fill Ralph in on what has happened."

They all got a cup of coffee and sat down. Ralph started to explain.

"I'm sorry I have deceived you all these years Chris, but it was necessary. Let me explain.

"Many years ago Bob and I were under your father's command in Iraq. We all knew each other before that tour and felt a strong camaraderie between us. Your father knew that he was retiring after Iraq, and that Bob and I were getting out after our enlistment. We all knew that civilian life could be difficult after the Corps and we wanted a way to stay in touch and watch each other's back.

"One night in the desert of Iraq, we made a pact that we would stay close and always be there for each other. However, we wouldn't reveal our relationship to others, unless we absolutely had to. It was felt that it might be easier to protect one another if other people didn't know who the protectors were.

"I went to work for your father so I could be close, but nobody knew our relationship. That way I could watch his back without others suspecting me of doing so. Even though we believe your father was killed for not selling his company, I was able to continue there after his death and make sure it was not sold unless you made the decision."

"So," Chris interrupted, "You believe my father was killed as well?"

"Of course Chris, but he wouldn't let anybody get involved when he started getting threats. Both Bob and I wanted to help, but he told us to stay out of it. He said if he needed us, he would let us know. He believed he could handle it, and as you know, he was a stubborn man. But we loved him.

"That is why, when you sold your father's company, I came to you for a job. After your father died, my next duty was to protect his son."

"I guess I understand," Chris said, "but I wish I had known."

"If you had known, would anything be different?"

"I suppose not," Chris responded looking down at the table.

"That was another reason Bob always stayed down in the Peekskill area. It wasn't just that he had his parent's property. It kept him close to your father and me. After your father died, Bob and I discussed the matter as Bob wanted to get out of the area and build further up north. I told him I would remain in the area and stay with you, and he would still be close enough if the need arose."

"So, let me get this straight," Chris interrupted. "You and Bob have been watching my back ever since I was young. Even after my father was killed, you have continued to do so without my knowing it. And now you are both willing to put your life on the line for me. I wish I had gone into the Marine Corps because I have never seen such dedication or loyalty for friends in my life. I am truly humbled by your faithfulness to each other and the pact you took. It is a very rare thing today."

"When you are in combat together," Bob interjected, "It isn't about patriotism as some would like you to believe. Sure, that is why you got involved. But when you are out there, it is the guy next to you that you are willing to die for. You trust each other with your life and that my friend makes for a strong bond, that can't be broken."

"So Ralph, when I told you I needed to locate a Bob Armstrong, you already knew who I was looking for and led me to him?" Chris asked.

"Of course Chris. I obviously couldn't say anything to you, or ask any questions, but I did have words with Bob. I didn't know what it was about, but I knew if Bob was involved I would be kept in the loop. That way you had another set of eyes on your back, without your being aware of it."

"This all sounds like a spy thriller, but I must admit that I am very happy to have two individuals like you as friends. God knows I would hate to have you as enemies," Chris concluded, smiling for the first time since the conversation began.

Ralph looked at Chris and asked, "So are we good; I mean us as friends."

"Of course, "Chris responded.

Ralph turned to Bob.

"I can't believe how much you've accomplished since the last time I was here."

"And you haven't seen it all yet Buddy," Bob said smiling.

"You have been here before?" Chris asked Ralph.

Now it was Ralphs turn to smile.

"Of course, where do you think I was when I went on vacation?"

"I can assume it wasn't the Adirondacks?" Chris answered smiling along with both Ralph and Bob.

"I was here helping Bob pour the footings and walls for this fortress," Ralph said raising both arms in the air.

"And Buddy busted his ass working here," Bob interjected. "It wasn't much of a vacation but his help was truly appreciated."

"Why do you keep calling Ralph, Buddy?" Chris asked with a quizzical expression.

"Oh by the way, meet Buddy Owens," Bob replied. "That is his alternate identification name. I use it to keep in practice."

"Damn," Chris said, "Everybody has two names but me."

"We'll come up with something for you," Ralph said, and he and Bob both laughed.

* * *

At the same time Ralph and Bob were explaining their relationship to Chris, the DTTF was holding a mission briefing for the raid on Sunday, the following day. Max Archer had selected four agents for the raid and had them assembled in the briefing room.

"Alright, settle down," Max Archer commanded.

The agents settled back in their chairs and gave their full attention to Archer.

"Tomorrow morning, at eight o'clock, we will be conducting our first domestic terrorist raid down in the Peekskill, New York area. As you know, we normally conduct surveillance on a place before we go in, and normally raids are conducted in rural areas. However, it has already been determined by outside sources that this place has various violations to the new code pertaining to domestic terrorism.

"We will travel to the location in two vehicles. You four agents will be in one vehicle, and I will be in the other as a command post. We are to move in swiftly and try to apprehend the owner who has been identified as Robert Armstrong, who uses 'Bob' as his first name. We are hoping that, being it is early on a Sunday morning, he will be home. If he is not, we are to enter the residence and setup surveillance in an attempt to capture him when he returns.

"Agent Keegan, this is where your expertise in 'methods of entry' will come in. You will pick the lock to the residence, or gain entrance in another manner, without destroying any property. When, and if, Armstrong returns, we don't want him suspicious."

"Aye sir," Agent Keegan replied.

"The following is how a surveillance will be conducted, if required. One man will remain inside the residence. All vehicles will leave the area and be staged at the Westchester County Sheriff's Office repair garage. I will provide you with the directions after the briefing. The agent on surveillance will be relieved every eight hours, if another agent can be exchanged. It is our understanding that this residence is surrounded by a wooded area and we should be able to insert, and exchange an agent, through those woods without revealing our presence.

Agent Davis, you will take the first shift if a surveillance is required."

"Aye sir," Agent Davis replied.

"One more thing, it is our understanding that this Robert Armstrong is very close friends with another individual by the name of Christopher Hughes, who is under investigation for other acts of domestic terrorism. If he is found on the premises, he is to be captured as well.

"If either of these individuals are captured, we must use normal protocol. They are to be bound by both hands and feet with flex cuffs, gagged, and blindfolded using the usual black bag. They are to remain in that condition, without any conversation until they are delivered to our headquarters. At that point, I will be the first one to interview them. Are there any questions?'

With no questions being raised, Archer concluded the briefing.

* * *

Having filled Chris in about how Bob knew Ralph, it was Ralph's turn to be apprised of the current situation.

"OK," Ralph asked. "Who is going to fill me in on where we stand?"

Bob was the first to speak.

"You know from our previous conversations about Chris making a recording of the CANE Conference. I know you understand his reasoning for doing so, although neither of us necessarily thinks it was a good idea.

"You also know about Chris caching the flash drive and needing me to retrieve it. And you know the copy I provided you was just in case the others were lost.

"Well, yesterday, a guy came to my house right after Chris showed up to retrieve the copies I made. This was just shortly after I met you with the extra copy."

"And am I thankful for that other copy," Chris interjected.

"Anyway, all of a sudden this guy tries to kill me and Chris with a suppressed 1911. I took him out, but didn't kill him, like I would have in the old days."

"Well, we all get old," Ralph said with a chuckle.

"Yea, screw you," Bob continued smiling.

"I knew that if Chris hadn't told anybody but me, and only the three of us knew, then the only way these people could have known was through a technical intercept. That reminds me, you can assume that Chris' house and your offices at ZeRho are bugged."

"Nice to know," Ralph said with a frown.

"Once the attack took place at my house, I knew we had to get out of the area and hide until we could figure out how we were going to handle this situation.

"I had Chris follow me to Stewart Airport, and he parked his car there in long term parking with his cell phone plugged in, for obvious reasons. He then booked a flight to Vegas, came out of the terminal and we headed up here.

"On the way up here, we stopped at a diner to eat. When I went to the head, Chris was conned by some woman who allegedly dropped her purse behind his seat, and while assisting her, an apparent accomplice grabbed Chris' pack which had the flash drives in it. When I returned and noticed Chris' pack was gone, the two working together were nowhere to be found.

"When I got up here, I called you to the rescue. Now you are filled in," Bob concluded with a smile.

"Well, it sounds like you guys had a busy day yesterday," Ralph responded. "The question is what do we do now?"

They all sat there for a few minutes until Bob spoke first.

"I have an idea I was thinking about, so let me run it by you, and see what you think

"First of all, I don't believe that these people can be negotiated with. They apparently know what Chris did and obviously want him dead, and myself now as well."

"Maybe we can negotiate with them," Chris stated. "If I tell them I will destroy the recording and sign a non-disclosure agreement to never reveal its contents..."

Ralph interrupted, "No offense Chris, but that train of thought is very naive, and will get you killed. This isn't a business deal gone bad and we can call in the lawyers to help. These guys are serious and have a lot to protect. You and Bob being dead is their only assurance that the recording won't be revealed."

"OK, I guess it was pretty fucking stupid," Chris replied. "This was supposed to be my getting back at them for my father. It wasn't supposed to involve, or endanger anyone else."

Both Bob and Ralph just sat for a moment looking at Chris.

"What?" Chris asked noticing the stares.

"Nothing," Ralph replied. "I just never heard you swear before."

"Well it doesn't mean I don't know how," Chris replied.

"Let me continue," Bob interjected shaking his head. "As long as they know that we have the recording, they will continue to hunt us. But what if the recording was revealed, say on the nightly news, with the fact that the recording was made by Chris. We explain how Chris got naively involved with CANE thinking it would be good for his business, as he was told it would be. But after becoming a member he realized they were an evil organization. He made the recording in order to expose their intentions which were to hurt regular people. He could end up looking like a hero. CANE will obviously deny this but the recording directly links them and their plans. Even if nobody buys the story, Chris' name is out there, and if they try to kill him, it will only confirm he was telling the truth. It just might result in a détente. If nothing else it should give us some breathing room."

"How do we get this on the nightly news?" Chris asked.

"This is my idea," Bob replies.

"I hope to talk to Dawn Garrity at Wolf News. We know Wolf News is a conservative cable network and would be more likely to air something like this."

"Is this the Dawn Garrity who has her own show at night called The Garrity Report?" Chris asked.

"That's the one," Bob replied.

"How do you plan on getting to them and getting them to air it?" Ralph asked.

"Let me explain," Bob continued. "I knew Dawn long before she was on television. She was a waitress and bartender at her Father's pub in Peekskill, called Garrity's Pub, when she attended college for journalism and even after she got her first job as a reporter for a small news agency. I have frequented that pub for many years and became friends with Dawn. We even dated on and off but our relationship never became serious enough to take it any further. However, we have remained good friends to this day.

"I have her cell phone number. I will send her a text message and ask that she call me, when she has some privacy. I will obviously use the number from my alternate cell phone. So she knows it is me, I will sign the message 'Big Bob,' which is what she usually calls me."

"Well you old dog you," Ralph said smirking.

"We all have our secrets," Bob retorted.

"But Dawn Garrity," Chris remarked.

"No big deal, just a good friend, as I said. She calls me that because when we first met she thought I was real tall. But then as she grew up, I wasn't that big anymore. She continues to call me that as a joke. Anyway, may I continue while you two latent adolescents conjure up lewd images in your mind?" Bob said with a snicker.

For a moment, Bob thought of Dawn when he would see her on Wolf News. At five foot eight, she always appeared as a cultured beauty. Her well coiffed red hair worn shoulder length, and immaculate makeup, applied by professionals at the studio, seemed to accentuate her large brown eyes. Although dressed in professional attire, the apparel she wore invariably seemed to reveal just enough of her lovely pair of legs and breasts that were neither too large, nor too small, for her stature. The high heels, which always matched her dresses, provided her calves a tight sensuous uplifting. Whenever Bob saw her on television, he was amazed at how she was presented, because he knew another Dawn.

A pretty little redhead with puppy dog eyes, he met her when she was still tending bar and waiting tables at her father's pub. Always in flat shoes and a green apron with "Garrity's Pub" embroidered across the front in gold, she was a sight to behold. . . just a different one. However, in Bob's opinion, she looked best when they were hiking in the Catskill Mountains. Dressed in jeans, hiking boots, and a hooded sweatshirt, she was the epitome of the country girl Bob craved. He always felt it was a shame that their desires had led them in different directions.

Bob continued, "When she calls I will explain our dilemma. I will ask if she will at least listen to the recording and determine if there is a way to work it into her show. She loves to go after bad guys and the government. She can even say the recording has not been verified as authentic, and is being investigated. But, like they say, once something is hanging out there, it is hanging out there. I trust her, so even if she can't get it on the news, she will be investigating it for sure. It is a shot in the dark, but the only one I can think of, for the time being."

"If she is willing, how do we get the flash drive to her?" 96Ralph asked. "We certainly can't take the chance of using any of our emails."

"That's where you will come in Ralph. Chris can't go anywhere until we solve this problem. However, you can still move around, as nobody knows you are involved. I thought we could use a dead drop."

"What is a dead drop?" Chris asked.

"You don't read enough spy thrillers," Ralph responded with a laugh. "It is where you hide something at a place, and then leave a signal that it is there. The other person goes to the place, sees the signal, and picks it up. That way neither person is there at the same time, and don't even have to know each other's identity."

"Exactly Ralph," Bob said. "I know that Dawn drives by her father's pub everyday on the way to work. I figure Ralph could go to the pub as nobody knows him there. He can have a drink or two and then go to the men's room. In the hallway, back by the rest rooms, there is a large fake plant, like a bamboo tree or something, that has been there for years. It was still there several weeks ago when I stopped for a quick beer and a hello to the father.

"Anyway, Ralph could hide the flash drive in the pot under the artificial grass stuff like they use in Easter baskets. When Ralph leaves he will mark the post office pickup box that sits out front of the pub, on the north side with a big "X" using chalk. Dawn drives by the north side in the morning, and when she sees the mark, she will know the flash drive is there.

"I'll explain all of this to Dawn of course. Once she has the flash drive she can review the recording and take it from there. Chris and I will stay in hiding here as long as we can. If this place is somehow compromised, we will bug-out and head for the woods.

"Ralph, you remember the place just inside the Catskill Park about twenty miles from here, where we used to go camping on weekends? It is very secluded and as long as we lay low we should be able to hide there. If you need us, or get word that it is safe to come out, you will know where to find us."

"I know where it is," Ralph replied. "The plan sounds good, if this Dawn is willing to help. Bottom line is any plan is better than no plan. Now is anybody else hungry other than me," he concluded with a smile, rubbing his stomach.

"Why are we going way up into the Catskill Park when there are all these woods right here to hide out in?" Chris asked.

"If they determine that we are here, it means they traced me through my aunt. It will also mean they will know she has over twelve-hundred acres here. They will most likely search them first, before moving the search circle out. While they're wasting their time here, it will allow us more time there.

"I get it," Chris replied.

"Then let's fix up something for a late lunch. Then we have to get a bunch of copies made of this flash drive. I have about a dozen IronKeys in the communications room."

"The communications room?" Chris said with a puzzled expression.

"You'll see," Bob said. "But let's eat."

"I have some great sirloin steak and we might as well enjoy them outside," Bob said. "I also picked up some huge baking potatoes. I'll fix up a nice salad and we can all sit out front and relax a moment. It's been a hectic couple of days and we could all use it. I also have a nice Trapiche 2013 Broquel Malbec that goes great with sirloin. I'll get a bottle from the wine cellar."

"You have a wine cellar?" Chris asked with a look of disbelief.

"Doesn't every sophisticated man?" Bob answered with a wink.

Bob asked Ralph to go out to the garage and roll the Weber gas grill over to the front of the house.

"I'm on it Bob," Ralph replied as he headed outside.

"Is there anything I can do?" Chris asked.

"Yes, out in the garage there is a patio table. Once Ralph gets the grill out front, you could help him carry that over to the front as well."

"I'm on it," Chris said smiling, trying to be one of the guys.

Bob washed the potatoes, stuck them with a fork in several places, and laid them on a rack in the hot oven. He then got some makings for a salad from the refrigerator and prepared a bowl.

Ralph came in and said the grill and table were in place.

"Anything else I can do?" Ralph asked Bob.

"Not now, but when the potatoes have been in a while, I'll have you fire up the grill. What is Chris doing?"

"He's just sitting out front. He was saying how great this place is. Even with our problems, he feels safe."

"Well that may not last long," Bob said looking concerned. "But I will deal with that if and when it occurs. Let me go get a bottle of that wine."

Bob went through the small pantry to the large room behind it. To the left he opened a metal door which provided access to his small wine cellar. Grabbing a bottle of the Malbec, he returned to the kitchen.

When Bob got back, Ralph was still standing by the counter.

"These potatoes take about forty minutes to bake," Bob told him, "so you should fire up the grill in about twenty minutes. While you're grilling the steaks, maybe Chris can gather some dishes and utensils and take them out to the table in front."

Once the potatoes were baked and the steaks were grilled, Bob took the bowl of salad out to the table along with a bottle of Italian dressing. He then grabbed the bottle of wine, three acrylic wine glasses, and a cork screw and returned out front.

"Getting awful fancy with crystal wine glasses ain't you Bob?" Ralph teased when he saw Bob set them on the table.

"Actually wise ass, they are acrylic and are unbreakable."

Ralph picked one up. "Wow, these are light, yet they look just like crystal."

Bob lifted a glass from the table, holding it with his pinky finger sticking straight out.

"Would you expect anything less from a refined and cultivated individual such as myself?" Bob said, lifting his nose in the air.

Everybody laughed and Bob opened the bottle of wine and poured each of them a glass. Then they all dug in and it was evident they were all hungry.

The meal was consumed with small talk about Bob's new place and the beauty of the surrounding area. It was obvious they were all trying to forget the stress created by the events of the last two days, knowing there was more ahead of them.

When everybody was finished, the dishes were carried to the kitchen, and with the concerted effort of all three, they were washed, dried, and put away, in short order.

"Let's get a bunch of copies made of that recording," Bob suggested when they were done."

Bob grabbed the IronKey flash drive that Ralph had brought with him and headed through the small pantry, with Ralph and Chris right behind him. He walked to the right side of the storage room, and first pulling the storage unit forward he opened the metal door into the communications room. Upon entering, he flipped a switch on the wall just inside the door, and an array of small LED lights came on around the inside perimeter of the room. It provided more than enough light to see.

"Boy, this looks like a mini NASA command room," Chris said after a short whistle.

"Very nice Bob," Ralph said upon entering. "You have really put a lot of work in here."

"It is my only high tech room, so I tried to make it as user friendly as possible," Bob replied.

Bob then walked over to a large "L" shaped counter that had several high back roller desk chairs in front of it. On the left side of the "L" there was a large computer monitor that had two smaller monitors, stacked one over the other, on the left side, and one medium sized monitor on the right side.

"This here is the main computer," Bob explained as he bent over and turned it on. It is connected to the internet via a satellite dish. As soon as it fires up, we can copy the flash drive onto some extra IronKeys I keep on hand in the fireproof file cabinet.

"In the mean time, I'll explain some of the other features in here. This monitor on the left bottom is for a computer that never goes on line, which I use for confidential information that I don't want anyone to have access to. This monitor on the left top is for a DVR (digital video recorder) system I plan on installing soon, which will have a thirty-two camera input."

"A video system?" Chris asked.

"Yes, it will be just like the one I have at my other house. There will be multiple cameras around the house and outside on the property. It will be live at all times and record on the computer, as well as upload to a cloud real time. I will be able to access it from anywhere using my iPhone, or a tablet. Of course, if I am here, I can just review the video on the computer.

"As you can see, the walls and ceiling are covered with charcoal gray panels. The panels are made from a semi rigid Porous Expanded Poly Propylene (P.E.P.P.) that is called the 'Sound Muffler.' It is basically a lightweight, dual-function, acoustical panel used in recording studios. It both blocks and absorbs sound, and as you can see, can be attached to both walls and ceilings. It can actually be painted, or covered in fabric, but I like the looks of it as is.

"The bright LED lights illuminate the room providing adequate lighting, using little power from my solar system. These computers, the video system when it is installed, and all the communications equipment are powered by twelve volt.

"Let me quickly describe some of the communications capabilities," Bob continued obviously proud of his room.

Bob showed some of the equipment on the right side of the "L" counter, pointing out the various types of radios he had and elaborated on a few.

"Of course I have various dual band radios for AM, FM, weather band, and shortwave, both in here and out in the house. But some of this stuff is for more special use.

"This ham radio is a Kenwood TS-2000 100 watt transceiver that is connected to a long wire antenna outside. This is a Galaxy DX-2547 AM/SSB CB Base Station, which is connected to a fiberglass Gain Master antenna mounted on a mast outside.

"Some of the newer scanners on the market have the 'Trunk Tracker' and 'Close Call' technology. The Trunk Tracker allows you to monitor two-way 'Trunked' radio using Motorola trunking, EDACS (Enhanced Digital Communications System), and LTR (Logic Trunk Radio) systems. The 'Close Call' feature lets you know if someone is transmitting close to your location by locking onto the signal automatically, allowing you to listen in. I have one of these newer digital scanners which has both features, which is connected to a wideband Discone antenna, also on a mast, which provides excellent omni-directional reception.

"Unfortunately, the 'Close Call' function does not work that well and adjusting the sensitivity is difficult. So I use an old standby that I got many years ago.

"Ralph, you will appreciate this as you probably recall when I got it. This is an old Scanlock surveillance receiver. They were developed by a company in the UK called Audiotel, back in 1978, and were one of the original bug finders developed and built. Audiotel is still making equipment today. This one here is a receiver that automatically searches for transmitters within a room, using a novel technique at the time, and was called a harmonic receiver. The reason I have held onto it, is because of its sensitivity. If the squelch is set properly, it can determine if someone is using a radio around my property. Even though the scanner is supposed to do that, this old Scanlock does it better."

"What do you use it for?" Chris asked.

"If anyone keys a radio mic anywhere around my property, this thing automatically locks on the signal and I can hear them talking. It lets me know if hunters are around because they will often stay in contact with each other with those inexpensive FRS or GMRS radios. Once I know they are around, I go down to my small range below the garden area and shoot off a few rounds. That usually scares off the game as well as warns the hunters.

"Oh, and just so you know, I have external speakers for the Scanlock in several locations in the house, one in the garage, and a few around the property. This is so I don't have to be in here in order to hear somebody on a radio. I probably should have warned you in the event one of the speakers came alive last night," Bob said with a chuckle.

"I also have a handheld CB that can be powered from the vehicle and used with a magnetic mount antenna, as an option.

"There are several wide band receivers here, to include my old ICOM R100, which is a full band receiver without the blocks for cellular, and an old AOR-8000 handheld communications receiver which provides mobility.

"All of the wide band receivers, scanners, and the Scanlock, are also connected to the mast mounted wideband Discone antenna, using an eight port VHF/UHF receiver multicoupler.

"Over there," Bob pointed to a small bench, "is my test bench. It provides me a place to work on various electronic projects and make repairs to equipment. I have two soldering stations, a regular and a micro, and a quality bench mount multi-meter. I have a DC power supply providing two to twelve volts, and an SWR meter to indicate the degree of mismatch between my transmitters and antennas, and evaluate the effectiveness of my impedance matching efforts. I also have an old AVCOM portable spectrum analyzer which I always liked because it runs off twelve volt. A metal Kennedy machinist's chest keeps all my electronic tools in one place. It's not a lot, but it will keep things running around here.

"I also have several Motorola Talkabout MR350R, combination FRS/GMRS radios that also have the weather band in them. They can be used for us to stay in contact while we are on the property, or when bugging-out. However, if we have to bug-out we won't be taking any radios."

"Why not?" Chris asked curiously.

"The DTTF might have DFing capabilities."

"What is DFing?"

"It means direction finding. If they have the capability, they can use our radio signals when transmitting to determine our location. It could lead them right to us, and we obviously don't want that."

"I have a lot to learn," Chris replied.

"Anyway, I have probably missed a few things, but that is basically my capabilities when it comes to communications.

"It should also be noted that I have several fireproof file cabinets along the wall over there," Bob said pointing. "I have several faraday cages built into one of them and keep extra communications receivers as well as backup battery controllers, AC inverters, other components for the solar system, and, of course, a quality multi-meter," Bob concluded.

"The faraday cages are to protect the stuff from an EMP (Electromagnetic Pulse) right?" Chris asked. "We learned about that at M.I.T."

"That's correct Chris, see you are smarter than you look," Bob responded with a quick laugh.

Chris smiled, feeling like he was actually becoming one of the guys.

"Now we really should get some copies made of that recoding," Bob said as he walked over to one of the fireproof safes.

Reaching into the top drawer, Bob extracted four IronKey flash drives. He took them over to the main computer. Bob then plugged the flash drive that Ralph had brought him into a USB port on the computer. An "Unlock Screen" came up on the monitor. Having typed in the password, and clicking on the button, access was gained.

Next, Bob plugged one of the new IronKey flash drives into another USB port, and went through the same procedure to open it. First he had to set the new one up with a password. Once that was done, he was then able to copy the data from the original to the new one. He repeated the procedure for the remaining three IronKeys.

"We now have four new copies and the original that Ralph brought. I have used the same password for three of them, which is the same password as the original. The last one I used a different password, and that is the one we will send down to Dawn."

When Bob finished making copies of the flash drive, he informed Chris that they should get and stage their bug-out bags in the communications room.

"Won't that make them difficult to get to if we need to get out of here fast?" Chris asked.

"You didn't tell him about the tunnel yet?" Ralph asked smiling.

"That reminds me," Bob responded.

"Over here on the east wall, this section of the Sound Muffler panels hinges inward, as you can see," Bob said as he opened the section.

"That reveals this metal door which leads to a tunnel that exits to the east side of the property inside the woods line."

"You're kidding right?" Chris said. "You guys are pulling my leg right?"

Bob unlocked the door by turning a bolt lock, and opened it. Reaching in and flipping a switch, a long row of LED lights came on.

"Come over here and look," Bob said to Chris.

"Damn, this is just like some kind of James Bond lair," Chris said as he looked down the tunnel.

"When you get to the far end, there is ladder that brings you up to a hidden hinged door that is pushed up. You are then in the woods," Bob explained.

"Damn," was Chris' only reply.

Bob turned the lights in the tunnel back off, closed the door and locked it.

"As you can see, you don't need a key to unlock it from this side, only from the outside. Remember that Chris."

"Ralph, I still need to set you up for the night. I will get you a cot from the garage. You can bunk in my office, as Chris is staying in the living room.

"Chris, let's go get the bug-out bags while we are thinking about it and get them in here."

Ralph told Bob that he could go out and get the cot from the garage while they staged their bags in the communications room.

"Before you leave the supply room, grab a sleeping bag from the shelves over there," Bob told Ralph.

Ralph set his cot up in Bob's office while Bob and Chris staged their bug-out bags in the communications room. Bob loaded the magazines for his guns and placed them in the pouches on his tactical vest, and the two larger ones in the side pockets of the pouch for the KEL-TEC.

Having had a large late lunch, they all agreed to just having a quick snack before they all went to bed.

CHAPTER 19

The Set-Up

Sunday morning Bob arose at his usual time and went to the kitchen to make a pot of coffee; and Ralph was right behind him.

"Morning Buddy," Bob said to Ralph. "Old habits are hard to break ain't they?"

"Yea, I never was much for sleeping," Ralph replied.

"Were your accommodations OK?" Bob asked.

"A lot better than that tent we stayed in the last couple of times I was here," Ralph replied smiling.

"Once we get some coffee here, I'm going to send the text message to Dawn. Hopefully when she gets up she will see it and call me."

"If she doesn't, where do we go from here?" Ralph asked.

"Not sure, let's just wait and see if she calls."

Bob set out some cups and a sugar bowl.

"At least this morning we have milk for the coffee. We've been using the powdered creamer, and it just isn't the same," Bob said as he took the milk from the refrigerator.

"You're getting soft my friend," Ralph replied.

"Yea, look who's talking my executive friend," Bob said smiling.

"It really is good to see you Bob," Ralph said seriously. "I just wish it was under better circumstances."

"I know Buddy; when all this is over you will have to take another vacation and come up here and we will just chill out."

"I'll take you up on that," Ralph replied with a chuckle.

"I'll be right back, I'm going to run through the shower," Bob said as he headed for the bathroom.

When Bob returned to the kitchen, Ralph was sitting at the table drinking a cup of coffee. Bob fixed himself a cup and, with cell phone and coffee in hand, went out to the front of the house. Ralph followed.

"It's a beautiful morning out here," Ralph stated.

"Yea, I love it up here. Can't wait to move here permanently, which hopefully will be soon," Bob replied.

Bob set his coffee on the table and started writing out a text message to Dawn. When he finished and hit send, he could hear the whoosh as the message was sent.

"Well, all we have to do now is wait for her call."

"You know what I haven't had in a long time?" Ralph asked.

"I hope this isn't going to be sexual," Bob replied as he raised his cup of coffee.

"Screw you," Ralph replied. "I meant a good cigar, and I just happened to bring some Padron Churchill's. I should have thought of it last night, but with such a beautiful morning, I think I'll partake in one. You in?"

"I'm in," Bob replied. "Get them out here."

Ralph went into the house and returned with two cigars, a cutter, and a small box of wooden matches.

"You're the man," Bob said as Ralph sat down.

Bob and Ralph sat at the table in front of the house, drinking coffee, puffing on a cigar, and talking about old times. It felt good to relax, as they both knew things might turn to crap real quickly.

"Good morning," Chris said as he came out of the house with a cup of coffee in hand."

He was wearing jeans, his hiking boots, a sweatshirt, and a ball cap.

"Who the hell are you?" Ralph asked with a chuckle.

"I'm your worst nightmare," Chris replied trying to look intimidating, but feeling like one of the guys.

"Damn Bob, it didn't take you long to transform this poor man," Ralph declared. "And it is good to see you got him a real ball cap, not one of those stupid things with the flat bill."

"Marines have standards," Bob said with a wink.

"He's even wearing a Spec-Ops belt. Next he will be carrying a gun," Ralph continued.

"You guys are just a ton of fun," Chris said with a wide grin.

"We do what we can," Bob replied.

"You guys smoking a cigar this early?" Chris asked rhetorically.

"Well, we thought we would enjoy one now just in case we don't make it through the day," Bob responded.

"You're kidding right?" Chris asked looking worried.

"Of course Chris," Ralph replied. "Would you like a cigar?"

"No thanks; I don't mind being around them, but it is a habit I just never took up," Chris responded.

They all sat at the table enjoying the morning and refilling their coffee cups when required. If only every morning could be this peaceful Bob thought to himself.

The time was seven o'clock when Bob's phone rang. He got up from the table and walked with the phone out into the yard.

"Big Bob here," Bob said answering the call.

Bob heard a laugh at the other end of the phone.

"To what do I owe this pleasure early on a Sunday morning?" Dawn asked.

"I have a little problem and was hoping you could help. I know I can trust you, so, if after hearing the problem, you feel you can't get involved just say so. But I need your assurance that the information we discuss will remain confidential."

"This sounds serious," Dawn replied. "You know I would never do anything to hurt you Bob."

Bob laid out the situation in detail, and explained the reason the tape had been held so long. He filled her in about Chris' accident, the coma, and the loss of memory, and described what he hoped she might be able to do. He then told her about the dead drop at her father's pub and how she would know the flash drive was there. When he told her that the password for the flash drive was 'BigBob' she laughed.

"Of course I will do whatever I can," Dawn said. "But I can't give you any guarantees. However, I have been working on a story about the advantages of being self reliant, and yes, before you say anything; you have rubbed off on me."

Bob gave a short laugh.

Dawn continued, "It seems like the government doesn't want people to be able to rely on anything but them. It sounds like this recording will give me some real ammunition to prove my theory."

"Well," Bob stated. "Anything you can do is more than I have now. These people are serious as I explained. I have no choice but to keep Chris and myself hidden until the details can be made public. Even then, I can't be certain that they won't continue trying to find us. But it is the only chance we have of making them back off. I'm just not sure how long we can hide before they find us."

"When will the flash drive be in place?" Dawn asked.

"It should be there no later than Tuesday, but maybe before. You'll know when you see the 'X' on the mail box."

"OK," Dawn said. "I'll check it every day starting tomorrow, and Bob, be safe dear."

"I'll do my best Dawn, and thanks, I really appreciate it."

"Anything for Big Bob," Dawn said with a giggle as she ended the call.

Bob returned to the table where Ralph was sitting, still smoking his cigar. Bob picked his up from the can being used as an ashtray and re-lit it.

"Where's Chris?" Bob asked.

He's making us all some sausage and eggs for breakfast," Ralph replied.

"Well let's go tell him that the game is on."

* * *

Two vehicles had rolled out of the northeast DTTF facility in Albany, New York at six o'clock Sunday morning. The lead vehicle was a solid black Chevy Tahoe with heavily tinted windows, being driven by Max Archer, the facility's commander. He was dressed in full tactical gear. His vehicle was followed by a larger Chevy Suburban, also solid black with the same window tint. It contained four DTTF agents, all dressed in tactical gear as well. The vehicles proceed south on the New York State Thruway running as a convoy. They crossed the Hudson River on the Newburgh-Beacon bridge and from there proceeded south on Route 9. The convoy continued to Peekskill where Max Archer pulled over to the side of the road. The Suburban pulled over behind it.

Max Archer got out of the Tahoe and walked back to the Suburban. The driver's window went down.

"Ok guys, we are almost there. My GPS indicates we have about a mile to go. When we reach Bennett Road, you will pull around me and enter the property first. It is the first driveway on the left. I will follow at a short distance. As soon as we get there you are all to secure the perimeter. Remember, these guys are not supposed to be the violent type, but don't take any chances.

"Agent Keegan, you knock on the front door, and Agent Davis, you guard the side entrance which is supposed to be on the right side of the house. After knocking several times, if nobody answers, Agent Keegan will do his stuff getting us in without doing damage to the structure. Agents Douglas and Ramsey, you will secure the other buildings on the premises. If neither Armstrong nor Hughes are located and apprehended, we will initiate surveillance as planned.

"I also want photos taken of all structures and all devices that violate the new policy for self-reliance. If surveillance is required, the vehicles and other agents will be staged at the Westchester County Sheriff's Office repair garage, as we discussed at the briefing. When arrangements were made, I was assured we would not be bothered. Is everybody on track?"

All agents responded in the affirmative and Archer returned to the Tahoe. He pulled back onto the road with the Suburban right behind him. As the vehicles approached Bennett road, Archer pulled the Tahoe over slightly, and the Suburban drove around it.

As the Suburban drove up the driveway and approached Bob's house, it abruptly stopped. All agents exited the vehicle, with an M4 carbine on a two point sling. The M4 carbine, being a shorter version of the M16A2, was ideal for close quarter's tactical operations such as these. Each had a Glock 22 pistol in a drop-down leg holster and a rectangular patch on the back of their black tactical uniform emblazoned with the large letters "DTTF." They all wore a tactical FAST ballistic helmet equipped with the new Rail Attached Communications (RAC) headset and boom microphone, over a lightweight black balaclava. The helmets were wired to their radios which were mounted to the top rear of their tactical vests.

As each agent proceeded to their assigned positions, Archer pulled in with the Tahoe. He exited the vehicle with the same weaponry and tactical uniform as the other agents.

He watched as Agent Keegan positioned himself alongside the front door and Agent Davis went around to the right and positioned himself by the side entrance. Agents Douglas and Ramsey disappeared around the back of the house.

"Let's let them know we are here Unit Two. Over." Archer said upon keying the microphone of his radio.

Keegan knocked hard on the front door and yelled, "Federal agents, we are here for violations of the Domestic Terrorism Act. If anyone is inside, open the door slowly and come out with your hands in the air. All exits are covered."

Keegan stepped back to the side of the door and waited.

Archer radioed Davis at the side door.

"Unit Three, any movement over there? Over."

"Nothing sir. Over." Davis replied.

"Units Four and Five, any movement in the back yard? Over." Archer asked Douglas and Ramsey through the radio.

"Nothing yet, we are still searching the outbuildings. Over." Unit Four replied.

"Same here. Over." Unit Five replied.

"Let's gain access through that front door. Over." Archer commanded. "Unit Four, join us at the front of the house, Unit five, continue with your search. Over."

Keegan knelt down in front of the front door and removed a pouch from his tactical vest. From the pouch he withdrew a lock pick and tension wrench. Placing the tension wrench in the bottom of the lock with his left hand, he applied slight pressure with the middle finger of that same hand, so that the cylinder of the lock had tension on it. With his right hand, he inserted a pick into the slot of the cylinder and started picking the pins from the rear forward. As each set of pins became lined up with the shear line of the cylinder, his finger could feel the cylinder want to turn, which was almost imperceptible to the mind. As the last and forward most set of pins were picked, the cylinder rotated and the door was open. Total time on the lock was forty-five seconds.

Archer and Douglas joined with Keegan at the front of the house. When Archer radioed, "Go," the three entered one behind the other. Using the house clearing procedure, that they had practiced many times, they cleared each room as they proceeded through the house. As each room was cleared the words "Clear" could be heard over the radio.

When they reached the side door of the house they opened it. Davis was still there ensuring nobody exited through that door.

"The house is clear. Over." Archer stated. "Unit five, anything back there? Over."

"No sir, no signs of life. Over."

"Join us around the side of the house. Over," Archer directed.

As all agents came to the side of the house, Archer asked Ramsey what he had found. "There is a small building with just tools in it. There is another building that is a little larger that has all kinds of empty pots and stuff for planting. I found a whole bunch of packs of seeds and they all say 'Heirloom' on them. There is a large four bay garage and there are only two vehicles in there; an old beat-up pickup truck and a Smart Car. The other two bays are empty. No signs of anyone around the property," Ramsey reported.

"OK," Archer said. "Get some pictures of the solar panels, those water barrels, and the gardens. Photograph where you found those seed packets, then confiscate them and get them in an evidence bag. Let's move."

The agents did as Archer instructed and he walked around to the rear of the house examining the woods to the left. When the agents returned he explained how the surveillance would work.

"See those woods to the left over there," he said pointing. "When we set up surveillance inside the house, the relieving agent will come in through there. He will be discretely dropped off on the road that runs parallel to Bennett Road alongside the deli at the intersection. It is wooded and there are no residences until you get farther up that road, so dropping off an agent should be no problem. We don't want to be driving in and out of here every eight hours, which will be the duration of each shift.

"Radio contact must be made every hour by the agent on duty to confirm everything is status quo, and to ensure their safety. If you do not check in we will attempt radio contact with you. If you do not respond we will assume that you are down and we will respond immediately. Everybody understand those procedures?"

All agents responded in the affirmative.

"Agent Davis, you are up," Archer ordered. "You will remain in the residence until relieved, unless you see movement in the yard. If either Armstrong or Hughes returns, radio the team immediately and then apprehend. Do not screw this up."

"Aye sir," Davis responded and went inside the house to set up surveillance.

Removing his helmet and balaclava, Archer said, "Let's get out of here. You agents return to the staging area at the Sheriff's Office repair garage. I gave you all directions at the briefing. I will stop at a diner I saw on the way in here and pick up coffee and some breakfast sandwiches and be there shortly."

The three remaining agents, removing their headgear as well, loaded up in the Suburban. Archer got in his Tahoe, and left the property first, with the agents following. As they got to the end of the road, Archer turned right and the Suburban turned left, heading towards the designated staging point.

It was nine o'clock.

Archer drove a short distance, and turning his vehicle around, proceeded directly back to the Armstrong residence. Upon parking at the front of the house, he exited the vehicle and advanced towards the front door. Agent Davis, observing Archer's return, opened the front door as he approached it.

"Forget something sir?" Davis asked.

"Yes I did, follow me into the house."

Davis closed the front door, and proceeded to follow Archer.

As Archer walked into the living room ahead of Davis, he discreetly withdrew a suppressed Beretta 92FS compact from a slash pocket on his vest.

As Archer turned around he placed one shot to Davis' throat, just above his body armor. Davis fell to the floor clutching his throat. Archer walked over to his body lying on the floor and saw the anguished and questioned expression in Davis' eyes. Archer placed another round to Davis' forehead just below the helmet. The questioned expression left his face as death set in.

Archer exited the house, leaving the front door open, returned to his Tahoe and placed the Beretta into a tactical bag sitting on the front passenger seat. He then proceeded directly to the diner where he purchased coffee and breakfast sandwiches. From there he drove to the staging area and joined the other agents.

The time was nine-thirty.

As the agents were enjoying their coffee and sandwiches, Agent Douglas realized it was ten o'clock.

"Davis should be calling in shortly," he stated.

When the clock passed ten by five minutes, Archer directed Douglas to contact Davis by radio.

"Unit Two, this is Unit Four. Do you copy? Over."

No response so Douglas tried again.

"Unit Two, this is Unit Four. Do you copy? Over."

"Something's wrong," Archer exclaimed. "Load up, let's get the hell over there.

All agents jumped into their assigned vehicles and proceeded at top speed to the Armstrong residence. Pulling into the property, Archer pressed the microphone button on his radio.

"Unit Two, you will take the front door with me. Unit four, take the side door and standby there. Unit Five, secure the back yard. Over."

With the front door open, Archer and Keegan entered with Keegan going right and Archer going left. The body of Davis could immediately be observed on the living room floor with a pool of blood around his head.

"Agent down!" Archer exclaimed. "Secure the perimeter and make sure the assailant isn't still here. Over."

Archer and Keegan continued to clear the house and returned to the living room.

Keegan bent down over Davis' body checking for vital signs, but knew he was dead.

"He's dead sir," Keegan confirmed to Archer.

"Shit, apparently we underestimated this Armstrong character," Archer said to Keegan. "He must have been here hidden all along. How the hell did we miss him?"

"Unit One, this is Unit Five. Over"

"Unit One on. Over."

"Nobody found in or around the premises. Over."

"Affirmative, Unit Five, maintain perimeter security in back of the premises. Over."

"Affirmative Unit One. Over." Unit Five responded.

"Unit Four, you initiate perimeter security in front of the premises. Nobody is to enter the property. Over."

"Affirmative Unit One. Over." Unit Four responded.

"Keegan, we need to get a retrieval and forensic team down here from Albany. I'll get on the cell and make arrangements. We need to maintain the crime scene until they arrive. Get some photos of the body and surrounding area, but don't touch anything."

"Aye sir," Keegan responded.

Archer exited the house and returned to his vehicle. Using his cell phone, he made arrangements for both a forensic and retrieval team to proceed immediately from Albany to Peekskill to take over the crime scene and retrieve Davis' body.

Archer then went to Agents Douglas and Ramsey to inform them that Davis was dead, shot twice, and then returned to his vehicle.

While the agents maintained control of the crime scene, he placed another call to his superior, Director Drescher.

"This better be fucking important Archer," he said answering the phone.

"Sir, I am at the raid location. Neither Armstrong nor Hughes were located. However, after surveillance was initiated using one agent, he failed to check in after his first hour. Upon returning to the location, the agent was found dead with two shots, one to the throat and one to the head." I have both a forensic and retrieval team on the way from Albany.

"I can only assume that the agent was that son of a bitch Davis?"

"That's correct sir," Archer replied.

"This is what I want you to do. Discreetly leak the incident to PNN (the People's News Network) who will be there before your teams from Albany, I'm sure. They will have plenty of questions as well. Don't let them on the fucking property, but as the Agent in Charge, you should only indicate that an operation was being conducted and an agent was killed. Explain that you can't provide any further information at this time. However, once the scene is secured, you would be willing to conduct a press conference. They will eat that shit right up. You have the driver's license photos of Armstrong and Hughes in your file, which should be with you I assume?"

"That's correct sir," Archer responded.

"Don't give any real specifics, just that Robert Armstrong is suspected of the murder of our agent, and that Christopher Hughes is a known associate and is wanted for questioning.

225

Make sure you get those fucking photos on the news and ask that all agencies assist in locating the two suspects.

"I'll get right on it sir."

"Keep me the fuck informed," Drescher said as he hung up.

* * *

While the raid was being conducted at Bob's residence in Peekskill, Bob, Ralph, and Chris enjoyed the breakfast that Chris had prepared. They each had poured another cup of coffee and proceeded to the table out in front.

"Thanks Chris, That was good. I didn't know you could cook," Ralph said.

"When you are single, you can cook," Chris replied.

"I guess we all agree with that statement," Bob replied with a smile.

"When do you want me to leave with the flash drive for Dawn?" Ralph asked.

"I thought you might get out of here early afternoon," Bob said. "That should get you down in the Peekskill area in time to change your clothes, and visit the pub later in the evening."

"Sounds good to me," Ralph replied. "What shall we do until then, other than enjoy this beautiful weather?"

"Well I still think we are pretty secure here. Chris said he wanted to learn how to make a survival bracelet from parachute cord, so I thought we might do that," Bob answered.

"First the clothes and ball cap, now a survival bracelet. You ain't going native on us are you Chris?" Ralph asked.

Both Bob and Ralph laughed.

"No," Chris laughed as well. "I just figure if Bob and I have to bug-out it is a good way to carry extra cordage."

"Man Bob, you are really rubbing off on our friend here," Ralph said continuing to laugh.

"Well let me get some parachute cord and a small buckle and I'll get you started Chris," Bob said as he stood.

When Bob returned with the items he started showing Chris how to estimate the length of the cordage between the two buckle ends so that it would fit his wrist properly when done. "If you make these initial cords too short," he showed Chris," it will look like it fits, but once you get the weaving done over the top of those cords, it will be too tight."

Chris, looking at Bob's bracelet, said, "I really like the looks of the weave over top. Is there a term for that?"

"Well if you want to sound tactical," Bob replied smiling, "you will call it 'Cobra Stitch' and people will think it's really cool. But in reality it is just a basic macramé knot."

Ralph said, "Well I haven't worn one for years, so I guess I might as well make one too. Never know if I might need it."

"I'll get you a buckle," Bob said as he got up and went into the house.

For the next hour, they all sat at the front of the house talking, while Ralph and Chris each made a bracelet.

Suddenly, Bob's alternate cell phone rang, which was very unusual. Upon looking at it he saw that it was his Aunt Martha, who had both of his numbers.

"Good morning Martha," Bob said cheerfully when answering her call.

Bob listened for a minute as his aunt talked.

"Calm down Martha, I'll check it out immediately," Bob said. "And thanks for the call; I'll get back with you later."

"What's that all about?" Ralph asked as Bob got up from the table.

"She said I should turn on the PNN news channel immediately. Apparently they are outside of my property and are reporting that during a raid at my home this morning a federal agent was shot and killed. My aunt knows it wasn't me as she knows we are all here, but she is very upset. Let's get to the Comm room and put on the television.

Ralph and Chris followed Bob through the various hidden doors and they all entered the room. Bob turned on the television and turned it to the channel for PNN, which was known as a highly liberal cable news agency. Bob normally watched the Wolf News cable network, which was much more conservative, but honestly, you couldn't trust any of the news networks for the true story.

When the television came on, Bob said, "Shit."

There was a female PNN news reporter at the front of Bob's driveway with various other reporters and cameras. There was an orange tape across the front of the driveway that had the words "Crime Scene - Do Not Cross" emblazoned on it every few feet.

"I'm Leslie Reeves and I'm here at the residence of a Robert Armstrong and it appears that a federal agent of the Domestic Terrorism Task Force has been shot and killed during an operation here just hours ago.

"We have very little information at this time, but have spoken to the Agent in Charge, Max Archer. He indicated that this was some type of an operation in regard to domestic terrorism, and as a result of that operation an agent has died from gunshot wounds. He explained that he was not at liberty to provide any further information at this time, but will give a press conference at four o'clock this afternoon."

"This is bad," Bob stated with his eyes glued to the television screen.

"This is really bad," Ralph replied.

"How the hell could an agent be shot and killed at your house?" Chris asked, "Nobody is even there."

"Exactly," Bob said. "This is definitely a false flag operation."

"Agreed," Ralph retorted.

"What the hell is a false flag operation?" Chris wanted to know.

"A False Flag operation is usually a covert operation that is designed to deceive the public in such a way that they think the operation was carried out by someone else. Originally, it was a term used by the military when they would fly false colors, flying a flag of a different country, so the enemy would be deceived into believing they were fighting a different country. However, more recently they are used in peace time by both covert agencies and government entities," Bob replied.

"So, you've been set up," Chris stated confidently.

"Exactly," Bob responded. "This will make it much easier for them to find us. They will have everybody out looking."

"What do we do now?" Chris asked.

"Well the first thing," Ralph replied, "Is to stay calm."

"The first thing I have to do is get the video footage from the house to see what actually occurred. It just might help me prove I'm innocent," Bob said.

"How are you going to do that?" Chris asked.

"I explained that yesterday," Chris. "Everything recorded at that location is uploaded real time to a cloud. Unless they found the hidden room with the DVR it should still be uploading live video. Let's check the cloud."

Bob got the video footage from his other house which had been streamed to his cloud. As they all reviewed it, they could see a DTTF agent hiding in the house after the initial raid. But then, only minutes later, another DTTF agent entered the house, and right there in the living room, shot the other one with a suppressed handgun. He then shot him again and casually walked out of the house.

"They freaking shot one of their own guys just to get at us?" Chris asked incredulously.

"I told you Chris, these people mean business. Now they have a government agency trying to kill us. You can bet if they find us, before another agency does, we won't live to talk."

"We need to make a new plan," Ralph stated.

"I agree," Bob said. "The first thing we need to do is make copies of the video showing how the agent was killed. We will add that to all the IronKeys that have the audio recording on it. Ralph get the copy I made you for Dawn, and Chris, get the copies out of our packs. I'll get the others."

All three of them went in different directions and all came back with IronKeys. Bob immediately started adding the file he created with the video footage from the house to all the flash drives. He also made one extra copy on an IronKey so Ralph would have one to hide as a backup.

"Bob, you know something I was just thinking of?" Ralph added.

"What is that Ralph?" Bob responded without looking up from what he was doing.

"I have a friend in the FBI; maybe he can help us," Ralph replied.

Ralph used to attend a gathering many years ago at Camp Smith near Peekskill, New York, put on by the FBI-Marine Corps Association. It was an organization that was originated to foster the continued relationship between the FBI and the United

States Marine Corps, which has always been good. Many FBI agents were former Marines. Although you only had to be a former or present Marine to join, if you were an FBI Special Agent, you had to have been a Marine first.

It was an all day affair in the fall, starting out with shooting on various ranges in the morning followed by beer and chili, served outdoors. The highlight would come when the Commandant of the Marine Corps arrived, which he did every year. All the attendees would get in a formation and the Commandant would hold a mock inspection of the troops. This would be followed by a sit-down dinner in a large hall where the Commandant and others would speak. The hall was decorated with all types of Marine Corps banners and posters. It was a sight to behold.

Ralph really enjoyed renewing the "esprit de corps" shown by the members and getting to meet the current Commandant. The round tables in the hall were set up for twelve people each, and it was a grab a seat where you could type of affair. On one occasion Ralph hit it off real well with a former Marine, and current FBI agent who was sitting at the table he chose. Ralph and this agent became friends, meeting on occasion for dinner, or to shoot at a local range. He was transferred from the Westchester County area to a New York City office, but they still met on occasion for a drink or dinner.

"You have a friend in the FBI?" Chris asked.

"That's correct," Ralph said. "Now I know we didn't want to notify the police about this, but with this video recording, we can prove Bob didn't do the shooting. I'm not sure we can trust anybody, but we know this Domestic Terrorism Task Force is a scumbag organization as evidenced by them shooting their own people. I believe the FBI has more scruples than that."

"You might have an idea there," Bob said contemplating the FBI. "At least we would be working on two levels, trying to prove my innocence. Dawn, hopefully, can get something on Wolf News, and if the FBI knows I didn't do it, they might be able to call off the goons. They might also be interested in Chris' recording as it reveals this organization was formed for the purpose of helping big business, not the people. We will have to think this out, but in the mean time I will make extra IronKey copies."

Bob, Ralph and Chris discussed the situation. Although they didn't really trust anybody at this point, other than Dawn, they did need somebody else on their side. The FBI wouldn't necessarily be their first choice, but at least it was a federal agency, which would be better than some local law enforcement.

Bob thought that Ralph could perform the drop off of the flash drive for Dawn. He then could discreetly make contact with his FBI friend.

Bob indicated he would let Chris use his computer to email Ralph a copy of both the video and audio recording. This might be dangerous at this point, but at least Ralph wouldn't have to admit that he had actually been with Chris or even knew Bob. Chris' email should indicate that he was sending them to Ralph because he needed help revealing the information. Being Ralph was employed by Chris, he could say he wanted to do what he could for his boss. Chris should also state in the email that he, at this time couldn't reveal his location. Ralph could explain that he put them on an IronKey so he could provide the information to the FBI. Eventually they would suspect that Chris was with Bob anyway. It provided Ralph with at least a layer of protection, as well as Bob and Chris.

"We will have to get you out of here soon Ralph so you can get the flash drive to the pub," Bob said.

"The Press Conference is starting," Chris announced, "Can we turn this up?"

Bob grabbed the remote and turned up the volume on the television monitor. The three of them sat watching as it began.

CHAPTER 20
The Press Conference

More than a dozen microphones from various news agencies were set up in front of Bob Armstrong's driveway with the crime scene tape still stretched across it. A makeshift podium, with the front draped with the emblem for the Domestic Terrorism Task Force, was centered on the microphones. The microphone for PNN was prominently displayed in the middle.

Max Archer walked to the podium, looking much less intimidating without his balaclava and helmet.

"I am Agent Archer, the Facility's Commander for the Northeast Sector of the Domestic Terrorism Task Force," he began.

"During a routine operation against a suspected domestic terrorist, surveillance was being conducted on the suspect's residence. Sometime during that surveillance one of our DTTF agents was shot and killed. We believe it may have been the owner of the residence that killed our agent.

"The suspect's name is Robert Armstrong; he is the owner of this property. It is believed that he has little regard for government regulations, as evidenced by the violations of the Domestic Terrorism Act at this residence.

"Our initial investigation reveals that this Bob Armstrong is a former Marine and was with an elite unit called Force Recon, who fought in the Iraq war. It is also believed that he may be suffering from PTSD (Posttraumatic Stress Disorder), like the individual who shot and killed the Navy Seal sniper a few years ago. Therefore he is to be considered extremely dangerous.

"I have an enlarged photo of this Robert Armstrong taken from his driver's license, which was obtained from the Department of Motor Vehicles."

Archer held up the enlarged photo and it looked like a strobe light hitting it as camera flashes went off. Of course the photo showed Robert Armstrong with short hair, because the ponytail was not evident from the front, a clean shaven face, and the large black rimmed glasses.

"Of course, a digital copy of this photo will be made available to all news agencies after the press conference," Archer continued.

"It should also be noted that the suspect has a known associate, who we believe may have been with him at the time of this incident. His name is Christopher Hughes and he is being sought for questioning in this matter."

Archer held up an enlarged photo of Hughes obtained from his driver's license as well.

"We are still in the very early stages of this investigation, and I'm sorry but that is all the details I have at this time. I will take a few short questions."

"How did this individual get away, if indeed he did the shooting?" a reporter asked.

"That is still unclear," Archer answered. "All vehicles registered to him are still on the premises. However, we have not located the vehicle owned by Christopher Hughes, and we believe that may have been used to get away."

"Do we know if this Armstrong guy has had any past incidents of violent behavior?" a reporter yelled.

"Again, we are in the early stages of our investigation and are still obtaining information. We will provide more information as it is processed," Archer replied.

"Can you reveal the name of the agent that was killed?"

"No we cannot. We must first contact and notify the agent's family. Of course I'm sure you understand," Archer stated.

"What type of violations required a surveillance?" a reporter from Wolf News asked. "It is my understanding that the purpose of the Domestic Terrorism Act was to locate and apprehend individuals who violated new policy in regard to self-reliant behavior, which is usually in a rural area. How did you happen to raid a house in such an affluent suburban neighborhood?"

"I'm sorry, but that will be all for now," Archer announced.

Archer turned from the podium, and as he walked away, the reporters continued to shout questions.

* * *

"I can't believe they included Chris' name in the investigation. They definitely are getting input from CANE," Bob said sounding disgusted.

"Well I'm already a wanted man, and I haven't even been able to reveal the recording," Chris said dejectedly.

"Flip around the channels and see if this is only on PNN," Ralph said.

Bob started checking other cable news channels and it was on all of them, even Wolf News. They all had banners across the bottom with headings like, "News Alert," "Breaking News," and "News Flash."

"Well we are certainly stuck here for now," Bob exclaimed. "But I don't think we will be safe for long. Eventually they will trace me to this location."

"How will they do that?" Chris asked. I thought you said nobody but your aunt knows you're here?"

"And that is the weak link," Bob replied. "A thorough search is going to reveal she is my father's sister, and they will come asking questions. They always interview all family members, and often that is how they find somebody on the run."

"I better get out of here while I still can," Ralph interjected. "I need to be on the outside in order to help. Right now, nobody knows I'm involved with this, and it needs to stay that way. I have to get that flash drive to Dawn and try to contact my FBI friend."

"I agree Ralph," Bob said. "Let's get you out of here, and fast."

Just then, Bob's cell phone rang. He looked at the number and it was his aunt's.

"Hello Martha," he answered calmly.

"Did you see the press conference on the television?" Martha asked. "They are trying to make you out to be some type of nut. It's bullshit," she said vehemently.

"Yes I saw the press conference, and I agree, it's bullshit. I appreciate your standing by me on this. Just so you know, I have a video recording from the house proving I'm not the one that killed that agent. If you'd like, you can come up and look at it on the monitor."

"I believe you dear. How did you get that?" she asked.

"Modern technology," Bob responded with chuckle. "By the way, I'm concerned that eventually, and probably sooner than later, someone will come around asking you questions. Are you prepared for that?"

"I didn't get this old, and survive up here this long, by being a wuss," Martha replied. "I'll handle them."

"Thanks for the support Martha, I really appreciate it. I have to go, Buddy is leaving now."

"Give Buddy my love," Martha said as she hung up.

Just as Bob went to lay his phone down it rang again. He looked at the incoming number and it was Dawn.

"Well, you seem to have gotten yourself in a pickle haven't you?" Dawn started.

"I know it doesn't look good, but it is all bullshit, and I can prove it," Bob said sounding frustrated.

"And how will you do that?" Dawn asked.

"I have a video recording from the house showing that I didn't kill that DTTF agent," Bob retorted. "And you aren't going to believe this, but it was another agent that killed one of his own."

"And you have this on video?" Dawn asked.

"That I do, and I put a copy on the flash drive that we discussed yesterday. It will be heading in your direction shortly."

"I can't wait to see it," Dawn said sounding very interested. "This might be a good lead in to the other problem. Might show that they are after you to make sure you don't talk about the recording. If they can make you look like a nut, who in hell would listen to you."

"I agree, but they don't know I have the video. It should reveal they were trying to set me up. The audio recording will show the motive, and the video recording will show the attempt. Anyway, please retrieve the item as soon as possible and do what you can to help. I'm not sure how long we can stay hidden."

"I'll be there first thing in the morning," Dawn assured him. "The pub is closed then, but I still have keys. There won't be any questions that way."

"I really appreciate this Dawn," Bob said. "Just don't get yourself in any trouble."

"Trouble, that's my middle name," Dawn replied with a laugh. "You just stay hidden Big Bob until I can reveal this thing."

The phone went dead and Bob looked at the others.

"Ralph, you need to get out of here soon, and get that flash drive to the pub," Bob exclaimed. I want to take the Xterra down to my aunt's barn. If you would follow me down, you could bring me back in your car."

"No problem, let's do it," Ralph responded.

Bob drove his vehicle down and secured it in Aunt Martha's barn. Ralph, having followed him down, brought Bob back up to the house.

When they got back, Ralph asked, "One question though, where the hell do I get chalk?"

"I have some in the supply room that I use for marking fabric when I'm sewing," Bob said. "It washes out in the laundry."

"You can sew too?" Chris asked.

"Chris, Bob is a jack of all trades," Ralph answered for Bob.

"Yeah, and master of none," Bob added

Bob took Ralph to the supply room and gave him several large pieces of chalk.

"Just in case you need to do this again," Bob said while handing them to Ralph.

Ralph already had his pack ready to go and Bob and Chris followed him out to his car.

"Be careful Buddy, we really need you on the outside," Bob said as they shook hands.

"Yea Buddy," Chris said using that name for the first time. "We are depending on you."

"I know you guys are, and I won't let you down," Ralph replied as he shook Chris' hand as well.

Ralph then got in the car and headed for Peekskill, New York.

As Bob and Chris returned inside, Bob said they should grab a bite to eat and then recheck their packs making sure they were ready to go. He felt their time at their current location was limited.

Ralph arrived in Peekskill in plenty of time to freshen up and head over to Garrity's Pub. He walked in about ten-thirty that evening. He sat at the bar in front of a large flat screen television that was mounted behind the bar in a manner that caused a person to crane their neck to look up at it.

"What will you have tonight sir?" the bartender asked.

"I think I'll have a Guinness Draught," Ralph answered.

"Coming right up sir," the bartender replied.

Ralph sat sipping his beer trying to act like he was interested in the television program that he couldn't really hear. After about ten minutes had passed, he got up and headed for the restrooms. As he entered the back hallway leading to the men's room he observed the fake potted tree as Bob had described. Looking around he could see that it could not be observed from the front bar area. With his right hand in his trouser pocket, he paused at the tree, then extracted the IronKey. Looking around and not seeing anyone, he quickly lifted the artificial grass and dropped the IronKey in the pot. He casually proceeded on to the men's room.

Upon returning to the bar, Ralph sat back down and finished his beer.

"Have another one?" the bartender asked as he saw Ralph empty the glass.

"No thanks, just a quick one on the way home," Ralph replied. "I have an early morning tomorrow."

Ralph left the pub and making sure nobody was around, walked over to the mailbox at the curb and opened it, acting like he was dropping a letter inside. As he did so, he leaned over the side facing the direction that Dawn would be coming from, and marked it with a large "X" using a piece of chalk.

He then returned to his car and drove directly home. It will be nice to sleep in a real bed, he thought to himself, but being worried about his friends, he knew it would be a rough night.

When Ralph arrived home, the first thing he did was take the extra IronKeys that Bob had provided him, and secured them in the safe hidden in the wall of his den. He then turned on his computer and checked to ensure he had the email from Chris. It was there, so he opened and saved the files.

Ralph lay in bed that night trying to figure out the best way to contact his FBI friend, and then how he would approach him. He knew he had to be careful, yet at the same time, he had to get them involved. If he could get the FBI to at least consider that the DTTF was a rogue agency then he might be able to secure protection for Bob and Chris. He only hoped they would listen and not arrest him for being involved. If they did, he would be of no help to Bob and Chris, or to ZeRho.

CHAPTER 21
The Search Is On

First thing Monday morning, Ralph arrived at the offices of ZeRho like any other Monday morning. He showed no sign of stress or anxiety and went through the usual Monday morning banter with employees, before proceeding to his office.

* * *

While Ralph was entering his office at ZeRho, Dawn Garrity slowed as she approached her father's pub. She immediately spotted the large white "X" on the side of the mailbox out front. She pulled into the small parking area and stopped in front of a sign that read "For Patrons Only."

Dawn proceeded to the side entrance, which was for employees only, unlocked it and entered. The air smelled of stale beer, as it always did. She did not turn any lights on, as there was enough coming through the front windows, for her to see her way into the hallway by the restrooms.

Approaching the large fake potted tree, she lifted the imitation grass in several places until she saw the flash drive lying there. She reached in, grabbed it, and placed it in her purse. She then went to the bar and grabbed a small damp cloth that always hung behind it. Upon exiting the pub, she casually walked to the side of the mailbox where the "X" had been marked. Watching to ensure all cars had driven by, she leaned over, and subtly wiped the "X" off the box with the damp cloth.

Dawn returned to her car, and drove directly to her office. Upon entering, she turned on her computer, then went and got herself a cup of coffee.

When she returned to her office, she closed the door and withdrew the IronKey from her purse. She plugged it in a USB port, and when the "Unlock Screen" appeared she typed in the password "BigBob" and clicked on the "unlock" button.

She first went to the video recording file. As she watched, she was appalled at what she saw. This was unbelievable behavior, especially for a government agency. Having been at Bob's house, back when they dated, she immediately recognized that the shooting had taken place in his living room.

Dawn next listened to portions of the audio recording that was taken at the CANE Conference. She would listen to the entire recording when time permitted, but she wanted to get a flavor of the conversations that took place. This was definitely a case of abuse of power, both by big business and the government.

Now she had to figure out a way to get her superiors, and the legal department, to let her run with the story.

* * *

Even before the raid at Bob's residence, the DTTF had been busy conducting searches to obtain information on Robert Armstrong and Christopher Hughes. However, since the shooting they had definitely ramped up their investigation. They wanted any information they could find that might assist them in locating these two individuals.

Being concerned how they may have fled the area; a search was also conducted to determine if either had purchased a plane ticket. They found that a Christopher Hughes had bought a ticket for a flight to Las Vegas, Nevada from Stewart International Airport in Newburgh, New York, on Friday. But no flight was booked by a Robert Armstrong.

They next determined who Christopher Hughes' cell phone provider was, but couldn't locate one for Robert Armstrong. They contacted Hughes' provider, and indicating they had probable cause, requested an immediate GPS location for his phone. The coordinates provided let them know that the phone was at the Stewart Airport in Newburgh, New York. An agent was immediately dispatched to determine if Hughes or his vehicle were present. They provided the agent with a photograph of Hughes and the make, model, and license plate number of his vehicle.

Further searches for the next of kin for both individuals were being done in hopes that interviews could be conducted to obtain more information. However, they had not been successful as it appeared all direct relatives were deceased.

Sitting in his office in Albany, Max Archer's administrative assistant informed him he had an incoming call from an Agent Hammond.

"Max Archer," he stated as he answered the phone.

"Sir, this is Agent Hammond. I am at Stewart Airport in Newburgh and have found the vehicle owned by Christopher Hughes in the long term parking lot. It appears that the cell phone is sitting on the front passenger seat and is plugged in to a power outlet. I did a thorough search of the small terminal and there is no sign of Hughes. I asked at the counter if Hughes ever took the flight and they informed me they couldn't divulge that information without a court order because of the privacy laws. How do you want me to proceed?"

"Make arrangements for the vehicle to be towed to our impound lot and held for evidence," Archer directed. "Then get back to the office."

"Yes sir," Hammond replied.

As soon as Archer hung up with Agent Hammond he placed a call to Wolfgang Drescher, the Director.

"Drescher here," He answered.

"Archer sir, we have found Hughes' vehicle, with his cell phone in it, at Stewart Airport in Newburgh, New York. He booked a flight to Las Vegas, Nevada on Friday. They say we need a court order to determine if he actually took the flight." We have nothing yet on that god damn Armstrong. He seems to have just vanished."

"I want both of these mother fuckers found dammit, and soon!" Drescher yelled. "With all the fucking technology we have available to us, we should be able to find two fucking civilians."

"We're working on it sir, I'll contact you as soon as we have something," Archer assured Drescher.

"Well it better be soon!"

* * *

While the DTTF worked feverishly on obtaining information, a meeting was starting at the FBI headquarters building in Washington. Present were Director Wolfson, the Deputy Director Hernandez, and Director for the National Security Branch, Mitchell.

"I assume Mr. Mitchell that you have seen the press conference about the agent being killed during an operation?" Director Wolfson began. "Mr. Hernandez and I have been discussing it all morning."

"Yes sir, I have been following it."

"We want to know why we, the leading law enforcement agency in the country, are not being called in to help in the investigation," Wolfson continued.

"I wondered the same sir," Mitchell replied.

"I am bothered by the location of the operation. This agency is supposed to be going after domestic terrorist that are involved with self-reliant activities. Those activities normally occur in rural areas.

"How did they happen to conduct an operation on a residence in a very affluent suburban neighborhood? I mean, what would have led them there? Shit, even that reporter from Wolf News picked up on that.

"Something isn't right here, I just don't know what. They indicate an agent was shot during a surveillance, but don't explain why the agent was alone. We always run a minimum of two agents on this type of surveillance.

"I want to start investigating this immediately, whether they want us involved or not. It would be a real kick in their ass if we could find this Armstrong or Hughes before they do."

Just then, Mitchell's cell phone rang. He explained to Wolfson that it was his office, and they were instructed not to interrupt him in the meeting unless it was very important. Wolfson directed him to step out of the office and take the call.

Mitchell did as he was instructed. He returned after several minutes to rejoin the meeting.

"I hope that was important?" Wolfson said as Mitchell returned.

"It was about this situation," Mitchell replied

"Well, fill us in."

"We just found out the name of the agent that was killed, and it was Craig Davis," Mitchell announced.

"Isn't that the DTTF Agent that our Agent, what's his name, was meeting in an attempt to determine if we could solicit information from him?" Deputy Director Hernandez asked.

"Special Agent McDonald sir," Mitchell said.

"That's the one," Hernandez remarked.

"And how did we come about this information?" Wolfson asked leaning forward.

"Our undercover, Clint Robertson, Special Agent Kelly that is, was able to call in and inform us."

"And how did he find out?" Hernandez asked.

"He was informed because he is being transferred to the Northeast Sector office in Albany to replace the dead agent, Davis. He will be under the command of this Max Archer who gave the press conference."

"Well this blows our attempt to get Special Agent McDonald closer to Davis," Wolfson remarked. "It just seems strange that the one agent we were trying to get close to ends up dead on a surveillance without backup. I'm not saying it couldn't happen, but what are the chances?" Wolfson stated looking deep in thought.

"Maybe they found out about our agent getting close to theirs. Maybe this Armstrong guy is a patsy, used to kill Davis, and now they want him dead as well," Hernandez stated.

"Well, I don't want to get into any conspiracy theories at this point, but we need to get involved and fast," Wolfson interjected. "Let's get a team started on trying to find these two guys. I want them before the DTTF finds them."

"I'll get right on it sir," Mitchell replied.

"Oh, and Mr. Mitchell. I want you to contact our Assistant Director in Charge at the New York City Field Office, Franco Gonzalez. His office also handles the Westchester County area so let's get them involved as well. Also have him contact the Albany New York Field Office if he finds it necessary. Keep myself and Mr. Hernandez updated with any information you obtain Mr. Mitchell."

"Yes sir."

With that the meeting concluded and Alaister Mitchell returned to his office. He immediately formed a team and briefed them on the investigation. He also told them to stay low profile as they did not want the Domestic Terrorism Task Force to know they were involved. At least not yet.

* * *

While the meeting was ending at the FBI Headquarters, Ralph Cummings sat in his office at ZeRho. Taking out his cell phone he placed a call to his FBI friend, James Black.

"Special Agent in Charge Black," a voice answered.

"Hey Jim, Ralph Cummings here. How the hell you doing?'

"Hey Devil Dog, what's up?"

"Sounds like you got a promotion Marine. Moving on up are you?"

"I guess you could say that," Black replied.

"Well, Special Agent in Charge sounds pretty impressive to me," Ralph joked. "You now in charge of the New York City Office?"

"Not really, but it was a great promotion. Actually the Assistant Director in Charge, Franco Gonzalez, is in charge of the New York City office. He has six Special Agents in Charge, and I'm one of the six," Black answered.

"Well, it sounds like congratulations are in order my friend."

"Thanks Ralph, how is it going with you?"

"I'm glad you asked," Ralph replied. "I have a little problem and I was hoping you might be able to help."

"What's the problem Ralph, I'll do what I can, and you know that."

"It's something I really don't care to talk about over the phone. I was hoping we could meet for dinner and discuss it in private," Ralph said cautiously.

"Actually, I'm busier than a one-legged man at a butt kickin contest, but sure, when do you want to meet?"

"I hate to sound pushy, but as soon as possible," Ralph replied.

"I'll have to check my schedule, but you sound like this is urgent. Can you give me a hint?"

"I really hate to say anything on the phone," Ralph stated. He paused for a moment, and then said, "It is related to the agent that was shot yesterday."

"Ah, let's end our conversation here," Black said quickly. "How about eight o'clock tonight at Luigi's Italian Restaurant in Tarrytown?"

"Sounds great, and Jim, thanks," Ralph said.

"See you at eight," Black said as he hung up.

* * *

While Ralph was on the phone with James Black, Dawn was busy at Wolf News arranging a meeting with her boss, Harold Martin, the Senior Editor.

Martin was a stout man who stood five feet ten inches tall. Balding, he had a shrewd face and was known for flamboyant gestures when he became animated. Although he could be rough at times, he was always fair, at least with Dawn. She was used to calling him "Hal."

"I'm really glad you were able to meet at such short notice Hal, but this could be a big story," Dawn said as she entered his office, and closed the door behind her.

"Well get started," Hal said. "I ain't got all day."

"I have some very interesting information that has to do with that shooting of the DTTF agent yesterday. I wanted you to see it and maybe provide some guidance in regard to how we can get it out there."

"What kind of information?" Hal asked.

Dawn explained the video that showed that a DTTF agent actually did the shooting, not Robert Armstrong. She also told him about the recording from the CANE Conference. She explained that the Christopher Hughes the DTTF was also searching for had made the recording. Hal wanted to see the video, and listen to the audio recording. He had Dawn close the blinds to his office windows and they both watched the video and listened to portions of the audio recording in private.

"How did you come by these?" Hal asked.

"I retrieved them from a dead drop," Dawn replied.

"What are you a spy now? How did you find out they were there?" Hal asked sounding annoyed.

"I received a phone call telling me where they would be and when."

"And who is the person that called you, and told you about them?" Hal asked, now sounding exasperated.

"I have a right to conceal the identity of my sources, you know that Hal," Dawn stated.

"And you know that you can reveal a source to a Senior Editor and they are bound by the same confidentiality."

"For the time being, I'd rather not reveal my source," Dawn said stubbornly.

"OK, but get this straight," Hal continued. "This stuff is hot and if and when we use it, it will bring a lot of heat on us by both the government and big business. We have to make sure it's real."

"The video is real and the location is in Robert Armstrong's living room. I can verify that for a fact."

"And how can you verify that?" Hal asked.

Dawn paused for a moment and saw no way out of answering the question, without being truthful.

"I have been there," Dawn replied looking directly into Hal's eyes.

"Lately?"

"No, a couple of years ago when we were dating, but the place is the same," Dawn said adamantly.

"You dated this guy?" Hal asked looking dumbfounded.

"It's a long story," Dawn replied.

"Well you know I'm going to have to run this by our Head legal Council, Bernie Lambert. Being this shooting is all over the news, we might be able to get the video up. The Domestic

Terrorism Task Force will certainly have to defend their claims, which will be hard once we reveal the video."

"We also need to keep in mind that Robert Armstrong is in danger until the video clears him," Dawn interjected.

"I know, so I will get Bernie in here at once for guidance. In regard to the audio recording of the meeting, I find it very interesting, but I don't know how we can verify its authenticity. It would work well into the series you are doing on self-reliance though. I would suggest that you dig into this CANE organization. See if you can come up with a list of members somehow. If nothing else, start searching for video or audio clips of the members mentioned by name. These are prominent guys in business. There has to be something out there. We can then compare their voice and speech patterns to those on the recording. We may be able to verify their identity and therefore their attendance at the meeting. Do we know when this meeting took place?"

"It is my understanding that it took place a little over a year ago," Dawn replied.

"Why the hell did it take this Hughes so long to reveal the tape?"

"He had an accident shortly after he recorded the conference. He was in a comma and when he came out he had short term memory loss. It took almost a year for him to recall the recording and where he had hidden it," Dawn explained.

"And the plot thickens," Hal said with a wink. "I'll get right on this and let you know if and how we run the video."

"Thanks Hal, I really appreciate your help."

* * *

Wolfgang Drescher placed a secure call to Gray Mann at CANE Headquarters. He knew that if he didn't call soon, Mann would be calling him.

"What do you have to report," Gray Mann asked gruffly.

"Well sir, nothing good. We are still searching for those sons of a bitches Christopher Hughes and Robert Armstrong.

"We found Hughes' car at Stewart Airport in Newburgh, New York, with his cell phone inside. We determined that he booked a flight to Las Vegas on Friday. We have no idea where Armstrong went but we have a lot of people looking for him. We are doing various searches in hopes of getting something that will lead us to him. At this point he seems like a ghost."

"The shooting should make it easier to find Armstrong," Mann stated. "I'm sure there are plenty of people looking for him now. You should get some agents out to Vegas and see if Hughes can be located out there. If so, he should remain there. Bottom line Drescher, find them both, and quick!"

"We're on it Mr. Mann."

* * *

While Dawn was meeting with her Senior Editor, and Drescher was talking to Gray Mann, the Director for the National Security Branch of the FBI, Alaister Mitchell, placed a call to Franco Gonzalez, the Assistant Director in Charge at the New York City Field Office. He filled him in on the current investigation and asked that he get involved as soon as possible. He explained that time was of the essence in this investigation and they wanted to find both Robert Armstrong and Christopher Hughes before the Domestic Terrorism Task Force did.

* * *

Meanwhile, Bob and Chris stayed hidden at Bob's new place. They were ready to go at anytime; they just weren't sure when that time would be. Every so often, they would go into the communications room and check the news to see if Dawn had gotten the video or audio recording public. The longer it took to reveal the video, the more time the DTTF had to locate them. This also meant the less time they had before bugging-out.

Bob stayed busy teaching Chris various skills that would help both of them if they had to head out to the woods. The first was fire. Bob explained that starting a fire was easy, but building a fire took some expertise. He showed him that he first needed tinder, then kindling, then fuel. He explained that people often try to add fuel to a fire before they have a good set of coals from the kindling. He took Chris outside and demonstrated how to light smaller pieces of wood with the tinder that was started first.

"The smaller the better, to start," Bob explained. "Then start adding pieces of kindling that are a little thicker as the flames grow. Once you have a small bed of coals from the kindling, you can start adding small pieces of fuel. Just don't go throwing a log on a small flame or it will go out," he expounded.

Bob also demonstrated how to use the blowing tube he had included with Chris' supplies. Chris was amazed how it brought a small flame to life by simply blowing air through the tube into the bottom of the fire.

"This is like a small forge," Chris said.

"Just remember the fire triangle," Bob stated. "You need fuel, heat, and oxygen for a fire. What is often lacking, especially down at the bottom, is oxygen. My father used to wave his hat at the fire to get oxygen down into it. However, it blew ashes everywhere. This little tube with the flexible hose on it really allows you to direct the oxygen where you want it.

"Really great piece of gear," Chris said.

"One other thing, Chris. There will be a good chance that we won't be able to have an open fire, at least a big one, if we are hiding out in the woods. However, if we really need to cook or purify water by boiling it, I will make a Dakota Fire Hole. It allows us to place the fire in the ground and because of that, it burns below the surface of the ground, and that shields the fire from being seen, especially at night.

"Basically, it is a hole in the ground, with another angled hole that comes into the bottom of the first hole. As the hot air from the fire in the main hole exits up and out, a suction is created drawing fresh air down the angled hole and into the base of the fire. Having attended M.I.T. I'm sure you understand the Chimney effect, because that is what occurs here. As the fire gets hotter from more oxygen, it draws more air into the main hole, making it even hotter. Being the fire is more efficient it creates less smoke. And when we are done, it is easier to conceal the fact that we had a fire by simply filling in the hole with dirt and spread natural material around it."

"I have to tell you Bob, you do know your shit," Chris said smiling.

"Of course, during the day, we can always use the little gas cartridge stoves, but we are limited to the two small gas canisters each of us are carrying. They only last about forty-five minutes each, so we will have to be careful with them."

Bob also explained that they would not be able to make it into the Catskill Park in one day.

"The place I have in mind is about twenty-five miles from here and if we have to run, we will be doing it on foot. With the packs we will be carrying, the rough terrain, no trails, and you not being used to hiking, we will try to get half way there the first night. That is when we will use the hammocks.

"Hammocks are quick to setup and we don't have to be concerned with picking a good site that is level or has drainage if it rains. All we need is two trees about fifteen feet apart. We could actually stretch them across a creek if necessary, but it would make it rough getting in and out," Bob laughed.

Grabbing an extra hammock and tarp from the supply room, and selecting two trees, Bob spent a short time showing Chris how to use the ENO slap straps, which made connecting a hammock to a tree on each end, fast and easy. Bob showed how they were simply two lengths of nylon webbing with loops sewn in at one foot increments. The strap was easily placed around a tree and one end was threaded through the loop at the other end. Once it was pulled tight around the tree, the remainder of the strap provided the loops at the various lengths to attach the hammock, using the small carabiners supplied with the hammock. In only minutes the hammock was hanging and ready to use.

Chris had no problem putting up the hammock and indicated he felt the slap straps made setup quicker than having to use cordage at each end to tie the hammock to a tree.

One last thing Bob wanted to show Chris about the hammock was attaching drip lines. He showed him how to hang a piece of cordage off each end of the hammock. When it rained, and water ran down the straps holding his hammock, these pieces hanging down would direct water to the ground instead of into his hammock.

Bob also gave Chris a quick lesson on how to attach a ridge line over the hammock using parachute cord and a bowline knot on one end and a taut line hitch knot on the other end. Bob explained that the advantage of the taut line hitch was the ability to pull the ridge line tight, and then be able to easily keep it that way. He then showed how to place the lightweight tarp over the ridge line, and to stake it down over the hammock on each side, which would provide Chris with a readymade shelter over the hammock.

Bob spent some time showing the safe use of a knife and instructed him to always place it back into its sheath when not in use. "Never lay it down on the ground," he instructed. He reminded Chris that it was his second most important survival tool.

Lessons went on like this most of the day, as Bob knew time was getting short. At anytime, they might have to run.

* * *

Harold Martin, the Senior Editor for Wolf News, walked into Dawn Garrity's office with a look on his face that telegraphed what he was about to say.

"We can't run the video or the audio recording yet," he said bluntly. "The lawyers want to study this a little more and until we get an OK from them, we have to hold the story."

"You're shitting me, right Hal?" Dawn responded looking furious.

"What can I say Dawn, my hands are tied."

"Revealing this video is not only a top story, it might be the only thing that saves Robert Armstrong's life," Dawn stated emphatically.

"I know that, but I have a network to protect. I will talk to them again. The audio recording can wait, but I agree, this video is highly important. Once we get that out there, the other recording will be a good follow-up showing why they were after both of these men," Hal responded trying to appease Dawn.

"I am already writing that portion of the show. When you say go, I will be ready to roll," Dawn responded.

"I know you will, just hold your horses. We will make this happen kid,"

With that, Hal left Dawns office as quickly as he had entered. Dawn sat down at her desk and pulled her wallet out of her purse. Opening it, she pulled out an old photo of Bob. She touched it gently with her forefinger thinking; just hold on Big Bob, I'm doing the best I can. She then replaced the picture and went back to working on her show.

* * *

Max Archer was sitting in his office when an agent working on the investigation walked in holding a file folder.

"What's up Agent Brady?" Archer asked.

"We have been doing all kinds of searches on both Robert Armstrong and Christopher Hughes for relatives sir, and it seems as if all their immediate relatives are dead. It doesn't give us much to go on for interviews."

"Have you searched for siblings of them or their parents? If they had sisters, and they married, they would have a different last name." Archer stated.

"We did for Armstrong and Hughes, but not the deceased parents," Brady responded.

"Well get on it Brady," Archer said in a disgusted tone. "And another thing, has anybody been over to the Hughes' company, ZeRho I believe, to interview anybody?"

"No sir, not at this time," Brady responded.

"Well somebody there might know something. Get an agent over there and see what we can dig up."

"I'm on it sir," Brady said as he left the office in haste.

Agent Brady returned to his office and spoke to the investigation team he had put together. He explained how a search for siblings of Armstrong's and Hughes' parents should be initiated at once. He also assigned an agent to go to ZeRho the following morning to interview employees.

John D. McCann

CHAPTER 22
FBI Connection

Ralph dressed in a pair of grey flannel trousers, a light blue button down shirt, and a silk navy blue tie with miniature gold Marine Corps emblems on it. He slipped into a pair of Allen Edmonds 'Park Avenue' highly polished black cap-toe oxford shoes, and topped it all off with a Brooks Brothers navy blue double breasted jacket with gold buttons. He checked himself in the full length mirror, and satisfied with his appearance, he headed to Luigi's Italian Restaurant in Tarrytown, New York, with the Ironkey in his pocket.

Luigi's Italian Restaurant appeared as a nondescript little place on the outside, and sat on a side street off the main thoroughfare of Tarrytown. Inside, the decor was typical of many smaller Italian restaurants. The walls were covered in burgundy velvet flocked wallpaper with wall sconce lighting fixtures providing a low light atmosphere. All tables had clean

260

white tablecloths that were changed with a flourish after each party left, making the simple change more of a presentation than a mere replacement. There were several small side rooms for patrons who wished to have privacy. The food was excellent, as was the service.

Ralph pulled into the parking lot to the left of the restaurant at seven fifty, ten minutes early. He parked the rental car, which he had decided to keep for a few days, and proceeded inside. As he entered, he saw James Black sitting at the small bar which was located between the front door and the eating area. As Ralph walked in, James raised his forefinger in the air in a gesture indicating he saw Ralph. Ralph walked directly to him.

"Long time no see Jim," Ralph said jutting his right hand forward.

"You to my friend," Jim responded standing up and reaching out for a vigorous hand shake.

Special Agent James Black was a very muscular black man who stood six foot three inches tall. He had very short black hair, a chiseled jaw line, and a smooth complexion. With his large chest, yet slim waist, Ralph was always impressed with the impeccable fitting of his suits. He went through the Marine Corps Officer Candidate School at Quantico Virginia and they always told him that there were no white Marines or Black Marines, only green Marines. Jim used to joke saying, "I guess then I'm a dark green Marine."

"I have reserved one of the separate side rooms so we can have some privacy," Ralph stated as he released Jim's hand.

Ralph walked towards the hostess, who stood behind a small podium at the entrance to the eating area. She was an older Italian woman dressed in an outdated long black dress. A small gold Crucifix hung from a gold chain around her neck.

"Good evening Angela," Ralph said as he approached the woman. "I have a reservation for eight o'clock in a private room."

"Of course Mr. Cummings," Angela said with a strong Italian accent. "It is nice to have you back. It has been a while. Please follow me."

Angela withdrew two menus from under the podium and walked towards the right rear of the restaurant with Ralph and Jim following. She stopped at a small room with one table inside. Although the room didn't have a door, it provided more privacy than the main dining area.

"Please be seated," Angela directed as she placed the menus on the table. "I will have your server come right over. Can I get you a drink while you're waiting?"

"You have the nicest Italian red house wine," Jim stated. "Can we have a carafe of that? You OK with that Ralph?"

"I'm fine with that Jim."

"I'll have it brought right over Mr. Black," Angela said as she left the room.

Once Ralph and Jim sat down and studied the menu, they started with the usual small talk about how they had been and what they had been doing.

When their server arrived with a basket of fresh bread sticks, still warm to the touch, and a carafe of wine, she placed them on the table and asked if she could take their order? They ordered an appetizer of fried calamari and a small antipasto platter to share as they normally did. An entree was selected and the server left the room.

"I have to tell you Ralph, you have really peaked my interest," Jim said, turning the conversation to the business at hand. "What do you know about this shooting?"

"I know it wasn't done by Robert Armstrong as reported by that Domestic Terrorism Task Force," Ralph asserted flatly.

"And how do you know this?" Jim asked as he furrowed his brow.

"I have a video recording of the shooting that occurred in Armstrong's house and it clearly shows that the shooter was another DTTF agent, not Armstrong."

"You are kidding right?" Jim asked.

"No I'm not Jim, I'm as serious as cancer," Ralph replied staring directly at him.

At that point appetizers were being served and Jim and Ralph sipped on their wine until the server left.

"And how did you come by this video?" Jim continued as the server exited their private room.

Ralph explained how he received an email from his boss, Christopher Hughes.

"And this is the same Christopher Hughes named in the DTTF press conference?" Jim asked.

"The same one," Ralph replied.

Ralph then continued explaining how he had the video recording that was taken during the shooting inside Armstrong's house that had apparently been uploaded to a cloud and retrieved by Mr. Armstrong.

"How did your boss, Hughes, get it to send to you?" Jim asked.

"It's a long story, but you need to hear it all to understand," Ralph stated.

Ralph then explained about the audio recording that he also received in the email, and what was on it.

"This just keeps getting better," Jim said with a smile. "If I didn't know you so well, I would think that you were either pulling my leg, or you were ready for the loony bin."

"I assure you my friend, it is neither," Ralph exclaimed emphatically.

As the main course arrived, Jim poured them both another glass of wine, and they continued with their meal and conversation.

"I would assume you could provide me with a copy of this video and audio recording if I asked?" Jim stated.

"That I could," Ralph replied as he pulled the IronKey from his pocket and slid it across the table to Jim.

"And both of those items are on this?" Jim asked.

"Yes Jim, this is an IronKey which is an extremely secure flash drive."

"I'm very familiar with them, we use them at work," Jim said as he picked it up and placed it in his pocket. "What is the password?" Jim asked.

"It is capital 'K', small c, a, l, b," Ralph replied in a hushed tone.

"Very creative," Jim said smiling. "My last name backwards."

"Well I didn't want to make it too difficult," Ralph said smiling back. "I wouldn't want you to forget it."

"You are sure that the video clearly shows that this Robert Armstrong didn't do the shooting?" Jim questioned.

"I'm certain," Jim replied. "It clearly shows it was another DTTF agent, and it was clearly a murder. The first shot to the throat, a second to the forehead, and then he just walked away."

"You also believe this audio recording of a meeting clearly reveals that the members, from various large companies, wanted an agency formed that would have the appearance that they were going after domestic terrorists, but actually wanted to keep self-reliant people dependent on their goods and services?" Jim said, more as a statement than a question.

"Correct again my friend," Ralph replied.

"This video really has me interested," Jim said as he pulled the IronKey out of his pocket and stared at it. I know you live only a short distance from here, and I really don't want to wait until I get back into the city to see this thing. What do you say about heading over to your house to review it? I haven't been there in a while anyway."

"Let's get a check and get out of here," Ralph said with a smile. "We can have coffee at my house."

When the bill arrived, Jim picked it up stating that this was agency business.

"I do have a rather substantial income you know?" Ralph said trying to grab the check away from Jim.

"Now you don't want to be accused of assaulting a Special Agent of the FBI, do you?" Jim said kidding.

"OK, I guess it isn't often that I get something from the government," Ralph replied kidding back.

Once Jim paid the bill, they both headed to Ralph's house in their separate cars. When they arrived, Ralph put on a pot of coffee, and took Jim into his small office and turned on his computer. When the computer was up and running, he placed the IronKey into a USB port. When the unlock screen appeared he typed in the password. He went to the video file and had Jim sit at his desk.

Jim watched the video in amazement. He couldn't believe what he was seeing on the monitor. He watched it several times and finally turned it off. He then exited the program, clearing the IronKey for removal from the computer.

"This is unbelievable," Jim stated shaking his head.

"Well, I thought you might be interested," Ralph replied. "I only ask that you try to ensure that I'm not sucked into this thing. I simply received this from my boss who asked that I try to help. I am not involved in this thing.

"OK Ralph, let's have a quick cup of that coffee you made," Jim said as he extracted the IronKey from the USB port and placed it back in his pocket. "I have to get back to the city. I have a feeling tomorrow is going to be a long day."

"I'm sure it will Jim," Ralph agreed. "I'm not pushing you my friend, but please work on this as fast as you can. It would appear as though this Armstrong has been set up and if the DTTF finds him first, well the video clearly shows what they will do."

"I will be on this like stink on shit my friend," Jim assured Ralph with a smile.

The two of them enjoyed their cup of coffee and then Jim left. Ralph shut down the computer, hoping to himself that Jim would be able to help both Chris and Bob.

As Jim drove home he placed a cell phone call to his boss, Franco Gonzalez, the Assistant Director in Charge of the New-York City FBI Field Office. He briefly filled him in on the information he had just received. Gonzalez told him to be in his office in the morning at seven o'clock sharp.

* * *

At six fifty-five on Tuesday morning, Jim was standing in the outside waiting room of Gonzalez's office with the IronKey in his pocket. Even after the late night he had, Jim had risen early so he could copy the video and audio recording to another flash drive, which he placed in the safe at his home.

At exactly seven o'clock, Gonzalez's administrative assistant informed Jim that the Assistant Director would see him now.

"Good morning Sir," Jim said as he entered the office.

"Good morning Jim," Gonzalez said. "Have a seat and tell me more about these recordings we discussed briefly last night."

Jim explained how he had received the IronKey flash drive from a friend that worked for Christopher Hughes at ZeRho and how he had come about obtaining the information.

"You indicated that you have a video recording that clearly shows that Robert Armstrong didn't do the shooting as reported by the DTTF," Gonzalez stated, more as a fact than a question.

"That's correct sir. The video clearly shows another DTTF agent pull a suppressed handgun and shoot the other agent, first in the throat and then in the forehead. He then simply walks away."

"Let's get this video up and running," Gonzalez demanded.

Jim handed the IronKey to Gonzalez which he inserted into a USB drive on a computer connected to a large screen monitor on his wall. Jim initiated the video recording by inserting the password, then double clicking on the video file. It came alive on screen. Gonzalez watched it all the way through the first time, then went back and paused on the frontal view of the agent doing the shooting. "We will need to get this to the lab and have them perform a facial recognition scan on this face.

"As you know, we have suspected for some time that this DTTF is some type of a rogue agency," Gonzalez remarked. "This just might be our excuse to initiate a full investigation of their activities. How do we know for sure that this video was actually taken at the Armstrong residence?"

"We don't Sir; we could get an agent over there directly and verify the room the video was allegedly taken in."

"Let's do it," Gonzalez replied. "And if the DTTF tries to stop our agent, he is to inform them that the incident is now under investigation by the FBI."

"I saw a quick clip this morning on Wolf News and it looks like the scene is now being guarded by local law enforcement, not the DTTF," Jim offered.

"You said that this audio recording clearly indicates that some business organization discussed getting the government to start an agency to keep people dependent on their products and services, and to do that they wanted legislation that prevents people from being self-reliant. Is that basically it in a nutshell?" Gonzalez asked.

"Basically sir," Jim replied.

"Well this might go a lot higher than we think. But proving it might be another matter. We need to get every available agent we can on this. Set up a meeting in the conference room for eleven o'clock and we will have a briefing on the various things I want accomplished in short order. While you are doing that, I will contact the Director at FBI Headquarters."

"Can I have the IronKey so I can have the lab make a copy and start on the facial recognition?" Jim asked. "I will then get an agent over to Armstrong's to photograph the living room."

As Gonzalez handed the IronKey to Ralph, he said, "As soon as the living room is photographed, get the agent back here for the conference."

Jim left Gonzalez's office and proceeded directly to the lab. He had them make a copy of the video recording file from the IronKey and indicated that they should start a facial recognition scan on the face of the shooter. As soon as they had something, they should report directly to Assistant Director, Gonzalez.

Jim took the IronKey back and proceeded to his office. He called one of his Special Agents, Mark Whitaker, located in Westchester County. He directed him to get over to Armstrong's house immediately and get photographs of the living room. When done, he should drive them to the city right away for the conference at eleven.

Gonzales placed a call to Director Wolfson in Washington. He informed him of his meeting and conversation with his Special Agent in Charge, James Black.

"I had the video recording taken down to our lab to have a facial recognition scan done in an attempt to identify the DTTF agent doing the shooting. I also have an agent going to Robert Armstrong's house to verify that the video was indeed taken there," Gonzalez explained. "If it is, then we have a DTTF Agent murdering one of their own agents, and trying to set-up Armstrong as the killer."

"Excellent," Wolfson exclaimed. "This is exactly what we have been looking for. Between the video and audio recording you are talking about, we just might have the ammunition to, not only go after this DTTF, but prove they are nothing more than a rogue agency working for the power brokers of our country. I need you to get a copy of both the video and audio recording to me immediately.

"We really need to find both this Robert Armstrong and Christopher Hughes before anybody else does. If we don't, there is a good chance they will be killed and disappear. We want the DTTF, but let's make finding these guys a priority.

"We need to stay on top of this and I want updates as things develop. I'll fill in Deputy Director Hernandez and we will determine what we can do from this end," Wolfson concluded.

"I'll report as soon as I have something Sir," Gonzalez replied.

CHAPTER 23
The Search Continues

Tuesday morning, Ralph had not been at his office at ZeRho for more than fifteen minutes, when his administrative assistant, Darlene, informed him that an agent from the Domestic Terrorism Task Force was there and wanted to interview employees.

"Send him in Darlene; I'll take care of this." Ralph said.

Darlene led a man into Ralph's office that identified himself as Agent Swanson of the Domestic Terrorism Task Force. He stood about five feet ten inches tall with a strong build. He wore a blue suit that was assuredly not tailored and brown dress shows that had failed to see any shoe polish for some time. He had a clip on tie that had seen better days.

"How can I help you Agent Swanson?" Ralph asked as he stood and reached over his desk extending his right hand.

"As I'm sure you know, we are looking for the owner of this company, Christopher Hughes, in connection with an investigation of a shooting that took place Sunday," Swanson said as he shook Ralph's hand.

"Have a seat Agent Swanson," Ralph said directing him to a chair in front of his desk. Ralph then sat down behind his desk and continued.

"I am well aware of that situation, but what do you think you can accomplish here at his business?" Ralph asked.

"I would like to interview employees who might have some information in regard to his whereabouts," Swanson replied.

"And who are these employees?"

"Well, I don't know," Swanson stumbled.

"We have several thousand employees here at ZeRho. I wouldn't think that you would want to interview them all. Can you narrow the field a little?" Ralph asked.

"I want to talk to those who were close to him. Those who might know where he might have gone."

"Mr. Hughes is a very private man," Ralph stated. "He is a loner in his own right. As the Senior Vice President of this company, I barely know him myself. He has always treated me and the employees very well, but I have never known him to personally associate with any employee. As you can see, conducting any type of interviews here would be time consuming, and certainly yield little information, other than maybe what color car he drives. Such an activity would surely disrupt our productivity, and as the person in charge while Mr. Hughes is gone, I certainly couldn't allow that."

"Well Mr. Cummings, I can see that you don't understand the authority of a Federal Agent of the Domestic Terrorism Task Force," Swanson retorted.

"Mr. Swanson, I am very aware of your 'authority' and I am more than willing to help in any way I can," Ralph replied with a smile as he stood. "As soon as you return with the required search warrant, and a list of specific names of people you wish to interview. For now, I will have to ask you to leave the premises at once."

"You will be hearing from me again," Swanson growled as he got up from his seat.

"And I look forward to that Agent Swanson. Now if you will excuse me, I have work to do."

Ralph pressed a button on his phone and asked that Darlene have security escort Agent Swanson from the building and premises.

* * *

Upon arriving at the offices of Wolf News, Dawn Garrity proceeded directly to the Senior Editor's office.

"Good morning Hal," she said. "How are we doing on releasing the video for my show?"

"We're still on hold," Hal replied looking up from his desk. "The lawyers are still concerned that the investigation by the Domestic Terrorism Task Force is ongoing and our releasing the video might put us in a bad position."

"This is bogus Hal, and you know it," Dawn blurted out. "The video shows that the investigation is bullshit and they are trying to get to Armstrong so they can make him a patsy. If we don't get this video up, Armstrong doesn't have a chance. Since when do we wait for an investigation to be concluded before we report on it?" Dawn added looking pissed.

"I know that Dawn, and watch your mouth," Hal said pointing his forefinger at her.

"Sorry Boss, I lost my head," Dawn said apologetically. "It just seems like we have an important story here, and we can't run with it. This video, and then the audio recording, needs to be made public. It's news, and news worthy. We can't sit on it forever."

"I know that as well Dawn," Hal replied. "I will get an answer by the end of the day."

"I'll be waiting for the word," Dawn said as she left Hal's office, and proceeded to her own.

She sat at her desk reviewing the details of the story, and how she would report it, when given the go ahead.

* * *

While Agent Swanson was at the offices of ZeRho with Ralph, another agent at the Northeast Sector Headquarters located a relative of Robert Armstrong. He found a Martha Wagner who lived just northwest of the Catskill Park and was the sister of Richard Armstrong, Robert's father.

The information was passed on to Max Archer immediately, who instructed an Agent McCarthy to get to her residence at once, and determine if she had any information on Armstrong.

"You call me as soon as you leave there, you understand?" Archer instructed McCarthy.

"Yes sir, I'll call immediately upon leaving," McCarthy acknowledged.

"Well get the hell going," Archer said.

McCarthy checked a vehicle out of the motor pool and began the trip which, according to his GPS, should take approximately one hour and fifteen minutes.

* * *

Bob had been up at his usual time and had made coffee. Chris, getting used to rising when he smelled the coffee, had joined Bob in the kitchen. They discussed the skills they would work on that day.

Bob explained to Chris that he had to be ready to leave at a moment's notice. That meant having on the proper hiking boots, and anything else he planned on wearing when they left. Bob felt it had been too long, and he could feel in his bones that something would happen soon.

After finishing a quick breakfast, Bob took Chris out to cut him a walking stick.

"I personally don't use one of these often, but it can save your knees and help with water crossings if the current is strong," Bob told Chris.

"Isn't it just something extra to carry?" Chris asked inquisitively.

"You don't actually carry it Chris, you place it out in front of you then walk towards it, Bob explained. Once we get one cut, I'll show you how to use it for hiking, both uphill and downhill, and for crossing water with a strong current, which we may have to do, being we are hiking up the back way into the mountains. You will actually use it as a third leg centered out in front of you. Facing the current you will lean forward towards the walking stick. It will provide you with much more stability, sort-of like a tripod, so the current doesn't knock you over."

Bob cut a large sapling that would result in a walking stick of the right height when trimmed. He then instructed Chris on its proper use.

* * *

Agent McCarthy arrived at Martha Wagner's property just after ten thirty. He parked alongside the small house and ascended the front porch and knocked on the door.

"I'm coming," Martha yelled as she dried her hands and walked from the kitchen to the front door.

Looking out one of the three small windows of the door, she could see a man dressed in khaki tactical pants and a black polo shirt with some type of gold emblem over the left breast. He had close cropped hair, like Bob had when he was in the Marine Corps. Standing erect, with shoulders back, he waited for someone to open the door.

Martha opened the door and stepped out onto the porch.

"May I help you sir?" she asked.

"Yes, I am Agent McCarthy from the Domestic Terrorism Task Force. Are you Martha Wagner?" he asked.

"That would be me," Martha responded with a smile.

"We are trying to locate a Robert Armstrong and it is our understanding that you are his aunt."

"And how would you know that?" she asked.

"We are a federal agency ma'am," McCarthy responded. "We can find out anything."

"Well, what do you want from me?" Martha asked.

"Like I said ma'am, we are trying to find your nephew, Robert Armstrong."

"And what makes you think I would know where he is?" Martha asked.

"Well he is your nephew. When was the last time you saw him?" McCarthy pushed.

"Well let me see now, Robert, he's the tall one right?" Martha asked.

"I have no idea how tall he is, have you seen him and when?"

"Oh, now I remember, my nephew Bob. He's the only nephew I have you know?" Martha continued. "He is a nice boy."

"Do you know where he is at this time?" McCarthy asked.

Looking at her watch Martha said, "Well it is a little early for lunch, so he is probably at work. They are pretty strict about leaving from work early you know?' Martha stated still providing no information.

"Where does he work ma'am?" McCarthy asked.

"Oh he's in the Marines," Martha answered. "He's really something to see in his uniform, very dashing," she finished with a wink.

"Mrs. Wagner, Robert Armstrong has not been in the Marine Corps for many years. Now have you seen him lately?"

"That must be why he didn't wear a uniform when he was here."

"He was here?" McCarthy asked.

"Yes sir, last year he came up here hunting like he does every deer season. I have over twelve hundred acres so he has plenty of room to hunt. Didn't get anything though. Shame really, came all the way up here and had to go home empty handed."

"Have you seen him since then?" McCarthy asked getting exasperated.

"We're still talking about the tall one right?" Martha asked.

"Yes, the tall one." McCarthy responded.

"Well the next time I see him, I'll tell him you were asking about him. I have to put on my tea water and feed the cat," Martha said. "You have a nice day now," she said as she went back into the house and closed the door.

For a moment, Agent McCarthy just stood there. Then he walked down off the porch and returned to his vehicle. As he pulled out of the driveway and started down the road, he dialed the number for Max Archer.

Martha called Bob's alternate cell phone immediately, using one that he had provided her. He had told her not to call him from her house phone until this was over.

"Hello Martha, What's up?" Bob asked as he answered, seeing it was her that was calling.

"Some agent from that terrorist task force thing was just here asking questions," She said.

"What did he want?"

"He wanted to know if I knew where you were, of course. But I couldn't really tell him much, being so senile and all," Martha said with chuckle.

"You're a pisser Martha," Bob said with a laugh.

"Once I remembered you were now out of the Marine Corps, he wanted to know the last time I saw you. I told him I think it was last year during hunting season, but you didn't get anything," Martha chuckled again.

"Now what did I tell you about lying young lady," Bob said kidding. "How did you get rid of him?"

"I told him I had to feed the cat, walked back in the house and closed the door. He stood there a moment then drove away."

"Well this means they are getting close. I don't think it will be long and they will be checking out the property. If I see any signs of that, Chris and I will be heading out on foot. We will be hiking up to that place I told you about. We will have a better chance of hiding there if this place is compromised."

"If you have to run, be careful. Take care of that Chris guy."

"I will Martha. Thanks for the heads up, and hopefully I'll talk to you later. But don't count on it," Bob said as he terminated the call.

What was that about?" Chris asked inquisitively.

"Martha said an agent from the DTTF was just there asking questions. He wanted to know if she knew where I was, and the last time she saw me. Of course, she didn't give him shit. But, they found her, so it means they are getting close. I wouldn't be surprised if they start checking out her land. The first sign they are, we are out of here my friend."

"I'm ready when you are. I even have the walking stick staged alongside my pack.

"Let's make some coffee and sit out front and relax. You never know, it might be our last chance to do so."

While they waited for the coffee to perk, Bob checked the weather app on his cell phone to see what the weather was going to be for the next couple of days. It looked mostly clear with some possible rain that evening.

* * *

As Agent McCarthy left Martha's he spoke to Max Archer, by cell phone, and filled him in on the lack of information he had obtained.

"She was a real flake sir," McCarthy stated. "I think she is senile or has Alzheimer's or something."

"Did you get anything at all?" Archer questioned.

"She said Armstrong was on her property last deer season. She has over twelve hundred acres."

"I bet that son of a bitch is up there somewhere with that fucking Hughes. Did you just leave?"

"Yes sir, just left her house."

"Give me the coordinates of your location. I'm sending a chopper over there now to recon her property."

Using the GPS in the vehicle, Agent McCarthy provided Archer with the coordinates of his location.

"Now get the hell back here," Archer told McCarthy.

* * *

The eleven o'clock meeting at the New York City FBI Field Office was setup in the main conference room of the executive level. The Assistant Director in Charge, Franco Gonzales, was presiding. All six of the Special Agents in Charge were present; James Black, Peter Lindsey, John Fitzgerald, Larry McBride, Charlie Wong, and Kenneth Underwood. There were also other assorted Special Agents from the various departments involved, as well as Special Agent Whitaker who had gone earlier to Robert Armstrong's house to verify it was the location of the video. Gonzales started the meeting.

"OK gentleman, we have a lot to cover here today. The first thing I want to do is show you all a video recording that has come into our possession. You will see that not Armstrong, but an agent of the DTTF, was the actual shooter at Armstrong's house Sunday. Run that video please," Gonzales instructed.

On one wall were several flat screen monitors, and on the large one in the center, the video came to life.

When it completed, Gonzales instructed that it be shown one more time. After the second run, Gonzales turned back to the attending staff.

"As you can see, this is one of the most bizarre acts by a Federal Agent that I have ever seen. It reveals the type of agency this Domestic Terrorism Task Force is, and it's not good. We have had suspicions that this is some type of a rogue agency, and this video certainly doesn't help their case.

"Have we verified that this video was indeed taken at Robert Armstrong's house?" Gonzalez asked.

"Yes sir," James Black answered. "Special Agent Whitaker just arrived with digital photos and we can verify that the video was indeed taken in Armstrong's living room."

"Put those digital photos up on the monitors for everyone to see," Gonzales instructed.

"It appears that this Robert Armstrong is either being used as a patsy on this thing, or they want him for another reason and are using this as an excuse. Because of an audio recording we have received of a meeting that Christopher Hughes attended, it implicates the purpose of the DTTF further. As soon as we can, we will provide you with transcripts of specific sections of that recording, to clarify our suspicions.

"Although we are not certain of the relationship between Armstrong and Hughes we can speculate that the DTTF is not happy with either of them. Either way, if we don't find this Armstrong, and Hughes before the DTTF does, most likely they will not live."

Just then the meeting was interrupted by a Special Agent Melton from the lab. He stated that he was instructed to report as soon as the facial recognition scan identified the shooter in the video.

"And have you identified the shooter Special Agent Melton?" Gonzales asked.

"Yes sir, the face of the shooter in the video belongs to a Max Archer. He was formerly a Diplomatic Security Special Agent with the U.S. Department of State. Although unverified, we believe he is presently with the Domestic Terrorism Task Force."

"I knew it!" Gonzalez blurted out. "That freaking agency is bad news. We have suspected it all along, and this just goes to show the type of behavior they are capable of. We need to ramp up this investigation now, and we need to arrest this Max Archer. Once we get him, hopefully the bricks of that agency will start to fall. And we need to get out there and find these two other guys before the same thing happens to them."

Just then, Gonzales reached down and felt his side, feeling his cell phone vibrate.

"Hold on a minute, I have a call coming in from Alaister Mitchell, the Director for the National Security Branch. Maybe he has some further information we can use. Standby while I take the call."

Gonzales stepped out into the hallway to take the incoming call from Mitchell. Mitchell quickly told him about having an undercover agent inside the DTTF that was now assigned to their Albany facility, and had replaced the agent that had been killed. Mitchell had just received a call from him reporting that the DTTF was sending a chopper over a piece of property up by the Catskill Park that they believed Armstrong and Hughes might be hiding out on. "This is occuring right now," he said. "Our undercover indicates that his team has just been told to gear up for a possible raid if the aerial surveillance finds any evidence that the two are there."

Gonzalez was only gone a few minutes, when he quickly reentered the room.

"OK gentleman, I just received word that the DTTF has located a piece of property up by the Catskill Park that they believe Armstrong and Hughes might be hiding out on."

John Fitzgerald, one of the six Special Agents in Charge started to talk.

"Sir, just this morning our investigators found a sister of Armstrong's deceased father. Her name is Martha Wagner, and she owns property up by the Catskill Park. We planned to send a Special Agent up there today to interview her."

"Well when the hell were you going to fill us in Fitzgerald?" Gonzalez asked.

"The first opportunity I got sir, which was just now."

"How the hell did this amateur DTTF agency find her before us?' We better get our heads out of our ass and start performing like the number one investigative agency in the country." Gonzales retorted. It was obvious he was not only perturbed, but frustrated that the DTTF had beaten them at locating a relative.

"Let's get out there and do our job. I will reiterate; if the DTTF locates these guys before we do, we can kiss their butts goodbye. "Agent Black, stay behind after the others leave. I want to speak with you personally," Gonzales said as he concluded the meeting.

As the other agents left the conference room, Gonzalez approached James Black.

"James," Gonzales started. It was unusual for Gonzales too use a first name, but he was alone with him and felt it was appropriate. "I want you to contact your friend that we got the video and audio recording from. Determine if he can provide us with any other information about these two guys. Let him know we are not after him. We just want to find these guys before the DTTF. Maybe there is something he left out, or forgot to tell us. I know he is your friend but we need information now, and from wherever we can get it."

"I'll do my best sir."

James Black returned to his office and placed a call to Ralph.

"Ralph, how's it going jarhead?" James asked trying to seem nonchalant.

"You tell me Jim." Ralph replied.

"We just got word that the DTTF found an aunt of Armstrong's who lives up by the Catskill Park. They are conducting an aerial recon of the area as we speak, trying to determine if Armstrong or Hughes might be hiding up there."

Ralph paused, and then said, "Well I might have a little more information than I first led you to believe."

"Shit!" James exclaimed. "We need to meet now. Can you come into the city to my office?"

"If I have to."

"You have to," James stated, and terminated the call.

CHAPTER 24
The Escape

While the meeting was taking place at the New York City FBI Field Office, a black Bell OH-58D Kiowa Warrior reconnaissance helicopter approached the property owned by Martha Wagner. Having the coordinates of her house, they started over that location. It could immediately be observed that there was an old road leading from her house, up into the immense woods around her property. Flying as low as possible, the helicopter tracked those portions of the road that were visible, hoping it would lead them to something.

Bob and Chris had just checked the television and could tell that the video had not yet been released. If it had, it would be all over the news.

What the hell is taking so long, Bob thought to himself as he proceeded to go back out, with Chris on his heels?

"Get back into the house quick!" he shouted as he suddenly stopped in his tracks, with Chris almost crashing into him.

"Chopper," Bob explained pushing Chris back through the door into the house.

"I don't hear anything," Chris declared.

"I can hear 'em long before I see 'em," Bob replied." Get back into the kitchen, we can watch from there."

As they squatted down in the kitchen area, a black helicopter could be heard hovering directly over Bob's property. It then came so low that it could be viewed through the large windows on the south side of the house. It remained off the ground, but hovered as it swiveled in a complete circle obviously examining everything.

"Maybe it's going to land for a raid," Chris said.

"I doubt it, it's a reconnaissance chopper. It's not made to deploy troops. It's just checking us out."

"Well they know somebody is living here," Chris said.

"And I'm sure they are on the radio reporting what they have found. We need to get out of here now before they can get agents up here. As soon as that chopper raises back up, we get to the comm room, grab our bags, and hit the tunnel," Bob announced. "We can't take a chance going out the front in the event that thing comes back."

The chopper remained in its position for several minutes then rose up and out of site. Bob and Chris went through the back of the small pantry and proceeded into the comm room. Bob put on his tactical vest and strapped the drop-down leg rig to his right leg. He then quickly took off his belt holster and transferred the Berretta to the leg rig. He then put his knife sheath on his belt on the right hip. Turning his cell phone to vibrate mode, he dropped it into the cargo pocket on the left leg of his trousers.

Opening the entrance for the tunnel, they both grabbed their packs and put them on. "We want to move quickly to the end of the tunnel Chris. When we get there I will climb up the ladder and open the concealed hatch. It's kind of tricky. You follow me up when you see it open," Bob instructed. We will be under adequate cover from the air. But we need to move slow and make sure the chopper is gone. If it is still around, I'll hear it."

Bob moved to the end of the tunnel, after locking the door behind him, with Chris following close behind. Bob climbed the short ladder, and after a few movements with his hands, the concealed hatch hinged open. As Bob climbed up and out, Chris scurried right behind him, pushing his walking stick up and out first. Kneeling down on one knee, Bob closed the hatch and secured it in place.

"That looks like a rock," Chris quipped.

"It's supposed to," Bob replied. "It sounds like the chopper has left, but I can bet this place will be crawling with DTTF goons soon. We will move, staying under overhead cover whenever possible. You need to keep up with me Chris. It is already midday so we need to cover as much ground as we can before dark."

"I won't let you down," Chris responded.

"I know you won't Chris."

* * *

Dawn Garrity was sitting at her desk, putting finishing touches on the show she hoped would air soon, when her boss, Hal, strode through the door. Dawn looked up in anticipation.

"It's a go for the video," Hal said smiling.

"And I'm ready to go," Dawn said feeling relieved, her shoulders pulled back and exuding confidence in her expression.

"Just one thing," Hal interjected.

Dawns head dropped forward as she said, "Here it comes."

"No big deal, the lawyers just want us to conceal the faces of the two agents in the video, at least until they are both identified. Just use that circular blur effect software we usually use."

"Did they say anything about the audio recording?" Dawn asked.

"They are going to let us run some of it, to enhance the story. But of course only segments. They want to see how the story is put together first, and what segments we want to use. You can keep working on that, but let's get your video story up tonight. Put together a short intro to get the viewers interested, and get that up this afternoon.

"I'll get right on it and have it to you shortly."

* * *

As Bob and Chris were carefully but methodically moving through the woods, Bob could hear a chopper in the distance. He had Chris stop and they both knelt down under a large Hemlock. The sound of the rotors became louder and Bob could just make out a black Sikorsky UH-60 Blackhawk traveling south towards his place.

"That's a deployment chopper," Bob told Chris in a low tone. "It looks like they are going to deploy agents at the house. Good luck to them, we will continue to head north-northeast."

The UH-60 Blackhawk approached Bob's property and hovered directly over the open area by the gardens. The large door on the left side of the chopper, slid to the rear, and two large coils of black rope were tossed out. One end was attached inside the chopper, and the coils on the other end deployed all the way to the ground. As soon as the ropes were down, DTTF agents, wearing the same tactical outfit they had worn when raiding Bob's other house, with the addition of a pack on their backs, started to fast rope down to the ground, two at a time, one on each rope. As the agents landed they immediately started forming a circular perimeter facing outward. Eight agents total were deployed. When the last two landed, the ropes fell from the chopper, and the Blackhawk rose up and disappeared over the trees.

When all agents were down the lead agent keyed the microphone on his radio and said, "Let's move out. Over." They all looked around when they heard the command, not only through their earphones, but from speakers from around the property. They weren't sure what was going on, but they moved out anyway, in a circular manner heading towards the various buildings on the property.

Four of them headed directly for the house, while the other four proceeded to the garage and other small buildings on the property.

Upon approaching the front door, which was all glass like all the large windows on the south side, the first agent there noticed that the door was ajar. Bob had left it that way when leaving, hoping they would not smash the window in order to gain access. The lead agent pressed on the door and it opened inwards. He yelled, "Federal Agents" and at the same time keyed his mic and said, "Go, Go." The "Go, Go" was heard echoing through speakers in the house as they entered. They proceeded to clear each room and as they did, they would transmit "CLEAR" over the radio. Each time they did, it could be heard from speakers in the various rooms as well.

Each room having been cleared without finding anyone inside, the four agents proceeded back out of the house.

"What the hell was that re-transmitting of our radios about?" one agent asked.

"Beats the hell out of me," another replied.

At that point, the other four agents were also heading that way.

"Nothing," one of them said as he approached.

"Nothing here either," the lead agent stated. "I'll report in by cell to Commander Archer, everybody just standby."

After calling Archer with his report that nobody was found on the premises, the lead agent told him that there were two sets of dirty dishes in the sink that were fresh. It was evident that two people had been there earlier that day. They didn't have any proof that the place was Armstrong's, but it had the same type of setup as his place down in Peekskill.

"It's his place alright," Archer stated extremely annoyed. "I want these bastards found. Hit the woods in two man teams and call me when you have something positive to report."

Aye sir," the agent responded as the call went dead.

Bob continued leading Chris through the woods that became denser, but the terrain was still rather level with some up and down inclines. Bob was moving as fast as he prudently could, and at the same time making sure that Chris was staying with him. He was impressed that Chris was doing well without any complaint. Bob could see the determination on Chris' face and knew that he was serious about the bug-out.

At one point in some thick brush, Bob felt a tug at the left cargo pocket on the leg of his trousers, but it didn't seem like much, and apparently was just snagged by a sharp branch.

A short while later, Bob stopped and had Chris catch up to him. He withdrew a couple of mesh bags from his vest and handed one to Chris, while keeping the other one for himself.

"Hang this light mesh bag off your belt," Bob said. "Whenever you see an old can, and you will see plenty up here, stick it in the bag. I will be doing the same. Once it is full, you can stop."

"Are we trying to clean the woods as we go?" Chris asked. "This might not be the best time to be nature buffs," Chris added.

"I have another use for them, I'll explain later," Bob said with a smile.

* * *

While Bob and Chris were moving towards the Catskill Park, and eight DTTF agents were combing the woods around Bob's new house, a "Breaking News Alert" from Wolf News flashed on television screens around the country.

"Hi, I'm Dawn Garrity, and tonight on 'The Garrity Report' I will have a breaking story on the Domestic Terrorism Task Force agent who was shot last Sunday," Dawn announced as she stood in front of a large monitor in the studio, that showed a still photo of the tape across the front of Bob's driveway with the words "Crime Scene - Do Not Cross" emblazoned across it.

"Was the shooter really who they say it was? Join me tonight and we will show a video of the actual shooting, and let you decide. I'll see you tonight at eight o'clock."

* * *

Bob and Chris had been hiking for about four hours and, in Bob's estimate, they had travelled about ten miles. He was surprise they had covered such a distance, but initially the terrain had been somewhat uncomplicated. However, it was now becoming more difficult with steep grades, both up and downhill. At this point, being a good distance from his aunt's property, he felt they should stop for the night.

"Chris, let's hole up here for the night," Bob said as he stopped by a large stand of trees. This looks like a good place and we should be about half way to where we are going."

Looking a little bedraggled, Chris said, "I won't argue with that." He stopped and dropped his pack in front of him.

"How are your shoulders?" Bob asked.

"Well they have been better," Chris said forcing a smile. "It seemed like the pack got heavier the further we went," he continued.

"Well it will feel lighter tomorrow," Bob chuckled. "I think this is a good location. We are on higher ground and, having refilled our water supply back at that last stream, we should have plenty to get us through the morning. Those chlorine dioxide tablets we put in our bottles should have that water purified by now. We have lots of cover here so, unless someone was far off a trail, we should be hard to find. Let's get the hammocks up and we'll have some dinner."

"I'm glad we ate right before we left," Chris said. "I'm hungry as hell."

Bob and Chris selected two trees the appropriate distance apart and hung their hammocks up using the slap straps. Bob told Chris to lay his sleeping bag out in the hammock so it would be ready when they wanted to crash. They each erected their tarp over a ridge line, as Bob had shown Chris earlier, and so they both had a shelter over their hammock.

"Chris, you might want to take your headlamp out of your pack and put the strap around your neck before it gets dark," Bob suggested. "It will be much easier to pull it up over your head if you need it, then trying to find it in your pack. But remember, only if you need it so you don't poke an eye out with a branch if you have to piss at night, and make sure the red lens is in place. The red light can still be seen at night but from less of a distance than a white light." Again, only use it if you have to."

Bob opened his pack and dug around for the Aloksak that held his food rations. He instructed Chris to do the same. They each took out an MRE entree and a heater bag.

"What are you eating tonight?" Bob asked, announcing he would be having beef stew with potatoes and vegetables.

"It looks like mine says chicken and rice with vegetables," Chris replied looking at the label on the pouch.

Bob indicated that being he hadn't had time back at the house he would show Chris how to use the heater bag to warm up his entree.

Bob took his heater bag and showed Chris how to tear off the top. Then holding the bag, he instructed Chris that he had to hold the heater, that was inside the bag, up and away from a line that was printed on the bottom of the bag.

"You pour in a little water up to this line," Bob explained. "Don't overfill it though. Insert you MRE entree into the bag and slide it, and the heater, to the bottom of the bag. Now fold the top of the bag over onto the opposite side of where the heater is. With the heater underneath the MRE, hold the bag level like this," Bob showed Chris. "After about one minute the heater should soak up the water you put in the bag. Then stuff the entire thing into the carton the MRE entree was in, with the heater down, and lean it against something like this rock," Bob demonstrated, leaning his carton against a small rock jutting out of the ground. "In about ten to fifteen minutes we will be ready to eat."

Chris followed the instructions and quickly had his MRE leaning against a small log lying on the ground, heating up too.

After the meals were heated, the top of the meal pouch was torn off, and they both sat leaning against a tree eating with their long titanium spoons.

"So what do you think of MRE's?" Bob asked.

"Well," Chris responded, "it certainly isn't the best cuisine I've ever had, but as hungry as I am, it tastes pretty damn good."

Bob smiled and continued eating.

After finishing their dinner and drinking some water, Bob informed Chris that he needed to set out some trip wires for perimeter security.

"We don't have explosives on us do we?" Chris asked with a smile, raising his eyebrows.

"No, I just want to know if someone breaches the perimeter of our camp," Bob said returning the smile.

Bob directed Chris to get out the cans he had collected that day and put them in a pile along with Bob's.

"This is what I want you to do," Bob explained. "I want you to take your small folding knife that I gave you and using the awl, punch a hole in the center of the bottom of the cans."

Bob pulled out his own Victorinox One-Hand Trekker and showed Chris where the awl was located on the back of the knife.

"Once you get the holes punched, I want you to start collecting small pebbles that will fit down into the opening of the can" Bob continued.

Bob went back to his pack and pulled out a fishing kit. From that he extracted a wound bobbin that had olive green braided fishing line on it. Bob then found himself a stick long enough to break off five pieces of about two inches in length each. As Chris punched the holes in the bottom of the cans, Bob tied a length of fishing line to the center of the sticks he broke. He then strung the fishing line up from the bottom of one can and through two more, with a good length of fishing line left. The stick on the bottom held the cans on top of one another.

"Now start putting a few of those small pebbles in each can that is threaded onto the fishing line," Bob instructed Chris. "As I complete each set of three cans, put a few pebbles in them as well. You can slide the top and second can up to get the pebbles into all of them."

Working together, Bob had five sets of three cans on a length of fishing line completed in about ten minutes.

"Now all I still need are some stakes," Bob stated.

Bob then cut a few saplings that provided him with a "V" shape when cutting where a limb stuck out. This gave him a stake that had a short limb sticking out and down. He made five of those as well. He then used the straight parts of the saplings to cut five straight stakes. For this, Bob used his fixed blade knife, which was on his right hip, in a custom leather sheath that he had made himself.

The knife was one of his favorites, the Swedish Fallkniven F1-L3GGM. The usual Fallkniven F1 had black checkered Thermorun elastomer handles, but Bob's had green micarta handles, which is why it had the designation "L3GGM" after the F1.

"Now we are ready to set up those trip wires," Bob said to Chris, who had been watching with interest, what Bob had been doing. "Let's go get it done."

Bob then went around the perimeter of their camp, setting up trip wires in a manner where anyone who approached the camp from any direction would hit one.

Bob went to find a tree or sapling with a limb sticking out. He then walked a distance from it and hammered a straight stake into the ground, using a rock, and tied the braided fishing line to it. Next, he walked back towards the tree, and when he was under the limb, he hammered one of the "V" shaped stakes in the ground, with the bottom of the "V" pointing up. He then pulled the fishing line towards himself from the straight stake and placed it under the "V", where the small limb protruded, and then threw the remaining line up and over the tree limb. He then tied one of the three can sets, onto the end of the line dangling from the other side of the limb. The small pebbles in the cans provided enough weight to keep the line stretched between the stationary stake and the point where it went under the "V" stake, and up over the limb. If someone hit the straight trip wire with a foot, it would pull on the fishing line and the cans hanging over the limbs would rattle, indicating the direction from which the intruder was entering the perimeter. Bob set-up four more of these so that no matter what direction you approached the hammocks, the alarm would sound.

Bob and Chris sat around their camp, relaxing after their first day's journey.

"While we are sitting here, maybe I can check the news on my phone and see if Dawn has shown the video yet," Bob mentioned to Chris.

However, when Bob went to reach into the cargo pocket on his left leg, nothing was there.

"What the hell. My phone is gone"

"Are you sure?" Chris asked.

"Damn sure. I got snagged on some brush today, but I didn't think any more of it. It looks like it ripped open the bottom of the pocket and the phone must have dropped out."

"Well that can't be good, but I'm glad you did it and not me," Chris said trying not to smile.

"Yea, well funny man, we now don't have any communication with the outside world."

* * *

While Bob and Chris sat in camp, Dawn's show, "The Garrity Report" began. "We have an interesting, yet shocking segment tonight," Dawn started. "It deals with the shooting that occurred on Sunday in the peaceful suburb of Peekskill, New York. I must warn our viewers that as part of that segment, we will be showing a video that was taken at the location of the shooting, as it occurred. The video shows graphic images that may be disturbing to some people, and viewer discretion is advised."

"But first," Dawn said, "we have a segment on the ongoing developments of the teacher in Florida that has been accused of having sexual relations with a student." Dawn ran several segments, as she usually did, holding the main event until last. She always said that if you run the real good stuff first, the audience will leave early.

Dawn started her last segment. "We have obtained a video from a confidential source and it clearly shows that the suspected shooter at Robert Armstrong's residence was indeed not Armstrong. But who was it, you ask? Well let's take a look at the video recording."

The message "The following video shows graphic images that may be disturbing to some people, and viewer discretion is advised." was also flashed at the bottom of the scene in a bright red banner.

A short portion of the video was played with the faces of the two DTTF agents being blurred to conceal their identity. It was played in full, and then in slow motion at the point of the shooting.

"As you can see," Dawn continued, "The actual shooter was another agent of the Domestic Terrorism Task Force, a newly formed agency developed for the purpose of fighting domestic terrorism. You can clearly see him pull a silenced weapon from his vest, and as he turns around he shoots the other agent, first in the throat, and then in the forehead. We have blurred the actual wounds as they are extremely graphic. The shooter then calmly walks away.

"So what would precipitate one agent of a government agency, violently killing another agent in cold blood?' This video is very disturbing, both in content, and in the questions it raises. At this point, we don't know why. We don't have the answers. But you can be assured that we are searching for them, and they will be brought to you as soon as we have them.

"As always, I thank you for joining us tonight for 'The Garrity Report.' I am Dawn Garrity, and I'm looking out for your interest and the truth behind the news."

* * *

It was starting to get dark and the DTTF agents hadn't found Bob or Chris. Because the raid took place during the day, night vision goggles had not been part of their load-out equipment.

The lead agent radioed for instructions and was told to camp at whatever their current location was so they wouldn't lose any ground the following day, and to continue the search in the morning.

* * *

Within fifteen minutes of Dawn completing "The Garrity Report" Wolfgang Drescher was on the phone to Max Archer.

"Archer here," he stated as he answered his cell phone at his apartment.

"Have you watched Wolf News tonight?" Drescher asked.

"No, I've been directing the search for those two pieces of shit," Archer replied.

"Well you're fucked my friend, and maybe the rest of us too," Drescher said sounding annoyed. He then explained about the video that was just shown on Dawn's show.

"How the fuck did they get a video of the shooting?" Archer asked, incredulous that a video existed.

"How the fuck do I know. That Armstrong guy must have taken it. But it's out there now and you are in big trouble. If I were you, I would get out of the country tonight. I'll try to secure things on this end. Unfortunately, I'm going to have to tell them you were just a rogue agent. I have to protect the DTTF."

"I understand. I'm out of here," Archer said as he ended the call. He then went to his safe, withdrew his passport and several thousand dollars in cash. He got in his personal vehicle and headed directly north, crossing into Canada hours later.

* * *

Back in the Catskill Mountains, darkness had fallen.

"I guess we are set for the night," Bob said to Chris. "It's been a long day. Let's hit the rack so we are well rested for tomorrow. As soon as we have some light in the morning, we are out of here. Keep your night vision goggles right on top of your pack under the tarp. If we need to move out tonight for some reason, you don't want to be feeling around for them."

"Sounds good to me," Chris said agreeing.

Both Bob and Chris got into their hammocks, Chris having a difficult time doing so, but within minutes they were asleep.

CHAPTER 25
Exposed

Bob was awake before the first sign of light. He could smell that it had rained the night before. He slid out of his sleeping bag, and quietly climbed out of the hammock. Releasing a carabiner from one of the slap straps at one end of his hammock, he lowered it to the ground. He could now sit comfortably on the dry ground under his tarp.

Taking out his small canister stove and a gas cartridge, he set it up on a level section of ground under his shelter. He then got his cup, a Spork, and one of his coffee packets.

Bob fired up the stove easily with his BIC lighter and he had a cup of water boiling in only minutes. A coffee bag was set in the cup and the aroma filled his shelter. Adding the fixings after the coffee bag had steeped, and been removed, Bob stirred his first cup of morning elixir.

Enjoying the new day approaching, Bob heard Chris get out of his hammock and exit his tarp. He walked a short distance into the woods to relieve himself, and hit a trip wire on the way out. The sound of three cans rattling over a nearby limb, made Chris jump.

"Good morning Chris," Bob yelled out with a chuckle.

"I forgot about this damn trip wire," Chris yelled back. "All I want to do is piss."

"I sort of figured that," Bob responded.

Chris came back into camp and approached Bob's tarp. Looking in he said, "Man, you got coffee already?"

"Some things just gotta be done," Bob said lifting his cup to his lips.

"Did your hammock get wet last night?" Chris asked.

"Not at all," Bob answered.

"Mine did a little."

"Did you put the drip lines on the ends like I showed you?"

"Damn, and I thought I did everything right."

"You'll get better as time goes by," Bob said with a smile. "Get your stove and some coffee and join me over here, there's plenty of room for us both under this tarp."

"I'll be right back," Chris said as he headed back to his own tarp. Returning with his stove, cup, and coffee, it wasn't long before he was enjoying a cup along with Bob.

"Once we finish, we will boil up a little more water and have some oatmeal and a power bar," Bob said. "Then we have to get packed up and get going. I want to get more distance between us and my aunt's property."

* * *

The DTTF agents spent the night in the woods, and got up early to continue their search for Armstrong and Hughes. Each individual was responsible for feeding themselves and then continuing with the search. The team leader placed a cell call to the Northeast Sector facility command. He spoke to the Assistant Facility Commander, Brian Decker.

"Sir, the teams are up and moving out," the Team Leader stated. "We still have a lot of acreage to cover up here."

"I know you do, but we still need these guys caught. We have a lot of violations of the Domestic Terrorism Act by this Armstrong, and from what you have described, we have even more up there," Decker replied.

"We'll do the best we can sir."

"I know you will. But to make things easier on you, I'm sending another team up there later this morning. When they land, coordinate their efforts by radio. Get them out into areas you haven't reached yet," Decker instructed.

"Aye sir."

* * *

Dawn Garrity was working in her office when Hal, the Senior Editor, casually strolled in. Dropping down into a chair next to her desk he waited for her to look up.

"Morning Hal," she said with a smile. "Sorry I was engrossed in what I was doing."

"No problem. I would assume that you have checked the stats for your show last night?"

"I did, and it would appear it was a hit."

"It was, but I have some other news for you."

Dawn looked up concerned, "What now?"

"Well it would appear you now have permission to run with the audio recording."

"No shit, finally."

"But first I want you to try to interview, or at least get a statement from, the CANE Organization, and if possible some of the businesses that are involved in the conversation on the recording. Be very careful with any part of the recording you play on the air, and keep it short. Just enough to wet the viewers whistle."

"I understand; I'll get right on it. And Hal, thanks again for your support."

Hal got up and strolled out as smoothly as he had entered.

* * *

Through various sources, the FBI determined that Max Archer was the Facility Commander for the Northeast Sector of the DTTF and that the facility was located in Albany, New York. Some additional investigation provided them with an address for the facility.

At the New York City Field Office, Franco Gonzalez, the Assistant Director in Charge, directed that a tactical team of six Special Agents proceed to the DTTF facility in Albany and serve an arrest warrant on Max Archer. Being a "High Risk" warrant, Gonzalez instructed that the team be extremely careful. He felt that, even though they were going directly to a government facility, Archer might not be cooperative with the arrest, and become violent.

The team of six agents proceeded to Albany in a Chevy Suburban in full tactical gear. The facility was located, and it looked like a military installation with a high chain link fence topped with barbed razor ribbon, leaning outward at an angle from the fence. Large white signs were posted on the fence about every twelve feet, which read "Restricted Area - Keep Out," in large red letters.

The suburban pulled up to a gate that was manned by two DTTF agents. The Special Agent driving the Suburban rolled down his window and informed the agent, that approached the window, that they were there to serve an arrest warrant.

The DTTF agent went into the gatehouse and placed a call to his commander. He was told to let the vehicle enter.

The agent exited the gate house and directed the Special Agent of the FBI to proceed to the left side of the building straight ahead and he would be met by the Assistant Facility Commander, Brian Decker.

As the gate opened, the suburban pulled forward to a nondescript building that looked like a large warehouse. It did not have any windows. To the left of the building was a large section of pavement. Sitting side by side were a Bell OH-58D Kiowa Warrior aerial reconnaissance helicopter and a Sikorsky UH-60 Blackhawk. Two individuals in flight suits, carrying clipboards were walking around the Blackhawk conducting what appeared to be a preflight check, while a group of DTTF agents in full tactical gear stood to one side.

Upon pulling around to the left of the building, as instructed, a small entrance door was observed with a plaque that read, "DTTF Office." As the suburban came to a stop, the six FBI Special Agents exited the vehicle. As they did, the office door opened and a tall man with a sturdy build, wearing khaki 5.11 trousers and a black polo shirt, came out and started walking towards them in a non-threatening manner.

Extending his hand, the man said, "Good morning, I am Brian Decker, the Assistant Facility Commander. How can I help you?"

"Good morning, I'm Special Agent Savage with the FBI," Savage said extending his hand, thinking this might be easier than expected. "We have an arrest warrant for Max Archer. Is he here?"

"No sir, and we don't know where he is. We have not heard from him since yesterday. We have tried his various phones, and we have not gotten an answer. I would assume this is about the video shown on the news?"

"Does he have any relatives in the area, or friends?" Agent Savage asked.

"No sir, he has no family, and I'm not aware of any friends."

"And you are certain that he is not at this facility?"

"Sir, if he were, I certainly would not attempt to obstruct a federal warrant. After all, we all work for the same government," Decker said with a smile.

"It looks like you have a team going up. Anything important?" Savage asked casually.

"Just trying to find some guys that have violated the Domestic Terrorism Act. Can't let people get away with that shit or they won't take us seriously," Decker answered.

"Well, I thank you for your cordial assistance with this matter," Savage replied.

"If there is nothing else, I believe I have a ton of work to attend to," Decker concluded as he turned and reentered the building.

"Let's load up guys," Savage directed the other agents. As they headed back to the office, Savage placed a call to Franco Gonzalez and reported that the warrant had not been served. Savage also informed him that, it appeared, the DTTF didn't know where he was either, and that he didn't have any family or friends.

"I can believe that," Gonzales said with a short chuckle, referring to the no friends.

"They also have a tactical team going up in a Blackhawk. It was getting ready to take off while we were there."

"Any idea where?"

"No sir, they didn't seem to want to say. Just going after some guys who violated the Domestic Terrorism Act. Wouldn't give us anything specific."

"Ok then, get the team back here until we can get some more information."

"Heading that way sir."

Gonzales spoke to his staff at the New York City Field Office and directed them to contact the major news networks and inform them he would be giving a press conference later that day.

* * *

Bob and Chris had broken camp early and Bob made sure that the cans for the trip wires were taken with them. He showed Chris how to pack them in the mesh bags, stuffing leaves between them, so they wouldn't rattle as they travelled.

They continued on the trek towards the area where Bob wanted to set up camp. He knew the location was well off known trails and there were a lot of rock outcrops that would help conceal their position, once there. But they still had a distance to travel, and Bob hoped they could get there by midday.

* * *

Dawn Garrity and her staff were busy trying to contact the CANE Organization, as well as the various businesses that were identified on the audio recording. Dawn told her staff she would contact CANE personally, but they should each select a different business and try to get an interview, or at least a statement.

Upon contacting CANE, Dawn was told that Mr. Mann was not available, by his secretary, Helga.

"Do you know when he will be available?" Dawn asked.

"No ma'am, I don't," Helga replied.

Explaining that Wolf News had an audio recording taken during a conference at the CANE facility, and that they would be running segments from it on her show that evening, Dawn informed Helga that they would like to give CANE an opportunity to comment.

"If I could have your phone number ma'am, I will see what I can do."

Dawn provided Helga with her cell phone number, as well as her office number, and thanked her for her assistance.

Her staff was not having any more luck with the different business entities identified on the recording. They all stated they were not aware of any CANE Organization. When they tried to speak with the actual people named on the recording, they were isolated by executive assistants who suggested a formal request be forwarded.

About twenty minutes after Dawn completed her call with Helga at CANE, she was told by her staff that they had received a phone call informing them that a formal statement would be forwarded to her office by late afternoon.

* * *

At twelve noon, Franco Gonzales held a press conference in the front of the FBI New York City Field Office.

"Max Archer is the Commander for the Northeast Sector Facility of the Domestic Terrorism Task Force, in Albany, New York and is being sought as a fugitive from justice," Gonzalez began. "He has disappeared from his employment and is believed to be on the run, possibly trying to get out of the country. We are issuing an all points bulletin to all law enforcement agencies to collaborate in helping the FBI find and apprehend this individual."

Gonzales had a large photo of Max Archer, blown up from a photo in his federal file, displayed on an easel to his right.

"This is the most recent photograph of Max Archer and we are providing a digital copy to all news agencies. We ask that they broadcast it nationwide."

Gonzalez concluded the press conference stating, "Max Archer is considered armed and dangerous. If you have any information on his whereabouts, please call the number being displayed at the bottom of your screen."

* * *

Bob and Chris finally made it to the location Bob had selected for hiding out. At least until Ralph could let him know it was safe to come out.

"Well, this is the place Chris," Bob said stopping in a heavily wooded area.

"It should be hard to find us here," Chris said, looking around.

"As you can see, we have high ground, but not all the way to the top of the mountain. There are some nice rock outcrops over there," Bob said pointing, "and we can build a shelter right up against them. If we get a Dakota Fire Hole dug, and keep a small fire going, the rocks will absorb the heat from it and reflect it back to us at night. And right down that bank to our right, there is a good strong stream that will provide us with water and fish if it comes to that."

"Looks like everything two refugees could want," Chris said with a laugh.

"Well let's get these packs off, and start building camp."

"How about getting something to eat first?"

"I agree with that," Bob said nodding his head.

Suddenly, Bob heard the rotors of a chopper and as it approached and flew over; Bob was able to catch just a glimpse of it through an opening in the canopy.

'That's another Blackhawk," Bob said. "They must be bringing in another team. They are determined bastards. By the sound of the chopper, they seem to be heading down towards my aunt's property. Hopefully, we will still be safe up here in the mountains."

"I'm hoping too," Chris said looking worried.

Bob and Chris made a quick lunch with a cup of soup and a power bar.

"I know that wasn't much," Bob admitted. "But we have to conserve the food we have. We don't know how many days we will be up here. If we are careful, we should have no problem for two to three days. All that hiking does give you an appetite, but now that we are here, we won't be expending as many calories."

"And hopefully Ralph will come get us sooner than later," Chris tossed in.

"If all else fails, we can start trapping and fishing, and with the rice we have, we could survive longer."

Bob and Chris spent the afternoon setting up camp. The large rock outcrops on the north side of their area made an ideal location for a shelter that could be somewhat concealed. One of the large rocks jutted out at an angle whereby it provided overhead cover, and was about fifteen foot wide.

Bob collected a bunch of small downed trees, and large limbs, with Chris' help. He explained to Chris that they were going to cut this wood to lengths so it would allow them to lean it in at an angle, from out front of the overhang, to just under the overhang, whereby the wall they were making would lean in towards the outcrop. This would be done on the left and right side of the overhang, and also on the front. However, they would leave a small section of the front open at the center. Bob would use his tarp to cover the left front and side, and Chris would use his for the right front and side. This would provide a sleeping area on each side with room for their packs.

With the side and front walls leaning out at the bottom, and the tarps covering them, water would run away from their position if it rained. Using their folding saws and fixed blade knives, Bob and Chris went to work building the shelter. It only took them about three hours to complete it.

Next, Bob had them both collect boughs from coniferous trees, mostly hemlock, which was plentiful in the surrounding area, and place them on the ground in their sleeping areas. This would soften the ground and provide insulation from it. They also filled a drum liner with leaves and placed that on the boughs for further insulation. They could then lay their sleeping bags on the drum liner for a fairly comfortable bed.

After that, it was now time for a Dakota Fire Hole.

"Right here at the center of the shelter, where we left it open, we will dig a Dakota Fire Hole which we can use to cook on, and for warmth if we need it," Bob said to Chris pointing at the ground in the center of the shelter. "I somewhat explained this to you at the house. We are going to dig a hole right here about ten to twelve inches in diameter and we want it about a foot deep, so let's get started."

Bob with his Gerber Gorge shovel, and Chris with his U-Dig-It trowel made quick work of the hole.

"Ok, now we have to dig the angled tunnel," Bob said. "We are going to start about a foot from this main hole, which will be the main chamber for the fire. Normally we would determine the direction the wind is blowing from, and place the hole there, but in this case we want the hole straight out from the front of the shelter. Once a fire is built in the main hole, the suction of the fire should draw adequate air through the tunnel. We want this second hole about six inches in diameter and angled in towards the main hole, so it enters the main hole at the bottom. You have the smaller trowel, so you will probably do better, making the tunnel. Just be careful not to damage the ground between the main hole and the tunnel hole."

"Piece of cake," Chris said, and started digging the tunnel.

Bob supervised and helped pull the dirt from the tunnel as it was dug. When they were finished, Bob said, "Good job my friend," which brought a big smile to Chris' face.

"Before we fire this thing up, I think we should get the trip wires positioned around the perimeter," Bob suggested.

"I'll help. I watched you yesterday and it seems pretty straight forward."

Bob and Chris spent about half an hour getting the trip wires out and the strings of cans hung. They then returned to the main camp area.

"Well, it would seem as though we have prepared a nice little camp for ourselves," Bob declared.

"I'm actually liking it," Chris replied.

"We'll see how long that lasts," Bob chuckled. "I'm going to get a fire going in the Dakota Fire Hole. Why don't you go down the bank over there and collect us some water from the stream. Use the collapsible two gallon water bag in your pack."`

Bob collected some tinder and kindling and then some small pieces of wood for fuel. By the time Chris got back with the water, and using his blowing tube, Bob had a good fire going in the Dakota Fire Hole.

"That's some beautiful water down there," Chris said as he returned. "Looks clear enough to drink."

"It may look clear, but never drink water without purifying it," Bob interjected. "You don't know what is upstream and most problems you wouldn't see anyway. It could have cysts, like Giardia lamblia or Cryptosporidium, or bacteria. In some areas, even viruses. You can never take a chance out here. The last thing you need is the shits and pukes, and the dehydration that comes along with it."

"I didn't drink it," Chris said defensively, "I was just saying it looks clear."

"I know Chris; I'm just giving a kindly warning."

"I appreciate it."

Chris set the water down in camp and walked over to the Dakota Fire Hole.

"As we add more fuel," Bob said while dropping more pieces of wood onto the fire in the hole, "the hot air exiting up and out of the main hole is creating a suction that draws fresh air in through the angled hole. The more air it draws in the hotter the fire gets. The hotter it gets, the more efficiently it burns, and the less smoke it gives off. It's great for this type of a situation where we don't want a big swirl of smoke exiting through the trees above."

"So we can actually cook some real food tonight?" Chris asked.

"For sure. I thought we might cook up a pot of rice and add some of the tuna from the pouches we have. Then maybe we can make a small stick bread."

"Stick bread?"

"Yea, I'll cut a green stick and remove the bark. We will mix-up a little of the bannock and I'll wrap it around the stick. We can then cook it over the fire"

"That sounds great," Chris said with a grin.

"It won't be as quick as with a large camp fire, because the hole is only twelve inches wide, but we'll make it happen. Before we do that, why don't you put water in both of our titanium pots that fit over our water bottles and boil it? We can use that to refill our bottles. We will use some more water to cook the rice, and that will boil while we cook with it. I'll cut some green limbs to lay across the top of the fire hole so you can set the pots on them."

"Won't the green sticks burn?"

"They will eventually, but being green they will last longer than dried branches. I'll cut a few extra sets so when they finally start to burn, we can push them in the fire and add some more," Bob answered.

Bob and Chris got to work boiling water and getting the evening meal cooked.

* * *

The Dawn Garrity show had started and Dawn began her segment on the audio recording. She explained to the viewers that the recording was taken at a conference held at the CANE

Organization by a member, Christopher Hughes. He thought the organization would be good for his business, as he was told it would be. However, after becoming a member he became disillusioned when he realized the members, along with government representatives, were actually trying to hurt regular people. Therefore, he made the recording to try and expose their intentions

"This organization indicates it is a Consortium for the Advancement of Nonpartisan Equity, but it seems like it is actually some type of a lobbying firm that looks to members of our government to help them in their cause. And it would appear that their cause is to keep the American people dependent on the members' products and services. They are highly opposed to people being self-reliant, or having any capability to fend for themselves.

"The recording also indicates that a new government agency, The Domestic Terrorism Task Force, may have been a result of the requests made by the CANE Organization.

"Let me play a few selected excerpts from this recording."

Dawn then played various short sections from the recording that provided credence to her story.

"We have tried to contact both, the CANE Organization, as well as the various businesses that are named in the recording. None of the businesses contacted would talk to us, nor would they admit to knowing about CANE. After hearing the segments played here tonight, I think they might have a difficult time maintaining that position.

"Even though the CANE Organization would not talk to us directly, they have provided us with a written statement, which I will display on the screen and read." Dawn both displayed, and read the following statement.

"Membership in the CANE Organization is held in the strictest of confidence. Our organization is a Consortium for the Advancement of Nonpartisan Equity. We endeavor to assist our members businesses and, on occasion, lobby for their benefit. We do not make policy, or in any other manner, propose laws. The advancement of our members in the business community is attained through hard and fair work on their part as well as ours.

"In regard to an audio recording having been made during a conference at our facility, I must warn you that any such use of that recording will result in a law suit. Any recording of conversations within our facility is strictly prohibited, and if such a recording was made, it was done so illegally. Our members have never given permission for their conversations to be recorded and therefore, if indeed they were, it can be considered a criminal offense. Unless all parties to a conversation give permission to be recorded, it cannot be done.

"At this time, I request that the audio recording you refer to, and any copies thereof, be immediately returned to the CANE Organization so that we can ensure that they are destroyed.

Signed - Gray Mann"

After reading the statement, Dawn told the viewers that CANE is misinformed on recording laws.

"Yes, if you are in a 'two party' state, then all parties to a conversation must agree to the recording of that conversation. However, New York is a 'one party' state, whereby only one party to a conversation needs to give permission. In other words, as long as you are a participant in a conversation in a 'one party' state, you can record that conversation without any other participant agreeing, or even being aware of it being done. The audio recording we have was recorded by a member of CANE, at the facility, and this member was at all times present and involved in the conversation. So that bird just isn't going to fly.

"I hope you have enjoyed our report tonight and we will have future updates on this story. As always, join us weekday nights here on Wolf News for 'The Garrity Report.'"

* * *

Back at camp, Bob and Chris had purified water, cooked dinner, and were now sitting in the shelter around the fire eating stick bread.

"This is really good," Chris said with a mouth full.

"Sprinkle some of this cinnamon-sugar on it," Bob said handing a small container to Chris.

Chris sprinkled some on his bread and took a bite.

"Man, this is a little taste of heaven."

"I agree, but it's about as close as I want to get for a while," Bob said smiling.

When they finished their bread, they both got situated in their sleeping bags and readied for a night's sleep.

"This is really comfortable with this stuff under us," Chris said as he laid down.

"It's a lot better than being on the cold hard ground. You have those night vision goggles where you can get to them don't you?" Bob asked.

"I have them right next to my head," Chris replied.

"Well, unless something happens, I'll see you in the morning. Keep one eye and ear open."

"Goodnight Bob."

About an hour after they laid down, the sound of rattling cans came from the left side of the camp. In an instant, Bob was up with the KEL-TEC in hand and night vision goggles in place. With stealth, he exited the shelter and lay prone listening for any further indication that something was moving.

Not hearing anything, and staying low, he headed towards the original noise. Suddenly the cans rattled again, and he looked in that direction. He could see a raccoon hanging from the limb the cans were draped over, and it was pulling at the string.

Feeling relieved that the intruder was not human; Bob threw a stick at the raccoon and finally got it to leave the area. A couple of small rocks thrown in its exiting direction would hopefully deter it from returning.

Bob went back to the shelter, and climbed back into his sleeping bag.

CHAPTER 26
Unforeseen

The next morning, Thursday, without any further incidents, Bob was up bright and early and made a quick cup of coffee with his small gas cartridge stove. It wasn't long and Chris was up and making coffee as well.

"Did you keep that one eye and ear open last night like I told you?" Bob asked.

"Yup, I was ready if something went down." Chris responded.

"Well it was a good thing, if something did happen I wouldn't want you to sleep through it," Bob chuckled.

"What?"

"Nothing."

After having their coffee, they had some oatmeal and beef jerky. Bob said he was going to do a little scouting around the perimeter just to get a feel for the land.

"I've been here many times before, so I'm not going far. I just want to make sure everything is still the same. While I'm gone, maybe you can go down and get some more water and get it boiled. If we have to run, I want to make sure our bottles are full."

"I can do that," Chris replied.

Bob got up and headed out of camp with the Berretta on his thigh and the KEL-TEC in his hands.

Chris ate a couple more pieces of beef jerky, and put everything away in the Aloksak. He then grabbed the water bag and headed down the bank to the creek. As he did, he stepped on a moss covered dead tree, that had fallen years before, with his left foot. His foot immediately slid off the other side, and the weight of his body, pulled him over and down the bank. As he tumbled, he felt pain in his right ankle, and hitting several branches and rocks, he ended up at the bottom of the bank, almost lying in the stream.

At first he couldn't figure out what had happened, but remembered it all started when he stepped on the moss. He checked himself, and although he felt bruised and battered, it was his right ankle that was really hurting. He thought to himself that the last thing he needed was a broken ankle.

Chris pulled his trouser leg up and away from his right ankle so he could check it. It was swelling fast. He tried to stand, but there was just no way he could put any weight on his right foot. He felt something warm in his left eye and reached up. It was blood, but not a lot. He reached up and felt a scrape or small cut on his forehead and figured it must be dripping blood. It was the least of his worries he thought.

Bob came back to camp in about twenty minutes and didn't find Chris. He checked the shelter and around the area. Maybe he went to take a crap, Bob thought to himself, knowing he had done so while he was gone.

After about ten minutes, Bob got a little concerned. He started looking around and noticed the water bag wasn't hanging on the broken limb of a tree where it had been earlier. He walked over to the bank, and looking down, saw Chris sitting on the ground by the stream.

"What are you taking a break?" he yelled just loud enough for Chris to hear him.

"No, I fell down the bank. I think I either sprained my ankle real bad, or it's broke," Chris yelled back up. "It's swelling like hell."

"I'll be right down," Bob yelled as he started carefully down the bank. "How the hell did you do this?"

"Not sure. One minute I was climbing down the bank and the next I was at the bottom."

"Well you look like shit," Bob said smiling. "Let me look at this ankle."

Chris pulled his trouser leg up and Bob could immediately see that the right ankle was really swollen.

"We have to get you back up to camp so I can check it further. I am going to have to try and carry you in a fireman's carry. With the steepness of that bank it won't be easy, but we will just have to make it happen."

Bob had Chris face him, standing on his good leg, and had him place his right arm up and over Bob's right shoulder. Bob reached up and back behind his own head with his left hand and grabbed Chris' right wrist, as he lifted Chris' weight, he pulled Chris' right arm around his neck,. When he was finished, he had Chris over his shoulders. Bob's right arm was around Chris' right leg, just under the knee, on Bob's right side, and he brought

Chris' right wrist down and across his chest and to his right side as well. He held it there with his right hand.

"This isn't gonna be easy, but I'm going to try and walk, or sort-of crawl, up this bank. You just stay up on my shoulders and your ankle should be OK. I only have my left hand to help me so we are going to take it slow and easy."

"This sucks," Chris said feeling helpless.

"Yea, I agree, but we have to get you up to camp."

It took about ten minutes of unique climbing by Bob, but he got Chris to the top of the bank. While he had him in the fireman's carry, he took Chris right over to the shelter and set him down on his sleeping bag.

"Let me get a better look at that ankle."

Chris pulled his trouser leg up again, and Bob did some examining.

"Does this hurt?" he asked as he moved the ankle, already knowing the answer from Chris' painful reply.

"Well I'm no doctor, nor do I play one on television, but I don't believe it's broke, and if it is, not bad," Bob said smiling. "I have instant ice packs in my first aid kit. Let me get them."

Bob went to his pack and pulled out a good size first aid kit. From inside he withdrew two ice packs. He then pulled his shemagh from his pack.

"I'm going to activate these and wrap them in the shemagh, being I don't have a towel. With the two of them we should be able to get one on each side of your ankle. I want to see if we can get the swelling down before we remove your boot. If something goes down, just stay in the shelter and I'll take care of it."

Chris did as he was told and held the ice packs around his ankle.

Suddenly, Bob could hear what sounded like numerous people approaching through the woods from various angles. He knew it was not stray hikers, as they would be on a trail and they would all be coming from the same direction. He didn't believe that the DTTF would get this far this quick. He wondered if he had miscalculated, or had they maybe dropped another team in this area?

"I think this is it," he told Chris. "If this is who I think it is we're going to have to fight it out, because I'm not giving up."

"You know I can't help on this Bob," Chris said looking defeated. "Why don't you just get the hell out of here and save yourself? With your alternate ID you should be able to make it to Canada until this blows over."

"You haven't understood a thing that Ralph and I have told you, have you?" Bob stated looking pissed. "I made a pact with your father and I'm not about to break it for you or anyone. Do you understand that?" Bob said with his teeth clenched.

"I understand," Chris said meekly. "But it doesn't mean I like it."

"I wish I had more time to setup a better fighting position, but I don't. We have the ledge behind us." Bob continued, "I will crawl out to that small outcrop in front of the shelter which will give me both cover and concealment, at least from the front. With the trip wires out, I will know when they are getting close, and from what direction. There can't be more than eight or ten of them if they deployed from a Blackhawk."

"If and when the shooting starts, I want you to stay in the shelter. With your injury, I don't want you moving around," Bob instructed. Bob thought to himself that he wished time had been available to teach Chris the basics of shooting so he could defend himself, however, never having shot before, a gun in his hands now might be more of a hazard to Chris, than not having one. Damn, I wish Ralph was here.

Then it happened; Bob heard cans shaking in all directions and knew the agents were approaching. Bob tapped the magazine on his KEL-TEC to make sure it was seated and prepared for the fight.

Suddenly Bob heard someone shout, "Armstrong, You can come out now."

"Fuck You!" Bob shouted back. "I'm not stupid. If you want my ass, come and get it. But prepare for a fight."

"This is the FBI, not the DTTF," another shout from ahead. "We are not here to kill you."

"Send someone forward to prove you are the FBI," Bob yelled.

An agent approached from the front in tactical gear with his weapon hanging from its sling. The agent stopped, and with his hands stretched out to the side, turned around so his back was to Bob. Emblazoned on the back of his tactical vest were the letters, FBI.

"I'll surrender, but you should know, beyond popular belief, I didn't kill that DTTF agent," Bob yelled again.

The agent in front of him turned back around so that he was facing Bob's direction.

"We aren't here to capture you Mr. Armstrong, we are here to rescue you," the agent said smiling.

Bob lowered his rifle slightly and said, "What?"

At that point Ralph came forward with Special Agent Black.

"Hey Bob, How's it going?" Ralph said smiling. "They know you didn't do it. They even know who did. You're cleared ole buddy."

"No shit? What took you so long?'

"No shit," Ralph replied. "I've been trying to call you on the cell phone. Where is Chris?"

"He's over there in the shelter. He has a bad sprained or broken ankle so I told him to stay hidden in the event this turned into a firefight."

Special Agent Black yelled, "Let's get a medic over here!"

Bob got up and walked over to Ralph and they shook hands.

"Good to see you Buddy," Bob said sincerely.

"You too," Ralph responded. "I'd like to introduce you to a good friend of mine. This is Special Agent, James Black, from the FBI," Ralph said motioning his hand towards Jim. "He was a leatherneck too."

"Nice to meet you Agent Black," Bob said holding out his hand.

"Call me Jim, your buddy here does."

Bob and Jim shook hands and Bob suddenly felt a load off his shoulders.

"If you guys are done playing soldier, maybe you can introduce me," Chris said, sitting up and sticking his head out of the shelter.

"We're Marines, not soldiers," Bob said.

They all laughed as the medic headed to attend to Chris' ankle.

* * *

Dawn had a taped interview with Helen Ferguson from Thursday afternoon, and played it on her show. "Good evening, I'm Dawn Garrity and this is 'The Garrity Report.' Today I interviewed Representative Helen Ferguson at the Capital Building. Here are the highlights."

"Good afternoon Representative Ferguson, I understand that you are the Committee Chairman for the Committee on Oversight and Government Reform."

"That's correct Dawn."

"And this is a bipartisan organization created by Congress to review, monitor, and supervise federal agencies, programs, activities, and policy implementation," Dawn continued.

"Yes, and I am also a member of the Committee on Ethics."

"What is your position on the incident involving the Domestic Terrorism Task Force, and the controversy surrounding its creation?" Dawn asked.

"Well Dawn, let me be perfectly clear. We in the house are appalled at what has taken place with this incident. We are investigating and will be holding congressional hearings in the near future. As soon as we return from the recess for our reelection campaigns, we will be introducing legislation to ensure this never happens again. The people can trust that their representatives are looking out for the good citizens of the United States of America."

"Thank you Representative Ferguson, and I thank you for joining us today."

Epilogue

Wolf News continued to run with both stories, trying to get the people concerned, not only with a federal agency that would kill one of their own employees, but with the loss of freedoms in regard to being self reliant. They continue with that agenda.

PNN, the People's News Network, ran the initial story about the shooting, but did not follow it. When they broadcast the story about the audio recording, they presented it in a way in which they asked their viewers whether they felt that an individual should be allowed to record unsuspecting persons, even if legal. "Maybe this law on the 'one party rule' of recording should be changed," they suggested to their viewers. "Would you want to be recorded without your knowledge?" they asked. They quickly dropped the story to follow another about a domestic terrorist that was trying to threaten our way of life. Apparently, this person had been saving seeds from his heirloom vegetables and was covertly sharing them with other gardeners in his rural area. Unable to pay the substantial bail, he sat in jail pending prosecution.

Because of the outrage of the American people over the Presidents Executive Order establishing the DTTF, and the new regulations pertaining to domestic terrorism, the Supreme Court reviewed it to determine if it was legal. They found that there was no indication that is was not a legal order.

The House and Senate couldn't directly vote against an Executive Order, unless it was found to be illegal. They did pass a bill to change it; however the President vetoed that bill. Congress was able to override the veto with over two thirds of both chambers, buy convincing those who opposed, that the reason they wanted the new bill was because the President's Executive Order didn't go far enough.

After another special meeting of the People's Representatives, they were then attempting to pass a law that basically replicated the initial Executive Order except it included banning wood burning stoves in homes, and a restriction on the use of cash. The Domestic Terrorism Task Force was in limbo as an operational agency until the new legislation was passed. All employees were on temporary leave with pay.

The FBI was still not happy about the DTTF, but for the time being, it appeared their hands were tied. They had ordered an investigation of those businesses that were named in the audio recording, to determine if any lobbying laws had been broken, or laws pertaining to restraint of trade. They felt if they could prove that any of the businesses involved had tried to eliminate or stifle competition, create a monopoly, or otherwise tried to hamper or obstruct the natural course of trade, as it would have gone on if it were left to the control of natural economic forces, then they could be persecuted for restraint of trade. The FBI felt they just might get a foothold with that last item.

Archer, as a fugitive from justice hiding out in Canada, was located by the Canadian Royal Mounted Police. When they attempted to apprehend him, he came out shooting and was killed in a hail of gunfire. His body was returned to the United States, and without family, it was buried in a Potter's Field outside of Albany.

Wolfgang Drescher attempted to avoid being involved by claiming Archer was a rogue agent. However, the FBI undercover agent with DTTF indicated that Wolfgang gave the order for Archer to take care of Davis, however it had yet to be determined how he got that information. In order to avoid possible prosecution, Drescher fled the country and went to live in Argentina under an assumed name

The CANE Organization never did figure out how Christopher Hughes recorded the conference. After going through the video of the day of the conference multiple times, which is always surreptitiously recorded, their scrutiny had failed to reveal the one anomaly. The set of keys on a key fob sitting on the table in front of Hughes.

In an attempt to prevent an audio recording in the future, they updated their countermeasures by installing an advanced audio masking system. This system was an Active Countermeasure system utilizing a masking source that generated a signal that was non-stationary Gaussian random. The system mixed this signal with an overlay of classical music whereby the output signal was equalized, amplified, and fed to the various transducer and speaker maskers that were installed within the conference room. As used in many government and military installations, the non-stationarity of the resultant signal provided an added degree of protection against known signal recovery techniques.

The CANE Organization had not changed, nor their membership, and it continued in its efforts to control both industry and government.

Agent Craig Davis' family was still trying to sue the government for the death of their son. However, the government maintained that, because Davis was shot and killed by a fellow employee, the incident was being considered workplace violence, and therefore no liability existed on their part.

Being New York State was a one party state when it came to recording, charges could not be brought against Christopher Hughes as a result of him recording the CANE Conference, however his membership in the organization was terminated.

This event had a transformational effect on Christopher Hughes' life. He realized that money without purpose, and close friends, yielded little for the soul. Bob Armstrong had indeed rubbed off on him, and his eyes saw a new future. The friendship between Bob and Ralph, and their dedication and loyalty to a promise made long ago, made an impression on him and he realized he needed a change. He needed true friendships. He had attained the monetary success that many never reach, but unlike Bob, he had never understood true freedom, and that is what he sought.

Hughes sold his company, ZeRho, to a large power company for an undisclosed amount, and split the money with Ralph. Neither of them would ever need to work again, nor be wanting for anything.

Both Chris and Ralph ended up building individual passive solar houses on portions of Aunt Martha's property which she leased to them for one hundred years. The single old logger's road remained the only access for Bob, Ralph and Chris. Chris adopted the assumed name of Christopher Logan. Bob Armstrong's Aunt Martha remained the Gatekeeper of the property.

Because of the video evidence, Bob Armstrong was cleared of the shooting of the DTTF agent, got his life back, and returned to his new home to continue his self-reliant lifestyle. He was presently seeing Dawn Garrity again, basically on weekends at his new home. Lying together in Bob's bed one night, Dawn hugged Bob gently and placed her mouth next to his ear.
"You know this will never work out don't you?" Dawn whispered.
"Yea, I know." Bob replied.

John D. McCann

About the Author

John D. McCann is a true advocate of self-reliance. He continues in his endeavor to learn and practice the skills necessary to enhance his knowledge and abilities for a self-reliant lifestyle. John is the author of seven books. He has written over a hundred articles and has been published in "Field and Stream," "Wilderness Way," where he was featured on the cover, "Self-Reliance Illustrated," "Survival Quarterly Magazine," and others." He has appeared on the "Martha Stewart Show" teaching how to build a survival kit. He also has various YouTube videos teaching survival and self-reliance skills. He is the founder and owner of Survival Resources, a company that designs and builds custom survival kits, and sells products related to survival and emergency preparedness. He can be contacted at SurvivalResources.com.

John D. McCann

Other Books by John D. McCann

Novels

Wake-Up Call

Non-Fiction

Build the Perfect Survival Kit - 2nd Edition

Stay Alive! - Survival Skills You Need

Practical Self-Reliance - Reducing Your Dependency On Others

Bug-Out - Reality Vs. Hype

The Layers Of Life - Thoughts on Nature, Living and Self Reliance

Signed copies of John's books are available at SurvivalResources.com. Other copies are available at Amazon.com and wherever fine books are sold.

John D. McCann